Battlemind

A Max O'Donnell Novel

Michael Waddington

Michael Waddington
4581 Weston Road, Suite 384, Weston, FL 33331
Battlemind/ Michael Waddington -- 1st ed.
ISBN-13: 978-1712187845 (printed version)

Dedication

*To Mom and Dad, for teaching me to
fight for justice in the face of adversity.*

BATTLEMIND - A soldier's inner strength to face fear and adversity with courage, self-confidence, and mental toughness.
-United States Army Definition (2005)

CHAPTER 1

The woods outside my childhood home were as treacherous as an Asian rain forest to my brother and me. After school and during summers, we crawled elbow over elbow on our bellies along our jungle floor. We pressed tight against the trees, holding our breath as we stalked the enemy. We knew every frame and line of *Rambo* as completely as we knew the trees and streams around our house. We never fought over who would be Rambo; we both were.

One thing that made it possible for me, Max O'Donnell, a scrawny little kid, to see myself as this insane, badass, ex-Army soldier, was the knife my dad gave me for Christmas when I was 10. My older brother, Ricky, got a knife that Christmas too. His was a Ka-Bar, an official U.S. Marine Corps fighting knife, with a thick blade and a leather handle. Mine was flimsier, but it was a replica of Rambo's. It had a nine-inch curved steel blade with top edge serrations so sharp, they could cut through barbed wire.

When I, like Rambo, escaped the prisoner of war camp and crept through the forest, I got my bearings from my knife's compass. I started fires with matches from its secret watertight chamber. I loved that Rambo started off alone, with no chance of surviving, and took on a hundred Russian soldiers with nothing but his brains, his brawn, and his knife.

We weren't the first members of our family to stalk these woods. Our great-great-great-great-grandfather, John

O'Donnell, fought in the Revolutionary War battles of Trenton, Long Island, and Brandywine as part of the First Pennsylvania Rifle Regiment. After the war, the government was too broke to pay the soldiers, so they gave them each 360 acres of Pennsylvania's western frontier. O'Donnell was among the veterans who made their way up the Beaver River in 1794 to claim this bounty.

By the time my brother and I defended these woods, time and generational financial troubles had whittled the family territory down to two acres, and the frontier had shifted to the playground at St. Francis Catholic School. On that postage stamp of asphalt, it was the Italians versus everybody else.

The downfall of American manufacturing in the 1980s hit Westfield hard. The steel and tin mills on the banks of the rivers running through the town moved to Pittsburgh and then overseas. The city quickly fell to ruin, as the industry collapsed. In my fourth-grade year, there were 40 kids in the class. The next year - the Rambo knife year - there were 15.

Around town, we saw fathers who had gone from working the factory lines and then the picket lines, to cleaning the grounds of the county jail in their inmate jumpsuits. When you can't feed your family, you do what you have to do until you get caught. Many of the nice kids "went south" (as my dad would say) and became thugs.

In Westfield, when I was growing up, you didn't have to go looking for a fight, a fight would always come looking for you. Some guys are born fighters. Others, like me, had to learn the hard way. Mornings at St. Francis School were brutal. The basketball stars, all Italian kids, lined up around the outside lunch tables with their slutty girlfriends draped over their shoulders. They stood loose and relaxed as if they were standing in their own backyards, wearing shiny tracksuits with gold crucifixes plumped up on their budding chest hair. They'd taunt all the other kids from the moment they entered the yard.

Often, one of them would step in front of a kid and say, "Wachyou lookin' at?" Or worse, "You gotta problem wit' me?"

By the end of my seventh-grade year at St. Francis, these morons, and my dad's orders to "never back down," had combined to make me miserable. My older brother wasn't around to help defend me anymore, so I attended morning mass to avoid having to brawl it out in the schoolyard. Church felt depressing. Nothing made any sense, and I began to have doubts about God.

The nuns, the Catholic teachers, and everybody else knew that the supposed coolest kids in school were terrorizing the weaker ones. The priests would tell us to turn the other cheek, to forgive. For me, that wasn't an option. That asked for more trouble. I knelt in church every morning, chanting and bowing so that I wouldn't have to fight every day.

Hunkering down in the church wasn't enough, though. One afternoon after gym class, I saw Donnie Fiorello push a buddy of mine into a wall.

"Hey, cut it out," I said.

"So, you think you're tough?" Donnie thrust out his chest. I didn't reply.

Donnie and I stood face to face. A middle school standoff. His overly made-up, under-clad girlfriend giggled. I'll never forget the sound of her high pitched "he-he-he-he," as she stood there with her poufy hair, chubby face, and gapped teeth.

She tittered, "Kick his ass, baby."

Donnie slapped me, and I snapped. I grasped his hair and slammed his face into the gym's metal door. He dropped to his knees, dazed.

"Donnie!" she cried.

I walked away feeling like a big man, but as Rambo says in *First Blood*, "Nothing is over."

At three o'clock, the school bell rang, and Donnie's gang of friends approached me. "We're gonna take this outside," one said.

"You're dead meat," another threatened.

When I walked into the street in front of the school, I found out I was fighting four guys, and none of my friends dared accompany me. We walked to an alley behind the church. There I stood with my back to a chain-link fence, my stance wide, arms tight at my sides, fists clenched. I scrambled into the fight, and my untied sneaker lace caught on one of the chain links. I fell to the ground. Then, all four of them started kicking me in the face and ribs. The metallic taste of blood filled my mouth.

"You guys stop! Stop it right now!" A mother. Salvation. "You guys have a game tonight," she said. "You don't want to hurt your shooting hand. Let's go! Do not argue with me, Joey Pavano. Let's go." I knew this woman, a leader in the Catholic Youth Group, and I was one of her students. She pointed at my battered face as she walked away and said, "You boys can deal with this later, but not on church property."

I'm not going to describe every fight I got into, just the ones where I learned something. I learned something then. I learned that when you're heading into trouble, make sure your shit is tied down before you get into it and never count on backup. That applies to everything in life. I also learned that not every bully is standing on a corner, smoking a cigarette. They must have someone in power supporting them, or they can't survive.

That night, during family dinner, Dad noticed my black eye. "Who won?" he asked.

I didn't answer. I scurried to my room, while Dad ranted about me being "a goddamn weakling." The next day I signed up at a local boxing gym. Run by the Fraternal Order of

Police, it had become an after-school refuge for people like me. Kids trying to deal with life's problems, whether it be poverty, abuse, or bullies, by using their fists.

Sergeant John Mullarkey, a retired Pittsburgh cop, ran the gym. He and Dad grew up together, but I did not want Dad involved. So, I asked the sergeant to keep my boxing a secret, and he agreed. Mullarkey had a gentle way of motivating me. Though he was anything but soft. I had to give 100 percent, or he would say, "O'Donnell, I can tell ya' don't want to be here. Go home, quit wasting my time." These words hit me harder than any name-calling ever would.

Mullarkey had me working the heavy bag until my knees buckled. I moved on to the speed bag, combos, and footwork. Every day, I owed him 200 pushups and 50 pull-ups before I could head home. In a few months, my strength, speed, and skill had increased, and I could hold my own when sparring with the other kids.

X

Redemption came on my thirteenth birthday. Dad and I went to see my brother Ricky's baseball game. I proudly wore my vintage Roberto Clemente Pittsburgh Pirates jacket. Mom was born in Ponce, Puerto Rico. Her loyalties had a rock-solid order of priority: God, family, and Clemente. The jacket, sporting a block "21" on the sleeve, had been one of the last gifts she gave me before she succumbed to breast cancer.

Halfway through the game, my dad was sitting in the stands waiting for my brother's team to finish. I was goofing around on a hill next to the field, playing tag. I saw Chris Tomassi too late. Classic bully. In my grade, but two years older and twice my weight - he was the perfect combination of stupid and mean.

"Nice jacket, you fuckin' spic," he said, and he took my jacket. I tried to snatch it back. He whipped it at me, and the zipper clawed my face. I started bleeding. I ran to my dad, like a whimpering puppy. My dad doesn't talk much. Our conversations are short, no bullshit. He asked me what was going on. I stood there about to cry with him looking up at the hill, and then back at me. Meanwhile, Tomassi had stolen some kid's bike. He was riding around wearing my jacket, terrorizing other middle school children.

"What's going on?" Dad asked.

I lied: "Nothin'."

"Maximillian O'Donnell, where's the jacket your mother gave you?"

I shrugged.

"Get it back. It's your jacket."

"But... uh... I... how... not sure." My stammers were not making a lot of sense.

"Dad?" I asked. "How?"

"Battlemind," he said, tapping his forehead with his right index finger. That was it. One word. "Pay attention. Your brother's up." Dad didn't take his eyes off the game. He just repeated, "Battlemind."

Hot with rage at my dad, at the kid, at myself, I went charging back up the hill. My mind went blank as I started punching that big kid in the face. I don't remember the blows that landed, only the ones that missed. Suddenly he was crying. I walked to the car, with my jacket wadded up in my bloodied, throbbing fist. I felt bad about it, but I also felt good. I had my jacket back. My dad didn't say anything. He'd left it all to me, even the victory. That kid never bothered me again. With that, I'd joined the fight.

It was more than that, for my brother and me, raised in this carved up, strip-mined, backwater on a diet of Hollywood heroism. We were not Rambo, and this was no Asian jungle. We were just a bunch of dumb kids slugging it out. There had to be something else, a place big enough for our ambitions. That place, we decided, was the Army.

We saw the military as a place where we could be as big as our courage, as big as Rambo. He lived by his own rules, made his own order. We didn't pick up the contradiction in the fact that what kept Rambo going was how much he wanted to go back and stab the bureaucrat who sent him there. Ricky and I both enlisted in the Army while in high school. I was later commissioned as an Army officer through the ROTC program.

At 18-years old, the Army assigned me to a Reserve Military Police Unit in Pittsburgh. There, I thought I'd meet some real heroes: guys who'd fought in the first Iraq war and who could tell me what it was like to be a warrior.

Imagine my surprise when it turned out that the unit was basically a drinking club. One weekend a month each soldier got a $100 check that they mostly spent on half-price booze at the Army liquor store, the Class 6. These were the soldiers our nation held in reserve, paid to be ready at any moment to save our country.

Were we going to go on maneuvers? No, we didn't have enough gas for the vehicles. Well, how about if we shot off some rounds at the firing range? They didn't have any ammo to shoot, and their weapons were rusted. Our job was what they called "vehicle maintenance."

One time, some soldiers and I were sitting in an Army vehicle listening to the Steelers game on the radio. During commercial breaks, I was reading a book called *Rogue Warrior*, by an ex-Navy Seal. Our commanding officer approached.

"Put the book down, Private O'Donnell," my sergeant said as the officer neared.

"Huh?" I was confused.

"You're making us look bad."

"What?"

"If you're sitting in the vehicle, he'll think you're testing it, but if you're reading, he knows you're not."

So, this was the military? These were the heroes? Where was the fight? Yes, I wanted the fight, but I still wanted something worth fighting for. What was that?

Justice. I decided that I wanted to be a JAG.

Getting into the Army Judge Advocate General Corps isn't easy. Candidates from the best law schools in the country compete for a handful of openings. From the moment I arrived at the University of Virginia in Charlottesville, for the four-month JAG course, I was told again and again about the JAG Corps' proud tradition as America's oldest law firm, started by General George Washington, no less.

I quickly learned the irony of looking for justice in the military. There is an old joke that "military intelligence" is an oxymoron. "Military justice" is another one. In the Army, a vigorous defense of your client is not considered a smart career move. I was frequently reminded that as Army lawyers, we were "all in this together." I was advised to "not rock the boat" or "burn any bridges."

At my first trial, I saw the prosecution's shotgun approach to charging the defendant. Courts-martial charge sheets are typically three or four pages long, usually with the same conduct charged repeatedly in a variety of ways. The strategy was to overwhelm the defendant so that he had no choice but to plead guilty. In many cases, the soldiers were made to feel guilty even when they were not.

As the wars in Iraq and Afghanistan wore on, more and more soldiers were accused of war crimes. Most of these men weren't killing machines that turned savage at the battle line. They were guys like me in many ways, who built a notion of American manhood from the scowls of their pissed off dads and the words of action movie heroes. They were men who had had the Greatest Generation shoved down their throats and were told they were too lazy and corn-fed to match that glory, men who saw 9/11 as their chance to prove themselves.

The fight on the ground in Iraq and Afghanistan was not so straightforward. Often, it wasn't clear who the bad guys were. In the War on Terror, your instincts, vague rules of engagement, and conflicting orders could easily betray you, and when the Army needs someone to blame for a mishap, it charges the enlisted man.

As an Army lawyer, I had a memory of myself getting picked on in school. The truth was, that by this point, I liked to fight. I had been doing it for so long. It didn't feel right not to be defending something, even if afterward hardly any of those battles seemed worth it.

Facing an opponent in the moments before the first punch, my mind was sharp, a clarity I found nowhere else, except for the courtroom. At that moment, some part of me stretched back to John O'Donnell, making his way up the river knowing the woods were full of enemies, and the other boats might be too. That state of hyperawareness was also a state of calm, the absence of fear in a stillness where movement and thought were one. This is the state my dad called "Battlemind."

CHAPTER 2

Sangar Air Base, Afghanistan - August 2002

Sangar Prison pounded the nose with a mixture of sweat, the ammonia of stale urine - and something else. At Sangar, you could always smell fear. Prisoners without clout and men without boundaries combined for a toxic cocktail of mistreatment.

The "guests" of Sangar deserved to be there, most of them. They'd been stalked, captured, caged, and labeled "enemy combatants." They were men without freedom, men without rights, and men without hope.

The political climate after the collapse of the Twin Towers on September 11, 2001, engendered a gunslinger approach: "shoot first and ask questions later," or "just beat the shit out of someone because the feel of knuckles on flesh unleashed your inner rage, and it felt good."

X

Sangar Air Base lay shrouded in a perpetual smog of smoldering feces. Commandeered by the U.S. Military in December 2001, a single 10,499-foot runway bisected the massive compound. Military and contract personnel slept in tents, so it wouldn't look like a permanent occupation. Constructed in 1977, and used as a base of operations for the Soviet Union's ill-fated attempt to invade Afghanistan, Sangar was steeped in a history not even the clatter of construction or the whine of jet turbines could render irrelevant. A hodgepodge of Army Reservists served as guards at the secretive military detention facility located in the center of the complex.

At midnight, the metal doors of Sangar Prison, an aircraft hangar turned terrorist holding center, creaked open. It had cooled somewhat, only 79 degrees. A dry wind coughed its way past the buildings without offering any relief, and kicked up a small, protesting fog of dust and sand. Four bearded men, wearing fatigues, yanked a hooded prisoner through the doorway.

Specialist Aaron Strickland, the guard on duty, closed the *Hot Rod* magazine he was reading and reclined in his swivel chair. Behind him, a large dry-erase board sat on an easel. It was covered with numbers and dates, along with the letters "ISO" and "S-DEP," meaning "Isolation" and "Sleep Deprivation." Activities for the passengers of the S.S. Sangar. A radio chattered in the background - a guard reporting his status.

Strickland spit chewing tobacco into a Gatorade bottle and raised a hand in greeting. "Evenin', boys. What we got?"

"New guest," one of the bearded men said as he shoved the hooded figure toward Strickland's cluttered desk. "This one's a VIP." Dried blood seeped through the burlap bag covering Hamza Nassar's head. Five-eight or so, the prisoner wore traditional Afghan clothing and was built like a linebacker.

"What'd this raghead do?" Strickland asked, pointing. "Get caught fuckin' a goat?"

The bearded men did not laugh. They never laughed. They hunted men for a living. Low-level guards were not part of their club. "Soldier, get off your fucking ass and call someone to get this mother-fucker out of here," the leader said. "We don't have all night."

Strickland thumbed his radio. "Sergeant." A crackle of static. Strickland adjusted a knob on the handset. "Sergeant, we got a new detainee. Bring a welcoming party."

"Roger that," came the reply.

A few minutes later, five large Army soldiers entered the room. Rumor had it the Crash Team members, as they were called, had been specially trained to handle violent prisoners. In reality, they were just the biggest guys anyone could find.

One toted an elaborate assortment of chains and belts; another carried an orange jumpsuit and a Hannibal Lecter muzzle. The shackles clanked like sinister wind chimes as the soldiers encircled the new guest. No longer needed, the men from the hunting party headed into the night, searching for more prey.

The Crash Team members were friendlier. At least they talked. "What's up, Strick?" one of them asked, nodding at Strickland.

"Evening, Sergeant." Strickland nodded back.

Sergeant Rodney Cullen stepped forward. "Time for show-n-tell," he said as he snatched the sack from Nassar's head. The prisoner blinked continually, his pupils clawing for the right setting. Cullen put his face two inches from the prisoner's ear and shouted, "Welcome to Sangar Prison, bitch!" One of the Crash Team members started to translate, but Cullen held up his hand. "He gets it, Anderson. Jesus! A complete idiot knows when someone's bustin' his balls."

The prisoner's black eyes never left Cullen's face - studying it, memorizing it, in case there was another time, another meeting, another outcome. Finally, Sergeant Cullen backed away. "Jefferson." Cullen pointed at the detainee. "Do your thing."

Sergeant Tyler Jefferson, a refrigerator of a soldier, stepped forward and folded his arms. At 6 foot 4 inches, he towered over the prisoner. His tightly fitted camouflage uniform seemed somehow crisp and clean, even here.

Suddenly, the prisoner lunged. Not far, but enough to make Jefferson flinch. The room echoed with laughter and catcalls. "Aw, Big Jeff, he made *you* his little bitch!"

Jefferson regained his composure, re-approached the detainee, and dropped an orange jumpsuit at the prisoner's feet. "You are now the property of the United States. We own your ass-" The prisoner drove his knee into Jefferson's crotch, stopping him mid-sentence. Jefferson never saw it coming. He dropped to the floor and groaned.

In a violent frenzy, the other guards slammed Nassar face-first into the concrete floor and wrenched his arms behind his back. In short order, Nassar was stripped, cavity searched, shoved into the jumpsuit, shackled, muzzled, and snatched to his feet.

Strickland lounged in his chair, watching Jefferson rearrange his testicles, as the Crash Team dragged the detainee out of the room. When Sergeant Jefferson finally got to his feet, Strickland remained the only one close enough to hear him whisper, "I'm going to kill that fuckin' raghead."

CHAPTER 3

In the bowels of Sangar Prison were dungeon-like cells reserved for high-value prisoners in the War on Terror. Inside one of these cells, Hamza Nassar dangled from the ceiling, suspended by his shackled wrists. Only his toes touched the floor. After three hours, his arms were being pulled from their sockets. This was only the beginning. Nassar knew he would probably die in the hands of the infidels. Though not afraid, he was not eager to withstand the humiliations his brothers had endured. At least, not without a fight.

At 0515 hours, Nassar defecated in his jumpsuit and shouted for relief. The two guards on duty, Private Jessica Hart and Specialist John Bernard, were Army Reservists, freshly deployed weekend warriors. Hart was a single mother of two and a part-time college student. Bernard, a Walmart assistant manager in civilian life, joined the Army Reserve after 9/11 out of a sense of patriotism.

At Sangar Prison, most of the Reservists were careless, at least early in their tour. They had no experience guarding prisoners. Before mobilizing to Afghanistan, they enjoyed dull civilian lives. One weekend a month, the Reservists played soldier. They pulled gate guard duty during the day and drank cheap liquor with their buddies at night.

Hart gagged when she entered Nassar's cell. Bernard covered his mouth and nose with his hand, but it did not help. They had dealt with dirty diapers before, but this was a full-blown intestinal assault from a 42-year-old man. Nassar wailed pitifully, ashamed to look them in the face.

Bernard hefted the prisoner onto his shoulder while Hart unlocked the chains. The second his wrist was unshackled, Nassar whipped the four-foot chain left to right, then back. The open handcuffs swooped silently through the air, like a hawk seeking its prey. Private Hart didn't have time to scream. Jagged metal ripped through her face, splattering the wall with flesh and blood. She blacked out and fractured her skull on the concrete floor.

Nassar looped the chain around Bernard's neck and yanked him to the floor. Broken blood vessels erupted in his eyes, and white foam oozed from his purple lips. By the time the Crash Team arrived, he was nearly brain dead.

Sergeant Tyler Jefferson and the other Crash Team members stopped short when they saw the carnage, but only for a moment. Fanning out into a malevolent ring, they closed in on the prisoner whose right hand still clutched the bloody chain.

CHAPTER 4

The water wouldn't stop. The water choked him, gagged him, suffocated him. Hamza Nassar had spent his entire life in an area dying for water. Now, he was dying from it. The water would. Not. Stop.

Neither would the voices. Not the same ones, not the ones belonging to the men who had initially subdued him. These voices were calmer, more frightening, more professional. These menacing voices whispered in his ear. They screamed in his face.

"How you like that, asshole?"

"You still think 9/11 was a good idea?"

"Where's Bin Laden?"

"You want this to stop? Tell us, when's the next attack?"

He felt hot breath against his ear. He could not see well, but his blindfold had slipped enough to allow him a glimpse of one of the speakers' faces. His eyes were the color of slate. His pupils were tiny. Then, everything went black. The voice grew louder.

"Keep going until he talks." More water.

Twelve feet above, in an air duct, a soldier watched the waterboarding below. He was careful not to move. Those guys down there heard things. The slightest wiggle and they'd know he was there. His legs ached, and he needed to piss. Two hours was a long time to remain motionless. He had to stay quiet. If they found him, if they knew he saw them, he could disappear. The guy in the black cowboy boots was obviously in charge. The silver tips gleamed in the glare of the interrogation lights. The man on the table passed out.

"Give it a rest for a while," the man in the boots said.

"I can wake him up," his partner replied.

"Nah. He isn't going anywhere. Besides, I gotta take a wicked shit."

"You sure?"

"Fuck yeah? He'll feel worse in an hour."

The men moved to the door.

"Leave the light on," the boss said, "and crank the music."

The other man pushed a button. Guns and Roses' "Welcome to the Jungle" blared from a boombox.

Finally, enough noise to cover his movement. The soldier moved carefully through the air duct. He curled up in a corner, stuck a needle between his toes, sighed, and wet his pants.

✕

That night, the soldier returned to the cool, cramped duct. Peering through a small ventilation hole, he couldn't see everybody in the room, but he could hear everything they said.

Dumbasses have no idea I am here, the soldier thought.

A group of men occupied the room below. Some wore Army uniforms. A man in an orange jumpsuit lay motionless on the floor. "Get 'em up," a gravelly voice said.

Two soldiers yanked the floor dweller to a weak-kneed standing position. One of them was Sergeant Rodney Cullen.

"Give him some pep, Doc." The same voice.

Another soldier, Major "Doc" Needham, came into view, a syringe in hand. He approached the men propping up the prisoner. "Is this really necessary?" Needham asked.

"Shut the fuck up and stick him, Doc," the voice said. "Just jab him with half an amp of epi. A total retard can stab someone."

The soldier in the duct had seen a lot. He went there whenever he was off-duty. He liked to watch. He got off on two things: Afghan opium and pain. He liked to dish it out - pain. He had a hard time finding a girl who would take it, and usually had to pay some whore to let him slap her around. Sheila back home liked it, at least when he got her high. When high, Sheila would do anything.

Doc Needham held up a cylinder. "This is an auto-injector, so I can fire it through clothing. Epinephrine hits like a mule. His heart rate will shoot up toward 200. For about 15 minutes, he's going to be wired, so hold on tight. Got it?"

"Yes, sir," Sergeant Cullen said.

"Now, give me something to shoot at," Needham said.

Cullen secured the captive's limp arm, and the doctor jabbed the EpiPen. The slumping man locked his legs and gasped. The soldier in the duct heard a prolonged, sucking intake of air. Cullen and his partner hung on for dear life.

The soldier in the duct was beginning to cramp again, but he knew he had to stay still a little longer. Once they were gone, he could do a little skin popping with some lovely Afghan smack.

"Load him on the chopper," the voice said. The soldiers wrangled the prisoner out the door. Doc Needham picked up his bag and headed in the opposite direction. "Where the fuck are you going, Doc?" the voice again.

Needham turned and said, "It's late. I'm going to bed."

"Hell no. You're going with us," the voice said. "You're gonna jump-start this asshole's battery one more time when we land. He has to be semi-functional, or we don't get our guy."

Needham's face reddened. "You're talking about 45 minutes from now?"

"Yep. We'll stand him up, and you'll light a fire under his jihadi ass."

"That much Epinephrine in such a short period could kill him, explode his heart."

"Well, Doc, you better not fuck it up, 'cause if this one drops dead before the swap, I will personally see to it that you spend the rest of your professional life in Mexico doing pap smears on clap-riddled hookers." Needham shook his head as he moved toward the door and the distant, distinctive thump of helicopter rotors.

"That's a good boy, Doc," the voice said. "Now, do your fucking job."

The soldier in the duct waited until the men below were gone. He shimmied backward toward the spot where he could manipulate his "works." Before the heroin hit him, he had one more thought. *The voice . . . that was the guy with the cowboy boots.*

CHAPTER 5

Fifty miles outside of Jalalabad, Afghanistan, a trio of al Qaeda vehicles convoyed over the rocky landscape - a dusty pickup truck, a battered SUV, and an out-of-place Mercedes sedan. The pickup sported a 50-caliber machine gun in its bed. They proceeded, tentatively, as if someone could actually see them in the forbidding darkness.

Several miles away, a chopper pilot spoke into his mic. "Be advised, Phantom 31. Standing by."

The response came almost instantly. "Phantom 31, you are clear to your objective."

The pilot keyed his mic as the American MH-47G Chinook helicopter smoothly vectored toward the cluster of vehicles. "Roger that. Phantom 31, pushing. ETA, three mikes."

"Roger."

He did the things pilots do, the stuff so seemingly effortless to the untrained eye, so precisely timed and endlessly practiced. The pilot couldn't see the crafts on his flanks, but he could sense them. He felt better knowing he was chaperoned by a pair of AH-6J Little Bird helicopters, his brothers from the U.S. Army's 160th Special Operations Aviation Regiment (SOAR). Nicknamed "The Night Stalkers," these men were the Army's best aviators. They were known for their lethality and expertise at nighttime operations.

The Little Birds raced over the surrounding hillsides, searching for hidden enemies using Forward-Looking Infrared (FLIR) cameras. After scouring the area, they called, "All clear."

The Chinook's rotors twirled cyclones of dust into the air as it approached the landing zone. Small stones rifled across the ground where they came to abrupt stops after bouncing off the wheels, sides, and windows of the small, parked armada. The pilot flashed the Chinook's cabin light, twice. The headlamps of the battered Mercedes sedan returned the signal.

The helicopter's engine idled. The pilot was not about to power down the craft. He reached up and threw a switch, and the rear door of the Chinook gaped open. The moment the tailgate hit the ground, eight heavily-armed men disembarked and formed a perimeter around a hooded prisoner. Though the soldiers were American, they wore no insignia.

Simultaneously, the driver of the Mercedes shouted in Arabic toward the SUV. Two jihadists wearing headscarves opened the rear door, reached in, and dragged a second hooded prisoner from the SUV.

The Americans and the terrorists approached one another with caution. When they met in the middle, the American's cut their prisoner's plastic flex-cuffs. They yanked off his hood, exposing a startled Hamza Nassar.

In unison, several men from the convoy shouted, "Allāhu Akbar."

In exchange, the terrorists released their captive, Chief Petty Officer David Walker, a U.S. Navy SEAL. Dazed and dehydrated, Walker stumbled forward, into the arms of his comrades. It had been five weeks since his capture. His hair and beard were unkempt, and his face was swollen from daily beatings.

Once each side had recovered their respective prisoner, they backed away to their places of origin. The rear gate of the Chinook hummed back into place, and the rotors spun ever faster. The Little Bird gunships ascended from the ridgeline as if to say, "We are here, and we are watching. Don't fuck with us."

The Chinook lifted into the night sky with the ungainly grace of a pelican. The men left on the ground listened as the thump of the rotors steadily diminished. They watched with careful relief as the AH-6Js dwindled in size, then disappeared into the darkness. On the ground, everyone clambered into the vehicles of the automotive flotilla.

Carefully concealed on a distant hillside, a team of U.S. Army Rangers watched and waited. The Ranger team leader's voice broke radio silence. "Target is in the SUV. I repeat, he's in the SUV."

"Roger that, light 'em up."

"Roger, wilco."

One of the Rangers painted the SUV with an infrared laser. Silently, the Little Birds popped up from behind their cover and fired. Two Hellfire missiles sprung from the helicopters and raced toward the SUV. The AGM-114KII missiles featured external blast fragmentation sleeves designed to eradicate everything in a 50-foot radius.

At that moment, as planned, a guy in the passenger side of the SUV heaved two canisters from his window. The white phosphorus grenades exploded 30 feet away with a brilliant white flame, then immediately produced a cloud of thick smoke. Momentarily blinded by the flash, the Ranger painting the SUV flipped up his night-vision goggles and rubbed his eyes. The Hellfire missiles veered sharply and slammed into a mountainside, missing the convoy by over 90 yards.

One hundred and sixty-three miles into the velvet sky, a KH-11 Kennan satellite slipped through space recording images at the rate of seven per second. Commonly known as the "Keyhole" satellite, the $1.25 billion toy used electro-optical digital imaging to create real-time optical observation capabilities. Its flyover had been carefully programmed with the Strike Team's mission. No one was happy when they saw the images. "How the hell did you miss everybody?"

Chapter 6

One November night, three years later, Sergeant Tyler Jefferson pulled the silver Dodge minivan into the driveway of his Dallas home. Gabby, his wife, sat quietly in the adjacent seat. Aliyah and Elijah dozed in the back. It was late for a school night, but tonight was special.

After Elijah's pee-wee football victory, the Jeffersons had met up with four other families to celebrate Aliyah's sixth birthday. And was there any better place for a party than Grimaldi's? Great friends, great cheesecake, and fabulous pizza. The neighborhood seemed ready for bed as Jefferson turned off the ignition and got out of the van.

"Get on the ground, now!" The voice came from Jefferson's left. He pivoted as an indescribable agony shot through his body. Jefferson recognized the pulsating electric shock. He had been tasered before as part of his military police training. One of the requirements before receiving certification to discharge the weapon was to undergo what the instructors called "the experience." Once you felt the complete disruption of your own body's natural electrical system, you tended to exercise considerable restraint before using it.

Jefferson landed hard on the driveway, his head glancing off the side of the van. Warm blood oozed from his forehead. Knees dug into his back and neck. He felt the cold metal cinch of handcuffs, which immediately restricted blood flow into his wrists.

"Daddy!" Aliyah was frantic. Birthday balloons floated away, dancing merrily on the slight breeze. The sight of the bright Mylar bouquet starkly contrasted the horror show unfolding on the ground.

One of the six men in full body armor grabbed Aliyah's arm. Gabby reacted with the ferocity of a tigress. "Get your damn hands off my baby," she said. She snatched her daughter to her chest and shoved the business end of a five-inch heel into the man's calf.

"Fuck!" He reached for her.

"Dawson! Damn it! Dawson!"

The man stood rigid. "Yes, sir."

"Quit fucking around. Secure the prisoner and get in the vehicle."

"Yes, sir."

Gabby released her terror. "Who are you, and what are you doing to my husband?"

The man in charge spoke. "Ma'am, I'm Deputy Marshal José Rivera, with the U.S. Marshals Service. We are executing an arrest warrant on behalf of the U.S. Army."

"The Army? For what?" Gabby searched his face for answers.

"For murder."

"What? Are you crazy? He didn't murder anyone."

"Calm down, ma'am. I promise you no one will harm your husband unless he resists."

"Resist?" she said. "He can't even walk."

Without another word. The men tossed Jefferson through the van's side door. Motors revved. Tires spun on the pavement, and they were gone.

⚔

Shortly after that, at Fort Custer, 634 miles across West Texas, an officer answered his phone. "Colonel Paine, speaking." Colonel Covington Paine knew that no one from his staff was calling. No one on his team dared to ring after 2200 hours without a good reason.

The voice was pleasant, sure of itself, and female. "Colonel, this is Rose Sanchez. I am a blogger with the Independent Online Press, and I have a few questions."

"You're with whom? And, you are a what?"

On the other end of the line from a confused and increasingly irritated Paine, Rose Sanchez grinned a little. *At least the man knows his grammar,* she thought, *even if he doesn't know about blogging.* Blogs were still an oddity. The term "blog" had only been recognized by the Merriam-Webster Dictionary the previous year.

"It's a web-based log, sir, called a blog," Rose said. "I'm an independent news reporter."

"I'm sorry, I don't even talk to legitimate reporters, ma'am," Paine responded.

Before he replaced the handset on the receiver, he heard one word. "Sangar."

"What did you say?" he asked.

"Would you like to comment about the new prosecutions coming out of Sangar Prison?"

Paine clenched his teeth. Years of Army training immediately engaged. "I have no comment," he said.

"What are the charges?"

"No comment."

"Who are the defendants?"

"No comment."

"When are the trials?"

"Miss, what don't you understand about 'No comment?'" Sanchez kept firing questions. Paine's head began to hurt. "Ma'am. I need to apologize." Thinking she was about to get the scoop, Sanchez finally quit talking. "Manners cost nothing," Paine said. "I was ill-mannered, and I am sorry."

"Does that mean you would like to comment on my story about the atrocities that occurred at Sangar?"

"No, not at all. Goodnight," he said and hung up.

$$\mathbb{X}$$

Rose Sanchez closed her flip phone and sank into the couch. She knew how to get what she needed. Her source was unimpeachable, but she could tell by Paine's reaction she'd jumped the gun.

Rose did not particularly love writing. She hated the hours and the research, but the internet was making celebrities out of all sorts of people, and she might as well hop on the bandwagon. A little over a year ago, she'd decided to try her hand at a blog. Get enough suckers to follow you, and suddenly, advertisers were throwing money at you.

Recently, she'd uncovered a route to more exciting stories. Stories that might lead to more advertisers and bigger paydays. Rose did not care about journalism. She wanted notoriety. Her pursuit of stories was less than orthodox. Ten years as an aspiring gymnast failed to produce an Olympic career. A five-inch growth spurt when she was 14 torpedoed her chances on the uneven parallel bars. Still, she had developed certain physical flexibility she employed to pry information out of whatever source she could find.

She thrived academically in her four years at Georgetown University and developed a broad range of valuable connections inside the Beltway. Stunning eyes, long legs, and a fastidiously maintained physique were as valuable to her as dogged persistence was to Woodward and Bernstein. Male, female, single, married, no one held out long when Rose Sanchez achieved journalistic missile lock.

She heard the knock she'd been expecting. That would be her contact. Rose stood, slipped out of her panties, and walked to the door wearing only a casually buttoned men's dress shirt.

Chapter 7

Sergeant Jefferson fidgeted in the middle bench seat, as the van headed west on Interstate 20 from Dallas to El Paso. They had been driving non-stop for five hours. Next to him sat Army Reserve Sergeant Rodney Cullen. Cullen was arrested the same night as Jefferson. In the back of the van, a third man slumped alone. He sported an un-military growth of facial tumbleweed and unwashed, almost shoulder-length hair.

"What's your name, buddy?" Cullen asked the grungy man.

"Everybody calls me Greaser," the man said, raking his fingers through his hair.

"Where you from?"

"Around."

"Have we met before?"

"Maybe."

"Did you work at Sangar?"

"For a while," Greaser said. "They sent me home early."

"Weren't you in second platoon?" Cullen asked.

Greaser nodded, slouched down in his seat, and closed his eyes.

Jefferson leaned into Cullen and whispered, "You know that dickhead?"

"Yeah. He worked the front desk at Sangar Prison, the night shift," Cullen replied.

"Oh, yeah. I remember. His nasty ass always smelled like rotten meat," Jefferson said.

Aaron "Greaser" Strickland bounced around a lot as many junkies do, after returning from Afghanistan. His attendance at his monthly Army Reserve drills was sporadic. He used forged doctors' notes to avoid AWOL charges. Finding Jefferson and Cullen had been easy for the Army. Strickland, however, posed a bit more of an issue.

The night of Jefferson's arrest, the U.S. Marshals Service raided Strickland's last known address only to find a dozen illegal Mexicans occupying the one-bedroom apartment. The next day, they tried his mother's house on the outskirts of Fort Worth. No luck. Meanwhile, Jefferson and Cullen languished in a Dallas jail. Eventually, the Army learned that Strickland was already in custody, pending trial for a DUI. A local judge happily released him to the Army's outstretched, prosecutorial arms. Once all three men were collared, they began the nine-hour ordeal to El Paso in a 15-passenger van.

The van motored west as Jefferson settled into his seat and tried to get some rest. It was no use. His uncertain future, his bladder, and the throbbing pain caused by the tight handcuffs kept him awake and uneasy. "Hey, I'm about to piss my pants," Jefferson called to Private Bo Kaminski, the military policeman driving the van.

Kaminski, a kid barely out of Basic Training, was nodding off. His fourth Red Bull hadn't worked. "Alright, we'll stop at the next exit, but just long enough to take a leak and get some gas," Kaminski said over his shoulder.

Ten minutes later, Kaminski pulled the van into a 24-hour Shell station in Stanton, Texas, and parked at a gas pump. In the passenger seat slept his partner, Sergeant George Booth, a long-time MP. Sergeant Booth was a squat man in his late 30s, with a thick Afro nowhere close to being in line with Army regulations.

"Booth, get up." Kaminski nudged his partner. "We gotta get gas."

"Pump it yourself, Private," Booth mumbled, barely awake.

"What about the prisoners?" Kaminski asked. "They got to pee."

"Let 'em take a leak," Booth said. "But keep an eye on 'em."

Kaminski got out of the van and opened the side door. After the passengers crawled out, the group trudged toward the mini-mart. Inside, Kaminski bought another energy drink and a can of Skoal dipping tobacco. "Make it quick," he said to the captives, trying to sound authoritarian.

The prisoners nodded in agreement and moved toward the men's bathroom near the back of the dingy service station, their hands and feet still shackled. Kaminski turned and walked outside to pump the gas.

"This is typical Army bullshit," Jefferson said. "You see any officers in handcuffs?"

"Fuck no." Cullen gritted his teeth. "They always blame the enlisted."

Strickland, head lowered, growled into his tee-shirt. "I'm gonna get the fuck out of here. I'm not going back to jail."

"You won't get far," Cullen said. "We're in the middle of nowhere."

Strickland ignored him and shimmied toward the counter, his chains dragging on the floor. Behind the cash register, a skinny clerk in a pink halter top restocked the cigarette display. "Sweet tat," Strickland said, pointing to a purplish butterfly tattoo on her left shoulder. The clerk smiled, revealing mangled teeth, meth teeth.

Cullen watched the interaction from across the store. "That guy's got balls," Cullen said to Jefferson as he gestured at Strickland with his thumb. "He's hitting on that chick while wearing shackles."

"Fuckin' loser," Jefferson muttered as he slammed the bathroom door open and shuffled inside. Cullen followed. Jefferson used the toilet and walked out of the bathroom. On the wall, he spotted a payphone and dialed the operator. He struggled to lift the handset to his ear; the chain around his waist restricted his movement.

The phone rang. *Pick up, pick up, pick up.*

He heard Gabby's voice, distant and echoing. "Hello?"

"Will you accept a collect call from Tyler?" the operator asked.

"Yes! Yes!" Gabby said. "Tyler? Is that you?"

"Honey, don't talk. Listen. The MPs have me. We're headed to El Paso. They're going to court-martial me."

Gabby started to respond, but Jefferson cut her off as he focused on Kaminski, who was capping the tank. "Gabby, I gotta go. Love you."

He hung up as Kaminski hustled into the store and shouted, "Let's roll."

Jefferson pushed open the bathroom door and hollered, "Hey guys, we gotta bolt."

A toilet flushed, and Cullen exited. "Where the hell is Greaser?" Jefferson asked.

"I thought he was with you," Cullen said.

They did not have to search for long. Greaser was gone, and so was the clerk.

CHAPTER 8

"Fuck, fuck, fuuuuuuuuuuuuuuuck!" Kaminski dry heaved in his mouth.

"Calm down, Private," Booth said, as he rubbed his eyes. "Did you remove his shackles?"

"No, Sergeant. Absolutely not."

"No one expects you to hold his dick while he pisses. He couldn't have gone far. It's a flat area with no vegetation. Get in the van. We'll find him, and no one would ever know he'd been misplaced."

Kaminski's heart pounded. "Fuuuuuuuuuuuuuck." They rode around the streets of Stanton, where 2,500 people slept, hoping to spot Strickland. The streets were barren, aside from the occasional stray dog. Two hours later, when the van stopped at a red light, Kaminski turned to Booth and said, "Let's call it a night."

"No. We keep looking." Booth's bloodshot eyes glanced from side to side.

"You assholes better call for backup," Jefferson said from the back of the van.

Booth pivoted and locked eyes with Jefferson. "Shut the fuck up and watch it with the asshole stuff. You're in enough trouble." Jefferson rolled to his side and closed his eyes. At 4:30 a.m., Booth finally called Fort Custer to report the escape on his cell phone. "Local police are assisting," Booth told the MP dispatcher. Kaminski winced when he heard Booth lie.

"Let me speak to the police officer in charge," the dispatcher responded.

"My cell's at one percent," Booth said. "I'll have him call you." Booth hung up as if the phone had gone dead.

Jefferson sat up, laughing, and said, "You guys are so fucked."

The MPs ignored him. After a few minutes, Booth realized that Jefferson was right. So, he called 9-1-1.

At 5:15 a.m., a police cruiser slid to a stop in front of the van. Deputy Sherriff Louis P. Fuller lit a fresh Camel cigarette and climbed out of the car. Nothing ever happened in this town after midnight. Who knew it would be a lousy night to hit the Jim Beam? Fuller, a jaded, white man in his forties, hiked up his sagging pants, pressed his black cowboy hat onto his head, and strolled toward the Army van. Booth lowered the window. The essence of stale sweat, microwaveable burritos, and unbrushed teeth smacked Fuller in the face.

Booth and Kaminski sat in the van chomping away at their breakfast from the Shell station like they were cutting gym class in high school. Jefferson and Cullen slept in the back.

"How the fuck did you two dumbasses allow a dangerous prisoner to escape in my jurisdiction?" the Sheriff asked.

"He's not dangerous," Booth replied in a defensive tone.

"Is he any less escaped?" Fuller's eyes narrowed to crinkled slits.

"Officer," Booth said, "can you call in some backup?"

"It's 'Sheriff,' and I'm the only backup you got." Fuller pulled a notepad and pen from his shirt pocket. "So, who is this escapee?"

"His name is Greaser," Kaminski said.

"Son." Fuller pointed his gloved finger at Kaminski. "You go around this part of the world asking if anyone's seen 'Greaser,' you're lucky if you only get half your ass kicked."

Kaminski's body stiffened at the remark.

"Now, about what time did he depart your supervision?" the Sheriff asked.

"0225 hours," Booth said, attempting to sound efficient and military. The crumbs on the front of his shirt didn't help his case.

Fuller cocked his head. "What in God's name have you been doing for the past three hours?"

"Lookin'," Booth said.

"Lookin' my ass." The Sheriff waited for some sort of reaction from Booth. He didn't get one. Fuller took a slow drag on his cigarette and exhaled in Booth's face. "Boy, your prisoner's long gone."

Booth furrowed his brow as he slowly began to comprehend the shit-storm headed his way.

"Tell you what, I'll forward his info to the Highway Patrol." Fuller keyed his radio handset, then stopped. "I can't call in 'Greaser,' you morons. Does this guy have a real name?"

"Here it is." Booth flipped through the pages of his clipboard, trying to keep his composure. "It's Strickland. Specialist Aaron Strickland."

"What does this clown look like?"

"He's five feet nine inches," Booth said, "black hair, brown eyes, and a tattoo on his back."

"What type of tattoo?"

Booth pointed at the clipboard. "Says here, 'Marilyn Manson.'"

Fuller rubbed his stubbled chin. "You mean Charles Manson, the cult killer guy?"

"No, Marilyn Manson, the singer," Kaminski said as he rolled his eyes.

"Who the fuck is that?" Fuller asked.

"He's that satanic guy," Kaminski said, "the one with fake tits."

Fuller's cigarette dangled from the corner of his mouth. "So, you're saying the prisoner you lost in my jurisdiction is a damn Satanist?"

"I guess so." Booth shrugged.

Fuller whirled and walked toward his cruiser, unleashing a barrage of obscenities so foul it made Kaminski blush. Back at his car, Fuller relayed Strickland's name and description to the dispatcher. Before he closed his door, he hollered back toward the van, "He's got a three-hour head start. You assholes better keep looking because I'm going home. This is most definitely not my fucking problem."

Chapter 9

Back in Dallas, he picked up on the first ring. "This is Reggie."

A woman's voice, strained and agitated, shot from the earpiece. "Reggie? Is that you?"

"Who is this?"

Gabby had not spoken with Reggie Jefferson in over seven years - ever since he went to prison. "It's me, Gabby, Tyler's wife."

Reggie heard sobs. "What's wrong, sweetie?" Reggie asked. "You okay?"

"It's Tyler," Gabby said.

"Is he dead?"

"No. God, no!"

"Then what's up?"

"Some men took him a few days ago. We came home. They were waiting. They used a taser. They did it in front of my babies! They took him away in a van."

"What men?"

"Marshals."

"What'd Tyler do this time?"

"He didn't do nothin'," she said.

"What are they sayin' he did?"

"The Army says he murdered someone."

"Whoa. That's some serious shit."

"Reggie." Her voice trembled. "I need your help."

"Name it."

"Can you meet me at the kids' school, Lee Elementary, off Grand Prairie Road?"

"I'll be there in 30 minutes," Reggie said. "And sweetie?"

"Yeah?"

"Don't worry. Ain't never been no one tough enough to take me down - sure as hell ain't no one tough enough to take down my boy."

※

Reggie Jefferson pulled his black Escalade with illegally tinted windows into the Lee Elementary parking lot as Gabby walked out the front door with her children. Reggie lowered his window and waved. Mirrored sunglasses blocked his eyes, but not the three-inch scar that zig-zagged from his left eye to his left ear.

"Nice to see ya, Gabby." Reggie lowered his sunglasses. "It's been a while."

Gabby gave an apprehensive smile. "Thanks for meeting me on such short notice."

"Who's that?" Elijah pointed a small finger at Reggie. His voice was skeptical.

"Don't be rude." Gabby squeezed the boy's hand.

"I'm your gramps," Reggie said with a chuckle. "Didn't nobody tell you about me?"

"I thought you were dead," Elijah said.

Gabby, embarrassed, put her hand over Elijah's mouth and said, "You best shush your mouth."

Reggie roared with laughter. "I ain't dead yet, son."

The Jeffersons had told their children that Grandpa Reggie was a famous cop who died fighting bad guys. Their story was only partly true. Yes, Reggie was a former cop, but he was more infamous than famous. He was also alive and well.

Reggie had worked undercover in his past life, deep inside the West Side Scorpions, a ruthless local gang. One muggy summer night, years ago, the Dallas Police raided the gang's headquarters. A raging firefight erupted, and a blood bath ensued. When a police officer lost his life, the brass blamed Reggie, who happened to be in the house during the raid. The police claimed it was an ambush, and Reggie was their scapegoat. In reality, an overeager lieutenant prematurely launched the assault before their SWAT backup arrived.

In the aftermath, Reggie took the fall for an array of trumped-up charges and went to prison. Sergeant Jefferson decided to cut ties with him. He had never been much of a father anyway.

After Reggie served his time in the penitentiary, he found employment as a security consultant for gang-affiliated strip clubs scattered throughout Texas. His base of operations was Cheetaz Gentlemen's Club, a two-story building in West Dallas. Cheetaz had become legendary for having the most beautiful black strippers in Texas, a dinner buffet fit for a king, and the occasional stabbing.

Gabby and the kids hopped into their minivan and followed Reggie's Escalade. After a short drive, they pulled into the Cheetaz parking lot. Before Reggie had time to kill the ignition, Gabby had leaped out of her van and snatched his door open.

"You gotta be kiddin', Reggie," she shouted at him. "You brought my kids to a strip club."

"This is where I work, Gabby. Don't worry, we don't open 'til four."

Gabby shook her head and remotely opened the minivan door. Aliyah ran to Reggie. "Hi, grandpa," she said and hugged his thick leg. "I'm glad you're not dead."

"Me too," Reggie said as he bent down, gently scooped her up, and squeezed her. After he unlocked the side entrance, Reggie led them inside. He turned on some music and flashing lights - distractions for the kids. Reggie and Gabby sat at a table, as the children ran up and down the catwalk.

"Start at the beginning and tell me everything you know about Tyler's situation." Reggie folded his hands on the table and leaned back. Gabby recounted the night of the arrest as accurately as she could. Reggie listened intently; two decades of investigative experience started to process what he heard. "Where is Tyler now?" he asked.

"He said something about being taken to El Paso."

"Fort Custer. That's where they're going. That gives us something to work with. We gotta find out exactly what they're saying he did, and who is saying he did it."

Gabby was struggling to keep it together. "What should I do?" she asked him.

"Pack a bag and never go anywhere without your phone. When I call and say it's 'Go Time,' we won't have a second to waste."

CHAPTER 10

On my drive to work at Fort Arnold, South Carolina, I thought about how quickly my time in the Army had passed. It was November 2005, and my tour was coming to an end. Though my future employment plans were uncertain, I knew we were staying in South Carolina. With baby number three on the way, my wife, Annabelle, insisted that we live close to her family.

What made South Carolina challenging was its proximity to my in-laws, Sterling and Martha Hillyard. Sterling owned a commercial real estate company. Martha was a homemaker and four-time president of the local Junior League. The couple spent most of their leisure time at the all-white Hunter's Glen Country Club. There, they played golf, bridge, and tennis, and bragged about their grandbabies. They made sure that everyone understood their son-in-law was only "*half* Latino."

My dad still lived in Westfield, an hour north of Pittsburgh. He liked to keep to himself. Dad had been a bona fide door kicker, a grunt. He served 10 years as an enlisted infantryman, including two tours in Vietnam. Now, he was a taciturn man. The only way I'd ever found out anything about his Army career had been through his buddies.

He met my mother, Marisol Rivera-Pérez, while he was stationed in Heidelberg, Germany, during the Cold War. She was the daughter of his former First Sergeant. On the rare occasions we talked, he reminded me that I took the easy way out by going to law school: "Real soldiers spend their time in the field, not behind a desk."

I met Annabelle in college. I was a junior at Pitt, and she attended Chatham College, formerly Pennsylvania College for Women. I never did quite understand how Annabelle, a southern belle, strayed so far from her roots. Willowy and blonde, Annabelle radiated an allure of helplessness I later came to realize was carefully ingrained in "young ladies of genteel breeding," particularly in South Carolina. The "allure" could more accurately be called a "façade" because Annabelle was about as helpless as a female grizzly bear.

With her dropped consonants, doe eyes, flirtatious smile, and drop-dead beauty, the moment she accepted my fumbling offer to get a coffee, I never dated anyone else. Eight months after our wedding, Ethan arrived, followed 10 months later by his baby sister, Eva.

The autumn sun blazed against a searing, blue background, as I passed through Fort Arnold's entrance. A light breeze kissed against the Stars and Stripes, causing it to lap lazily against the flagpole. This morning, I was late for work, and the Army frowns on lateness. You can get locked up in the brig for being late. With 90 days and a wake-up before civilian life, I officially did not give a shit.

I worked for the Army Trial Defense Service. TDS, for short. A TDS lawyer is the Army's equivalent of a public defender. TDS is the dumping ground for JAG lawyers deemed rebels, and rebels don't last long in the Army. I took whatever cases they gave me, from desertion to pot-smoking, and every so often, a serious crime. I spent my days defending drunk and disorderly cases, dereliction of duty cases, and general "I'm a fuck-up, so I joined the Army" cases. After three years in TDS, I was burned-out, and I counted down the days until my discharge.

This morning, the parking lot was packed, except for the row closest to the building, which had a dozen empty spaces reserved for senior officers. I slid my hunter green Chevy Malibu into the vacant "Military Judge" spot. Her Honor was on vacation all week. She wouldn't mind. I hurried toward my place of duty, which was a Vietnam-era barracks converted into a law office. I used the rear entrance to avoid the inevitable crowd of soldiers waiting in the hallway.

Today was Friday: walk-ins, low-level, ash and trash cases. Soldiers that showed up and were willing to wait long enough were guaranteed a chance to tell a genuine, Army JAG lawyer the story of how their fuck-up was not theirs but somebody else's fault. It was the same story, over and over again. My advice rarely changed: "Suck it up, take your punishment like a soldier and drive on."

I was the office supervisor. So, the walk-ins went to my two junior colleagues. Both were fresh out of law school and brimming with the idea of "liberty and justice for all." Above my office door hung a sign: "Senior Defense Counsel," my official title.

As I unpacked my briefcase, I heard a knock on my door. It was my loyal but slightly neurotic, second-in-command, Captain Julia Myers. Everybody called her Jules. Five-foot-ten, athletic, with a plain face framed by hipster Ray-Ban eyeglasses.

Jules graduated from Brown University, where she was All-American in swimming, with a degree in Women's Studies. After graduating from Cornell Law School with honors, she joined the Army JAG Corps looking for adventure. Quickly identified as a misfit, Jules was sent to TDS. Apparently, she ranted one too many times to one too many superior officers about how women should be allowed in the Infantry. Now, she worked with me - the first one in and the last one to leave - every day.

"Captain O'Donnell," she said, "do you have a moment? It's urgent."

"Jules, don't call me Captain. We're the same rank," I said, not for the first time. "What's going on?"

Jules dropped a stack of manila folders on my desk. "You need to delegate these cases," she said.

Without looking at them, I handed them back to her. "Like I've told you before, split the walk-ins between you and John. You don't need to wait for me to assign these cases. And, Jules, this is not urgent."

"Yes, sir," she said and walked toward the door. Halfway out, she stopped and faced me. "Major Dill stopped by earlier." Her eyebrows arched. "He wanted to know where you were."

Major Richard Dill was my supervisor. He had not stopped by my office in months, though I didn't mind. Dill's slothfulness was exceeded only by his ignorance of trial practice. On the rare occasions he showed up, I heard the same lame story about his last trial, his only trial, over 18 years ago. I would smile and act interested.

"What did you tell him?" I asked Jules.

"I told him your kid was sick."

"Which kid?"

She rolled her eyes. "Does it matter? He's not sure if you have two or twelve."

I nodded in agreement. "What did he want?"

"He didn't say. He avoids this place like the plague, so it must be something big."

CHAPTER 11

I wasn't in a hurry to see Major Dill. I considered putting off the confrontation until after the weekend. Still, I did not want him popping back into my office unannounced. Dill's sole job was to supervise and train young Army defense lawyers. He did neither. He merely bided his time until he could retire at the 21-year mark. Dill delegated most of his duties to me and spent his days going to medical appointments for a variety of mostly imagined ailments.

I knocked on Dill's door, three times, in case he was asleep. From inside, I heard, "Yes?"

"Captain O'Donnell, reporting," I said.

"Get in here, Max," the voice said. I opened the door and entered. Dill's cluttered office smelled like a Burger King dumpster. Behind his desk sat a trashcan overflowing with fast-food bags, Doritos wrappers, and empty cans of Diet Pepsi.

A dedicated nail biter, Dill was 52-years old, single, pudgy, and balding. He lived alone, unless you counted his three Siamese cats. His face, discolored by years of off-and-on chain-smoking, wore a constant frown. His resentment for the Army grew every time the promotion list came out, and his name wasn't on it. Lieutenant Colonel was not in the cards for "Why do you think they call him Dick" Dill.

Dill wore a faded camouflage uniform and black boots that had not been shined in years. His shirt strained unsuccessfully to contain his beer gut. He didn't stand to greet me, nor did he shake my hand. He kept his feet on his desk as he flipped through a *Maxim* magazine.

I stood at attention and saluted. "Sir, Captain O'Donnell reporting."

"Enough with the high-speed shit. Sit." I sat, and Dill reached for a bowl of candy sitting on his desk. He fished around with his fingers, pulled out a piece of candy corn, and dropped it into his mouth. His chewing was loud and laborious. "Mmmm. Want some?" he asked.

I held up my right hand. "No, thank you, sir."

"Suit yourself," he said. "Halloween only comes once a year." I nodded as he chomped away. After he swallowed, he passed me the bowl. "Don't be shy," he said. "Take some for your little ones."

Dill was notorious for wasting time, so I grabbed two boxes of Milk Duds, thanked him, and cut to the chase. "Sir, why did you want to see me?"

Dill flipped through a stack of manila folders on his desk, then handed me a slim one. "Before you open that, be aware." Dill picked at his teeth with his left index finger. "This is delicate. Some reservists got into trouble in Afghanistan. Prison guards. They beat the shit out of some detainees. I'm sure it's all in the file. I only flipped through it. Been busy lately, you know, with the retirement. The VA takes forever."

I opened the manila folder. Inside, there were maybe 20 pages. "Where's the rest of the file?" I asked.

"The trial counsel will send it to you shortly."

I read the first page and closed the folder. "This is a premeditated murder case."

Dill didn't flinch. "The facts are cut and dry," he said.

"Cut and dry?" I drew in a deep breath and released it. "Sir, I've never done a murder case."

"You'll do fine, Max." I started to stand, but Dill's next sentence shoved me back into the chair. "Pack your bags," he said. "You got to get out to Fort Custer ASAP and get ahead of this situation."

"What?"

"You heard me," Dill said. "You're going to Texas."

"Sir, if this case is in El Paso, couldn't they find a lawyer someplace closer than South Carolina?"

"There aren't enough defense lawyers to go around."

"There are dozens of JAGs in Texas."

"They're all conflicted out, or they're otherwise unavailable."

I squinted hard. Dill's explanation made no sense. Though he wasn't clever enough to be making this stuff up. I had a much more pressing issue. "My wife is due any day now with our third child," I said, raising my voice.

"That's right!" Dill slapped his palm on his desk. "You already have two. Damn. Are you trying to start a basketball team? Ever give that girl a rest?"

What an asshole, I thought.

"Captain Julia Myers is perfect for this case," I said. "She's an excellent trial lawyer."

Dill didn't look up from his hot pursuit of another piece of candy. "I appreciate the glowing endorsement of your colleague," he said. "However, this case requires experience."

"Sir, I only have a couple of months left in the Army, and I haven't found a job yet." I waited for him to make eye contact. He didn't, so I continued, "You told me I could take my excess leave when the baby is born."

"Duly noted, Max. This case should be resolved well before that time."

The voice inside my head screamed, *let it go.* The voice out of my mouth had other ideas. "Sir, I don't want this case," I said. "Even if we get an expedited trial, which I doubt, I don't have time for this."

I prepared for an ass chewing. It didn't come. Instead, Dill smiled. "Ah, that's the catch. The prosecution is offering a once-in-a-lifetime plea deal. If your client takes a dive, he'll get a light sentence."

"Something's not right about that," I said.

"Meaning?"

"Meaning, I have not seen the evidence or spoken with my client, and they want me to cut a deal?"

"You can review the evidence later. Strike while the iron's hot. If you fly out there and save this man's life, especially without seeing the evidence, I'll put you in for an Army Achievement Medal."

"Why would they cut this guy a break?" I asked.

Dill tried hard to look wise. He folded his hands and leaned back in his chair. "These detainee abuse cases are getting too much media attention. Truth is, nobody gives a shit about these jihadi terrorists, except the media and left-wing liberals. The press acts like these prisoners are saints, while making our boys look like Nazis. They're making us all look bad. The Army wants to wrap this up quickly and with discretion. Nobody wants a messy trial. I am sure you understand."

I didn't. "Premeditated murder in the military carries a mandatory life sentence," I said. "Sometimes, murder gets the needle."

"Max," Dill interrupted. "These cases involve some half-wits who opened up a can of whup-ass on a prisoner or two . . . or five. I can't keep track of all this. I assigned you to one of them: Jackson, Jordan, something like that. Hell, I don't know, and I don't care. All I know is someone, somewhere, who has a lot more rank than I do, is trying to make a point. Plead the damn thing out and come home in time for your leave. That is all."

I sat silently in the chair, thinking of how I would explain this situation to my wife.

"What part of 'that is all' do you not get?" he said. "You are dismissed."

I stood, holding the file and my Milk Duds. "How do I contact my client?" I asked.

"Don't worry. The prosecution will get you that information in due course."

"Take something for the road." Major Dill pointed at the candy bowl.

"No, thank you. I have a PT test coming up."

"Good luck with that." Dill laughed. "I haven't taken one in 10 years."

I glanced back at him.

"You know, because of my bad hip," he said.

"Roger, sir," I said and walked out the door.

CHAPTER 12

The Pentagon briefing room felt energized. Reporters hoping for some kind of news story hurried to their seats. An intense man stood at the edge of the stage, repeating his lines, like a thespian on opening night. If ever a man were born to wear an Army uniform, it was Colonel Covington Spencer Paine.

Paine, 45, with a skeleton-like face, stood erect with a fresh high and tight haircut. A backup quarterback while at the Military Academy at West Point, he lost partial vision in his right eye when a mortar exploded near him during a training accident. Paine never fully recovered, so the Army sent him to law school. Upon graduation, Paine had been immediately promoted to Major. Though he had limited courtroom experience, he was named Chief Prosecutor at "The Home of the Infantry," Fort Benning, Georgia. He hit the ground running.

A model government hack, Paine followed the Army's unwritten mantra: Always Be Charging. He would indict anyone, charge anything, and, somehow, make everything so Velcro-like in its stickiness that defendants begged for mercy like nuns confessing their sins.

He took sick pleasure in destroying the careers of officers accused of minor military offenses, like fraternization. He hammered into his subordinates the idea that "perception is reality," and "where there's smoke, there's fire," whether sufficient evidence existed or not. Paine always found a way to tank the officer's career, even when investigators found only rumor.

After the shit from Abu Ghraib hit the fan, the Army hand-picked Paine to lead the Pentagon's newly formed War Crime Prosecution Team. Paine possessed enough savvy to recognize a potential minefield when he saw one. Yet, his arrogant confidence led him to *know* he would come through on the other side with nary a hair out of place.

At precisely 0900 hours, Paine walked to the podium and commenced a well-rehearsed speech. "According to the Uniformed Code of Military Justice and the Geneva Convention, all prisoners of war shall be treated humanely. This includes prisoners captured in the War on Terror."

Paine stopped to bask in his moment of glory as cameras clicked, and flashes popped. "Any American soldier caught mistreating prisoners will be investigated and prosecuted to the fullest extent of the law. As part of our commitment to these principles, we are announcing the arrest and impending courts-martial of several U.S. Army soldiers suspected of war crimes at the Sangar Prison in Afghanistan."

A hand shot up from the front row, accompanied by a female voice. "Colonel, Rose Sanchez, Independent Online Press."

Before Paine could respond, Rose pressed a question. "Colonel, what are the names of the accused soldiers?"

"Their names will not be released at this time."

"How were the detainees tortured, Colonel?"

Paine's eyes narrowed to slits. "No one used the word torture."

Rose's voice sliced toward the podium again. "Were these soldiers acting independently or following orders?"

Paine stopped and glared at her. His inability to control the rising color in his cheeks irritated him. "These guards were acting as rogue agents. Our policy is clear: All prisoners, no matter their background, will be treated humanely and in accordance with international law."

Unflinching, she followed up. "Are you saying that superior officers had no knowledge of these abuses? How is that possible?"

Paine had not planned on interruptions. He was an Army man, and, in the Army, no one interrupts when a ranking officer is speaking. Paine ignored her and took a breath to calm himself.

Rose continued, "Why did it take so long for charges to be filed? This sounds like a cover-up."

Paine gestured in a sweeping motion around the room. "Does this look like a cover-up to you?" His voice snapped like a bullwhip. "With God as my witness, these men will be brought to justice." Paine stood at attention, made a right face, and exited the stage.

CHAPTER 13

Back at my Fort Arnold office, I opened the case file and read it page-by-page. It contained a Charge Sheet, a document that listed the accusations against Sergeant Tyler Jefferson, some photographs, and one sworn statement. Jefferson was accused of abusing several detainees and murdering a prisoner named Hamza Nassar.

After scrutinizing the allegations, I flipped the page and flinched. A bruised, bloody face leered at me, the prosecution's opening salvo. Behind it were eight more photos in ascending order of gruesome. Behind the images, I found a sworn statement made by Sergeant Jefferson. He reportedly told investigators that Nassar had "struck him in the groin and had to be subdued by force." Jefferson went on to explain that "Nassar was a violent man who had repeatedly attacked guards. I helped teach him some respect."

The file had no other information about Jefferson, so I Googled him. I found more than a few listings for Tyler Jefferson and T. Jefferson, but nothing about the Army, much less about prisoner abuse. Then, I typed in Hamza Nassar and my screen filled with articles that detailed how Nassar masterminded dozens of terrorist attacks across the Middle East, Africa, and Europe.

Well, I thought, *if this Nassar guy is involved, at least I may get a sympathetic jury.*

A half dozen years ago, this case might have gone under the nearest rug - the Army likes a clean image. Abu Ghraib changed everything.

Before the 2003 Iraq invasion, few Americans had ever heard of Abu Ghraib. In early 2004, the military announced an official investigation of improprieties at the 280-acre prison located 20 miles west of Baghdad. By and large, the mainstream media yawned. Then, on April 28, 2004, *60 Minutes* stunned the world with photographs of Iraqi detainees being humiliated and abused by U.S. Army soldiers. Unforgettable images of American troops taunting naked Iraqi prisoners led to international outrage and headlines about "the shaming of America."

In one photo, a female private and a male specialist posed beside a pyramid composed of naked prisoners piled on top of each other like slabs of bacon in a buffet tray. The two soldiers, standing arm-in-arm, grinned while giving the thumbs-up sign. In another photo, the same female, a cigarette dangling from her mouth, pointed at the genitals of a naked, hooded Iraqi being forced to masturbate. One of the most infamous photos showed a hooded and robed prisoner standing on a box with wires attached to his fingers and toes.

The shocking details were contained in a devastating, 53-page report written by Major General Antonio M. Taguba. The report, though never intended for public distribution, found the light of day with alarming speed. Throughout 2005, charges were brought against 14 soldiers amid relentless media coverage. Most soldiers received minor sentences, but one drew 10 years in prison, and another eight. A colonel was relieved of his command. Brigadier General Janis Karpinski, commanding officer at Abu Ghraib, was demoted. Secretary of Defense, Donald Rumsfeld, later revealed he had twice proffered his resignation as a result of the scandal. Still, President George W. Bush refused the proposition.

Though the Abu Ghraib cases were high profile, and the prisoners had been humiliated, harassed, and sexually abused, no one died. Then, the Sangar abuses went public, with dozens of victims of physical abuse, multiple dead bodies, sleep deprivation, and stress positioning. The torture seemed reminiscent of a medieval dungeon.

Afghan President, Hamid Karzai, demanded accountability and retribution. After the uproar over Abu Ghraib, the United States Government decided to accommodate him. Loudly proclaiming the United States did not condone prisoner abuse, the blame for Sangar Prison landed squarely on "unruly guards," most of whom were Army reservists.

CHAPTER 14

The voice sounded enthusiastic and loud. "Chop-chop, buddy." It was Captain Ryan Williams, an office colleague, standing at my door wearing shorts and a polo shirt. "We have a one o'clock tee time," he said, "and I want some more of your money."

I flicked off my computer and grabbed my clubs. On my way out, I poked my head into Jules' office. "Hey, I'm on the links," I said. "Keep the nation safe."

"Cool." She gave a thumbs up. "By the way, what did Dill want?"

"He assigned me a prisoner abuse case out in Texas," I said. "It'll be a quick plea deal."

Jules grimaced. "Good luck with that one."

"Thanks," I said, and walked out the door.

Ryan drove us in his red Mustang, the short distance to the course. The Fort Arnold Golf Course is one of the better Army tracks. Military personnel got preferred tee times and lower prices. The course is a little short for outstanding players. Still, the average GI isn't going to leave the military for life on tour, so playing 5,829 yards from the white tees provides a pleasant distraction.

Not so much that afternoon. The general sloppiness of my iron game was exceeded only by my miserable putting, *and* my total lack of accuracy off the tee. I lost three balls, which is hard at Fort Arnold, and shot 94, my worst score of the year. To make matters worse, because we rotated teams every six holes, I was the big loser and owed six beers by the time we finished the last hole.

Annabelle did not care for my weekly outing: "Those boys are so immature," she often reminded me. Well, so was I, at least every Friday afternoon.

After the game, I took a quick shower, changed back into my uniform, and headed home. I stopped at a mini-mart on the way for gum and a Powerade. Any whiff of alcohol would lead to a weekend-long argument about responsibility, drinking, fatherhood, respect, her parents, and who knew what else.

CHAPTER 15

We lived in Irmo, once a quiet little South Carolina town encircling one stoplight and a small general store, now a prosperous bedroom community of Columbia with easy access to the big city via I-26. Irmo offered affordable housing, safe neighborhoods (by anyone's standards), and excellent public schools (by South Carolina standards). On my drive home, I chugged the Powerade and chewed three pieces of gum to cover the Miller Lite scent. I figured all was well.

Annabelle and our children were waiting on the front porch when I got home. I hoisted the kids in my arms and hugged and kissed them as they giggled. For an instant, I felt guilty about playing and not telling her.

"Hey, Max," said Janet Grigsby. Janet, the neighborhood buzz-kill, reared her overly coifed head over the front rail - a prairie dog with a hair helmet. She sported an endless wardrobe of colorful Spandex that had never seen the inside of a gym.

"Hi, Janet," I said.

"Sorry I'm late." I kissed Annabelle's forehead. "I was working on a case."

Annabelle's return gaze told me she wasn't buying it.

"I bet you were," Janet said. "Bless your heart." Everything Janet said sounded cynical. Whenever I ran into her, I always felt a little dumber and a little closer to death.

"Work was fine," I said.

"Paul and I don't understand the whole being in the Army and being a lawyer thing," she said. "We just don't get it." Paul was Janet's husband. He went to law school but never passed the bar exam. After four attempts, he decided he was happier teaching paralegal studies at the local community college.

Janet held a real estate license but did not sell much. Annabelle and I suspected it was Paul's inheritance that kept the Grigsby family afloat. Mostly, Janet spread neighborhood gossip. We had known them since we moved to the neighborhood. Every time we met, which was too often, they asked me to explain, "Why are there lawyers in the Army?" and, "When are you going to get out of the Army and get a real law job?"

I ignored Janet and turned to Annabelle. "I'm starving. You want to order pizza?" Code for "time to ditch the stalker."

"I made chili," Annabelle said.

"I love chili." Janet flashed a fake smile. "Paul won't be home for dinner. He's working late, again. Would you like me to bring a salad?"

Yeah, right, I thought. We both know Paul's probably screwing one of his paralegal students at the Red Roof Inn. In Irmo, South Carolina, no secret lasted long.

"Gee, Janet. Another time," I said. "I've got something a little delicate to discuss with Annabelle tonight. Sorry about that."

Janet lumbered off the porch with a slightly bruised ego. "I understand," she said. "You two lovebirds need to talk about the new arrival."

Inside the door, I kissed Annabelle. "Ewwwww," Eva disapproved.

"It's okay, Eva," Ethan said. His voice was calm and confident. "That's how they get babies."

"Ethan!" Annabelle almost fumbled her sweet tea onto the floor.

I knelt. "Buddy, where did you learn that?" I asked.

"Disney, Dad." Ethan's face reflected actual innocence. "The king and queen always kiss, and then there is a princess."

"Well, where do little boys come from?" I asked.

"Don't know, Dad." Ethan was already headed for the kitchen. "They just show up and listen to the princess sing."

I smiled and stood. Annabelle's expression wiped the smile right off my face. "Tastes like you had a rough day at the office," she said. She turned and walked briskly into the kitchen. I followed her and changed the subject.

"I got assigned a new case today," I said. "It's in Texas."

"That's a long way, Max." Annabelle stared at the pot of chili.

"They ran out of lawyers."

Annabelle hated the Army. She hated my commanding officer, and I felt sure I might be inching my way onto her list. "Major Dill knows the baby is coming soon," she said. "I told him about the due date at the family picnic last month. Why didn't he assign someone else, like Jules?"

I agreed with her. Dill was an asshole. He consistently encountered "emergencies" requiring the cancellation of my leave. The last catastrophe was a PowerPoint presentation he delayed until the last minute and then delegated to me. I missed my brother's Army promotion ceremony as a result. "It'll be a quick plea," I said. "If not, someone else will have to replace me."

"You don't need to be going anywhere." Annabelle's blue eyes narrowed. "I need you here until the baby comes." She cut her eyes at the kids.

"Annabelle, I don't have a choice. I go where the Army tells me. You know that."

"I know, Max." Now she was checking her manicure. "We've lived in the middle of nowhere for almost four years."

I wanted to say, "You grew up here, and we chose Fort Arnold because *you* wanted to be close to your parents. I had wanted to be stationed in Germany or Hawaii, not South Carolina," but her lip started to quiver.

"I put my life on hold for so long," she said. "You've been promising we'd have a normal life. That's why I put up with this Army mess. They treat you like crap. You deal with scum. Worse, you deal with scum who don't pay you." Ah, the speech - the weeping, whining catalog of my sins and shortcomings. Annabelle failed to recognize that by Army standards, we were lucky. She lived near her parents, I was in a non-deployable unit, and I was home every night. "You could have asked Daddy to pay off your Army contract," she said. "He would have done it, you know."

That's not how it works, I thought.

"But no, you had to do it on your own. You could be on a partnership track by now with Uncle David's firm. We could be living in Shandon instead of Irmo."

God, I could do this from memory. I started to tune her out.

She suddenly changed tactics. "Max, you're not listening to me."

"This is a quick case. Piece of cake."

"Why can't Jules handle it?"

"It's a sensitive case, Sweetie. They want the best."

She finally made eye contact with me. Not a trace of affection in her face. "That's right. Sounds like a job for Jules."

Chapter 16

"Flight 239 to Atlanta now boarding at Gate 12," a muffled speaker announced at the Columbia airport.

Traveling on military orders was a hassle. The Army regulated my flight, hotel, and rental car. They used a contracted travel agency to book economy flights with multiple layovers and low-budget hotels in seedy areas. For some unknown reason, the travel agency charged the Army three times the commercial rate.

I was not looking forward to this trip to Texas. It didn't help that Annabelle was angry at me again, because of the Army. "I have a doctor's appointment tomorrow, Max." She rubbed her belly. "You promised you would go."

Orders are orders. Life in the military isn't fair, and it is, undoubtedly, not family-friendly. Dill had been crystal-clear. "I want you on the first flight out on Monday," he said. "Some General in Washington got a stick up his ass about this Jefferson case. The news coverage is not helping. Go shut this down. Then, you can go on leave and prepare for the baby. You got that?"

I boarded the first flight out of Columbia and found my seat in the back row, right before the rear galley and the bathroom. I opened the case file and flipped through the photographs. That was a mistake.

The man to my right let out a gasp. "Oh, my God. Is that guy dead?" He covered his mouth with his hand.

The full-color photograph showed a swarthy, dark-haired man, laid out on a concrete floor. Greenish-purple bruises covered his torso, arms, and legs. Dried blood, the color of wine, stained his swollen cheeks.

I covered the picture. "Sir, do you mind?"

"Oh, sorry," the man said. "What happened to him?"

"What does it look like?"

"Like someone beat him to death."

"Sure does," I said, and closed the file.

CHAPTER 17

When I landed in El Paso, I headed to Sunshine Rent a Car and picked up my ride. At 6 feet 2 inches tall, squeezing into the Toyota Yaris presented a challenge. After I'd left the rental car office, I realized that the air conditioning didn't work. For November, it was unseasonably warm. So, I hit the 4/60 temperature control. Four windows down at 60 miles an hour. In 15 minutes, I arrived at Fort Custer.

Fort Custer lies on a flat desert, flanked on one side by the Franklin Mountains. The Rio Grande and the Mexican border lie three miles south. On the other side of the border sits Ciudad Juárez, or Juárez to the locals. On my drive to the fort, I passed a billboard that said: "WARNING - Beware of kidnappers!" I had lived in some rundown places in my life. Even when near abject poverty and violent crime, I'd never seen a sign about people disappearing within the United States.

Juárez had become one of the deadliest cities in North America. The drug war between the Sinaloa and Juárez Cartels racked the city with violence. In 2005, the city averaged about 16 homicides a week, including many women, children, and police officers. The only thing separating El Paso from Juárez was a broken fence, a shallow river, and the Border Patrol.

After I cleared Fort Custer's gate, I drove past buildings that dated to the early 1900s, when General Pershing led an unsuccessful expedition into Mexico to destroy Pancho

Villa, the Mexican revolutionary and guerrilla leader. Before the Civil War, Fort Custer guarded the area against Apache attacks.

Colonel Paine's office was located near the parade field and easy to find. I parked my car and entered the building. Inside, the building appeared recently remodeled and well-equipped, with new computers and modern furniture. In comparison, my office at Fort Arnold had a copier that had not worked since I arrived, and my laptop was at least seven years old.

I approached a sergeant sitting behind a reception desk. "I'm Captain O'Donnell," I said, handing him my JAG business card. "I'm here to see Colonel Paine."

"Is he expecting you?" the sergeant asked.

"Yes. I have an appointment."

The sergeant picked up a phone and dialed. No one answered. "He's not available," he said in a flat tone. "Can you come back tomorrow?"

I'd flown from South Carolina to the Mexican border, and now some sergeant was busting my balls. I leaned closer to him. "I want to speak to him. Now."

"He's - not – here - sir." His voice was slow and accentuated.

"Where - is – he – Sergeant?" I responded in kind.

"He's training for an ultra-marathon." He let out a long exhale through his mouth as if he was annoyed. "Today is his long run day."

"It's the middle of the duty day." I glanced at my watch. "What time do you expect him back?"

"Can't say."

"Call and let him know I'm here," I said. "I'm flying back to South Carolina this afternoon."

The sergeant called someone. I could hear him explaining the situation. A minute later, he hung up. "Have a seat. Colonel Paine will be with you shortly." He motioned to a waiting room with a few chairs and a small TV playing Fox News. Typical Army bullshit. Hurry-up-and-wait.

"What about my client?" I said. "Can I meet with him?"

"Transport got delayed. They should be here soon."

I snapped. "Soon? How soon?"

"I don't know."

"I'll call him then. What's the number?"

"I cannot help you with that. You'll have to talk to Colonel Paine."

I sat in the waiting area. Sixty minutes later, Paine had not appeared. Across the room, I saw the sergeant standing with two other enlisted soldiers. They were bullshitting. I heard the sergeant say, "...after my tenth shot, the room got a little fuzzy..." That is as far as he got.

"Sergeant." I got up in his face. "Where's your fucking boss?"

He opened his mouth, but nothing came out.

"I'm flying back to Fort Arnold if he's not here in 10 minutes. You got that?"

"Roger, sir," he said, as he hurried to his desk. Two minutes later, the sergeant walked toward me as though crossing a minefield. "He'll be here in 30 minutes," he said.

I didn't respond and walked out of the building. I texted Annabelle that I'd be home by midnight, cranked the ignition, and left Fort Custer. My phone rang 10 minutes later. It was Paine. I declined the call, and he left a voicemail.

Paine's voice spoke with all the sincerity of someone reading the operating manual for a lawnmower. "Captain O'Donnell, Colonel Covington Paine. Sorry about the mix-up. I did not know you had been waiting for so long. Tell you what. To make up for my absence, I'll make your client a one-time offer. Jefferson pleads guilty to manslaughter and does a 10-year bit. Good behavior, he could be out in less. I must be crazy for doing this but consider it an early Thanksgiving gift. I need your answer in 72 hours. That is all."

The guy dismissed me over the phone. Incredible! Still, I'd reduced my client's sentence from life to 10 years without a single meeting. Not bad for a day's work. I ordered a Dos Equis at the airport bar, sat back, and waited for my flight.

CHAPTER 18

Two days later, after an uneventful weekend, I arrived back at my office. Jules saw me in the hallway. "Jefferson called this morning," she said, rolling her eyes. "Ten times." She handed me a stack of yellow sticky notes.

They all read the same: "Sergeant Jefferson - call back immediately."

This guy is going to be a pain in the ass, I thought as she walked away. I booted up my computer and sat down at my desk. Seconds later, my phone rang. I took a deep breath and answered. "Hello. This is Captain O'Donnell."

"Where have you been?" The voice sounded strident and loud.

I decided to irritate him further. "Who's calling?"

"This is Tyler Jefferson. Why didn't you call back?"

I waited for about 20 seconds.

"Hello?" he said. "Can you hear me?"

I kept my voice even. "You done?"

"What?"

"That's 'Sir' to you," I said.

I heard a sharp intake of air. Then Jefferson figured out what I meant. "Sir, this is Sergeant Tyler Jefferson, sir."

"Sergeant, in the future, call me once and leave a message. Don't call 10 times in two hours unless you're trying to piss me off."

"I'm sorry. I'm in solitary confinement at the Brig. You got to get me out of here."

I cut to the chase. "Sergeant, you're sitting in jail because you are accused of beating a shackled prisoner to death. In the Army, believe it or not, murder is a bad thing. There is no way in hell you're getting out of jail any time soon."

"Sir, I didn't kill nobody." He wasn't yelling, but he was getting close.

"Well, they usually don't charge innocent people with murder. Based on what I saw in the file, the evidence against you is strong." He didn't reply. Now was my chance to mention the deal I had already worked out. I figured he would weep tears of joy when he heard the offer. "Sergeant Jefferson, I've got some good news."

He stayed silent.

"First, as soon as we finish, I'll make a call and try to get you out of solitary. No reason you should be in there."

"Thank you, sir."

"There's more," I said. "What if I told you I could have you back to your family in less than 10 years?"

"Sir?"

I had his attention. This would be an easy sell. "I talked to the prosecutor," I said. "I think I can cut your sentence to 10 years." I was waiting for a "Praise Jesus" or a "Thank you, sir." No dice.

"Ten years for what?"

"For manslaughter."

"Hell no." Now, he shouted. "I'm not going to jail for some shit I didn't do."

"Sergeant, this is a once in a lifetime opportunity, and you can get paroled after you serve one-third of your sentence."

"Didn't do nothin' wrong. Not gonna say I did."

"If we lose at trial, it's a mandatory life sentence."

"Whose side are you on?" he asked.

"I'm on your side. I was appointed to defend you."

"It doesn't sound like much of a defense to me. Sounds like you're fuckin' me over."

I decided to let the language and the attitude go. "This deal is in your best interest. They've got a stack of evidence, and a line of witnesses that'll go around the courthouse. Plus." I paused for effect. "They have your confession."

Jefferson went ballistic. I put the phone down while he cursed and screamed. I didn't bother to follow his rant, but I got the gist, "I didn't fuckin' kill fuckin' nobody."

I picked up the handset. "Sergeant, go back to your cell and think about it. Talk to your wife. Better yet, talk to the chaplain."

"What if I want a different lawyer?" he asked.

Ah – the light. "You can hire anyone you want."

"How am I supposed to pay for a lawyer?"

"That's your problem."

"I can't afford no lawyer."

"I guess you're stuck with me." I hung up then reached for the intercom. "If Jefferson calls back, tell him I am out for the rest of the day."

CHAPTER 19

C herry paneling lined the office walls. Real wood, not the flimsy veneer. Law books rested in scrupulously arranged rows. Only three items hung on the walls: a diploma from the University of North Carolina - Chapel Hill, a degree from the UNC School of Law, and a certificate declaring L. Edward Williams as a member of the prestigious American Board of Criminal Lawyers, a small, exclusive fraternity of the nation's top defense attorneys.

The walls lacked decoration, but not the shelves. Row after row of barrister bookcases displayed beautifully framed photographs (many signed) of L. Edward Williams on the golf course, at dinner, hoisting a toast, or in full formal attire with former presidents, sports figures, captains of industry, and celebrities (both beloved and despised). In each, Williams grinned like Lewis Carrol's Cheshire Cat. With a bush of graying hair, he'd begun to look like Harrison Ford at 77.

"Mr. Williams, you have a call on line two." Gladys had a great voice. It was husky, sultry, and downright sexy.

"Who is it?" Williams drummed his fingers on his desk.

"He won't say."

Williams's eyes wandered across the room to the golf bag propped next to his private exit. "Gladys, I'm teeing off at the Governor's Club in an hour. I don't have time to talk to anyone, especially someone I don't know."

"Yes, sir. I know, sir."

Williams was three steps from escape when the intercom buzzed again. He moved closer to his desk to avoid yelling. "Yes?"

"He says he's a family friend."

Williams clenched his teeth. The Governors Club was the premier Jack Nicklaus course in the area. Despite his prominence, Williams did not get to play often. Apparently, many people didn't like associating with criminal defense attorneys, especially those who could get an NFL player (with a dead wife in the trunk) set free. "Well, what's his goddamn name, Gladys?"

The speaker went dead, then buzzed again. "He said, 'tell Terrance,' that's what he said, 'Terrance,' that he was an old friend from home, from Bass?"

"*Vass*," Williams said. "It's in Moore County."

"You've never mentioned that," she said. "I thought you grew up in Chapel Hill."

"Put him through. Come get me if I'm still on in five minutes."

"Yes, sir."

Williams picked up the phone and waited to make sure Gladys was not on the line. "This is L. Edward Williams. Who is this?"

"Well, she-it, this is your ole buddy, Ollie. Ollie Cullen, from Vass. Ya remember Vass? Lil' ole town where you and I used to get fucked up and do shit? Ya know, shit ya don't want no one to know about."

Williams could feel the pulse in his neck. "What the fuck do you want, Ollie?"

The voice continued, "Well, my boy's in some deep shit, and I believe ya owe me a big fuckin' favor." The next morning, L. Edward Williams was on a plane bound for El Paso, Texas.

CHAPTER 20

By 5 p.m. that same day, the loud buzz and click of the heavy metal door woke Jefferson. A prison guard pulled the door open. "Jefferson, follow me," the guard said. "Bring your gear." Jefferson grabbed his personal hygiene kit, which consisted of a shortened rubber toothbrush, a tiny tube of Colgate toothpaste, and a bar of soap. He ducked his head as he passed through the small portal and followed the guard. He was feeling disoriented. Even a brief stay in solitary confinement can do that to a man. "They're moving you to general population. You'll like it better over there."

"This is bullshit," Jefferson grumbled.

"It's a shame they are treating you guys like this. To us guards, you guys are heroes. Don't nobody care about those terrorists you killed."

Jefferson gritted his teeth. "I didn't kill nobody."

"I hear ya." The guard smiled and winked.

"Can I call my wife?" Jefferson asked.

"Now that you're out of solitary, you can pretty much do what you want, like the others. You just can't leave." The guard led Jefferson through a maze of corridors with walls painted flat white. At the end of the hallway, they stopped, and the guard spoke into an intercom. "I'm moving Jefferson to gen pop." Buzz, click. The heavy metal door opened. Once they passed, the greased bolt locked again.

Finally, Jefferson made it to his new home: Cell 12 of the Fort Custer Military Confinement Facility. It was an upgrade compared to where he came from. At least there were other humans to talk to. Guards kept watch from a control booth perched above. Below, prisoners played cards on glossy blue metal tables bolted to the floor. A small TV encased in plexiglass blared Fox News 24/7.

The guard recited the prison rules. "You're allowed a religious book, writing materials, and five photos." The guard held up five fingers. "Questions?"

"Where am I going to get pictures?" Jefferson snorted.

"Family, I guess."

Jefferson stepped away from the guard and cursed under his breath.

"Hey, Tyler," a familiar voice said. Jefferson turned around and saw Cullen standing behind him. "Where've you been, man?" Cullen asked.

"Fuckin' solitary."

"How was it?"

Jefferson scoffed. "How the fuck you think it was, asshole?"

"Well, I got some good news." Cullen smiled. "I talked with my dad, and he's working some things to help us out."

"Yeah? Like what?" Jefferson narrowed his eyes.

"He's got some heavy-hitting lawyer lined up," Cullen said. "He said he'd do whatever it takes to beat these charges."

"Shit. I can't afford no baller attorney. I got a wife and two kids."

"This guy and my dad are old friends. He'll defend us for free."

Jefferson stared at him in disbelief. "You think some big-time lawyer is going to take our cases for free?"

"Yeah. That's what my dad said. They're tight. Everybody knows we're getting a raw deal, so he'll hook us up."

"Thank God," Jefferson said. "The lawyer the Army gave me sucks." Both men laughed. For the first time in a week, Jefferson saw a glimmer of hope.

CHAPTER 21

I strolled into my office earlier than usual and checked my email, hoping I would hear back from some of the law firms I'd applied to. Unfortunately, my inbox remained empty. So, I called Jefferson at the Brig. I wanted to make sure he was released from solitary confinement.

This time, Jefferson's voice was different, lighter, damn near happy. A strange tone for someone looking at life in Leavenworth. "Morning, sir," he said. "I'm glad you called." He cleared his throat. "I'd like to start with an apology. The other day, on the phone, I was an asshole. Beg your pardon for the language."

"Apology accepted. I'm ready to move forward. If you want to fight, we will fight this."

"I appreciate your willingness to help, but there is something I want to tell you."

"What's up?"

"Well, I've been talking to Cullen, and . . . uh, well . . ."

"And what?"

Jefferson continued, "I think I need a different lawyer." This sounded like the song of the angels. I perked up. "I need someone with a little more firepower," he said. "No disrespect."

"Okay. The Army can appoint someone else."

"Nah. We got a real a heavy hitter in our corner now. We don't think we need any help from the Army."

Annabelle would be thrilled, but something didn't sound right. "Jefferson," I said. "Who's 'we?'"

"Me and Cullen."

"Sergeant Cullen? Your co-defendant?" This was bad. I was familiar enough with the case to know the prosecution could turn Cullen against Jefferson.

"Yes, sir," Jefferson said. "His dad is tight with a famous lawyer, a guy like Johnnie Cochran. You know, 'If it don't fit, you must acquit.'"

"I'm familiar," I said. "Why are you talking to Cullen about your case?"

"We've been friends since we were kids. He wants to help."

"He's charged with the same crimes as you. How is he going to help you?"

"His dad has connections. He got this big-time lawyer guy. He's going to represent both of us pro bono." Jefferson's voice grew more excited.

"Who is it?" I asked.

"L. Edward Williams."

I knew Williams. Knew of him, at least. "How did someone like Cullen get L. Edward Williams to defend him for free?"

"Cullen's dad and this guy go way back. High school ball and shit. Cullen said all his dad had to do was call, and it was all set."

Something wasn't right. "The judge won't allow the same lawyer to defend both of you," I said.

Jefferson snapped. "Man, you are so fuckin' negative." Then he caught himself. "Sorry, sir. Williams says we're getting railroaded. So, he's happy to help. Thinks this is a show trial. It's all politics. Williams plays hardball, you know, and he's all about helping the troops."

Relief slid across me like a freshly laundered sheet. "Easy enough. To release me, you need to fill out a form and sign it.

I'll fax it over as soon as we hang up. By the way, I still owe the prosecutor an answer on the plea deal."

"I ain't cuttin' no deal," he said.

"Well then, Sergeant, I wish you luck." Time to get off the phone and let this guy sail away into the sunset.

"Could you do me a favor?" Jefferson said.

The phone was already halfway to the cradle. I had to snatch it back just before I hung up. "Sure. What do you need?"

"Could you call my wife, Gabby. Tell her what's going on and that I'm okay."

"Why don't *you* call her?"

"I got no money," he said. "Inmates can't call anyone but their lawyers unless they buy a calling card?"

"Then buy a calling card."

"Can't, got no money."

"How much is the card?"

"The cheapest card is $30, and it's five bucks a minute."

"Alright, I'll call her."

Jefferson gave me the contact information, thanked me again, and signed off. After I hung up, I knew two things for sure. One, Williams would ride the free publicity as long as he could. Then, he would plead Jefferson out, and move on to whatever case would put him in front of the most cameras. Two, at that exact moment, I did not care.

CHAPTER 22

The moment Jefferson's signed release printed out of the fax machine, I drove to Major Dill's office and dropped it in his inbox. My children were playing on the living room floor when I got home.

Annabelle hoisted herself off the couch. "How was your day?" Her tone could not have indicated any less interest.

I tried to kiss her, but she turned her head and let me peck her cheek. "Great, actually," I said.

Sarcasm dripped from her next question. "Did you get a break in your big case?"

"Something much better," I said. "I'm not on the case anymore."

"What happened?" A bit more inflection.

"Jefferson called and fired me. He got another lawyer, some media hound civilian lawyer."

She narrowed her eyes. Skeptical, at best. "Did Major Dill approve your release?"

"Not yet. He'll sign it when he comes back from vacation."

"That's great, Max." A smile began to creep across her face. Then it broke into full bloom. "Now, you can focus on finding a job." Annabelle reached for her cell. "I'll call Uncle David right now."

After dinner, I read the kids some bedtime stories. This was always the best part of my day. I kissed them goodnight and tucked them in. Downstairs, I found Annabelle on the living room couch, reading a book. I sat next to her and sighed.

"What's wrong, honey?" she asked.

"My now-former client asked me to call his wife."

"How'd it go?"

"Haven't done it yet."

"Max, you get on the phone right now and call that poor woman. Think how crazed I would be if you were in jail." She caressed my thigh. "I'll make it worth your while." She gave me a wink and the first full-blown kiss I'd gotten from her in a long time.

"Yes, ma'am." I picked up the phone and called his wife. The phone rang three times.

"Hello."

"Ma'am, my name is Captain Max O'Donnell," I said. "I'm an Army lawyer. I am calling on behalf of Sergeant Tyler Jefferson."

She started crying. "What did you people do to my husband?"

"Ma'am."

Her voice turned from fear to anger. "You people attacked my husband, in front of my kids, you animals!"

"Ma'am. Stop!" I said in a forceful voice.

Suddenly, she became quiet, like she'd flipped a switch. "I'm, I'm so sorry," she said. "They came and took him away. I have no idea if he's okay. The kids don't sleep." Her voice faded.

"Your husband's okay. He asked me to call you."

"You're his lawyer? What is going on? We have to fight this."

"Your husband released me this morning," I said. "You should discuss that with his new attorney, L. Edward Williams."

"Who?"

"A lawyer from North Carolina. He's very experienced."

"We can't afford a lawyer."

"My understanding is that Mr. Williams will be representing your husband at no charge."

Gabby listened as I gave her a synopsis of the case. By the time I finished, she was a little calmer. Probably because I kinda, sorta led her to believe that Tyler had a fighting chance. Let someone else be the bearer of bad news. I hung up and sprinted up the stairs. Annabelle was naked under the sheets - and snoring like a buzz saw.

CHAPTER 23

David Weathersby Kline II was the senior partner at Stanford and Kline, Attorneys at Law, a position he had occupied in Columbia for almost 20 years, ever since dear old dad handed it to him - as his grandfather had done decades before. No one ever questioned whether Kline should ascend to such heights. No one ever questioned D.W. Kline about anything. In Columbia, South Carolina, he represented an unshakable pillar in the community, and he was a legend in his own mind.

Kline cared about three things. One, the law. Whether it was the prestige of leading one of the South's best-known firms, the money the position produced, or any sense of the beauty of justice, no one knew.

Second, Clemson University. The Kline family worshiped at the shrine of the Tiger Paw. Kline's office unabashedly displayed his adoration of all things Clemson. Pictures of Kline with Danny Ford, Terry Allen, Vic Beasley, and even an aging William "The Refrigerator" Perry, autographed and suitably framed, hung on the wall directly behind various footballs, which had been signed by every single member of the team, every, single, year. IPTAY, the Clemson booster association, might have started off as, "I pay ten a year," but for Kline, the acronym meant "I pay thousands a year."

Any associate invited to sit in Kline's box in Death Valley on a Saturday afternoon was tagged for the partnership track. No invitation after three years? Best to dust off the resume.

Last, but certainly far from least, Kline cared about his goddaughter, Annabelle Hillyard. "Sorry," he would always say. "I mean, O'Donnell." Kline and his wife of 30 years had never been able to produce a daughter. When his old friend, Sterling Hillyard, offered the opportunity to accept the "spiritual and social upbringing" of infant Annabelle, well, there was no hesitation at all.

It was Kline who taught Annabelle to drive in his Mercedes. Kline, who "called a few friends" on the occasion of Annabelle's "youthful indiscretion" that resulted in an arrest for underage alcohol consumption. The charges evaporated.

On her 16th birthday, Kline presented Annabelle with a giant red ribbon under which sat a gleaming, red Lexus convertible. "Anyone can drive a BMW," he said.

When Annabelle, age 18, appeared in tears at his office and sobbed through a sad story of a starry night, a magical prom, a dashing All-State quarterback, raging hormones, and a faulty prophylactic. "Uncle David" made all the appropriately discreet arrangements with an appropriately discreet doctor in an appropriately discreet clinic several hundred miles from Columbia.

Kline had initially been pleased when Annabelle called him and said, "Uncle David, I'm engaged!" She was elated. "Max this" and "Max that," and, "Max is so great." Until he met me at a barbeque. I wore a t-shirt with a Puerto Rican flag on it that said, "Boricua."

Kline pointed at my shirt. "What does that mean?" he asked and took a bite of his pulled-pork sandwich.

"It means I'm Puerto Rican."

He swallowed hard to avoid choking. "I thought your name was O'Donnell." Kline was honestly confused.

"It is. My dad's side is Irish. My mother is from Puerto Rico."

Kline stared. "But you don't look black."

)(

The interview was brief and uncomfortable. David Kline, the great man himself, three-piece suit, a silk tie with matching handkerchief, and a Rolex that would choke a horse, invited me into his office.

"Thank you for meeting me, Mr. Kline," I said. I was expecting, "Call me David." It didn't happen.

"Nothing's too good for my darling, Annabelle." Kline flashed a disingenuous smile. We chatted about innocuous things for less than four minutes, when someone knocked at the door. Kline said, "Come in," with a little too much zeal. A trio of suits entered. "These gentlemen will show you around," Kline said. The job interview was over. We shook hands. I could have sworn Kline flinched.

The three Senior Associates who led me to the Conference Room were as douche-i-fied as imaginable. Their names were Preston, Holloway, and Fleming. Who names a kid, "Fleming?" Also joining us was David Weathersby Kline, III (aka Trey), David's son. In high school, Trey's infatuation with Annabelle bordered on creepy, but she kept him squarely in the friend-zone. A few years out of law school, Trey was on the greased track to partnership at his father's firm. On the office tour, we talked a little about the actual practice of law, but mostly, "Who do you know?" (which was nobody they knew), and, "Does the Army let you fire anything that's full-auto?"

Before the scheduled lunch with "Uncle David," I fabricated an "emergency" and drove to Fort Arnold. I did not want to spend more time than necessary with any of these jokers.

CHAPTER 24

Inside his cell at Fort Custer, Jefferson waited with anticipation for his savior, L. Edward Williams. Jefferson only knew Williams by reputation, and what Cullen had told him, but he felt confident Williams would waltz him right out of the Brig like a debutante at her coming-out party.

Cullen and Jefferson had spent the prior evening talking about Williams's most famous murder case. A decade ago, the state police had stopped a BMW sedan doing over 100 mph on the interstate. Both state troopers recognized the driver. Everyone in the area knew the All-Pro receiver, and both troopers could spot someone high on cocaine. The football player grew agitated when they asked to search the trunk, so he took a swing at one of the officers.

Probable cause.

They popped the trunk and found the lifeless body of a woman who turned out to be the player's ex-wife. Within two days, L. Edward Williams had pounced on the case.

After a sensational trial, the player walked away scot-free. The moral giants of the NFL even hired him again. He signed a new contract with a massive bonus, destroyed his knee in training camp, and retired to Boca. Williams rode the hype like a rodeo cowboy. Now, every time CNN needed a "noted legal analyst," Williams's toothy grin dominated the screen.

"He got that guy off, our case should be a cakewalk," Jefferson said.

"Fuck, yeah." Cullen fist-bumped Jefferson. "These Army prosecutors are gonna shit themselves when he shows up."

"We're going to sit back and enjoy every minute of it."

"Amen, brother," Cullen said. "This is gonna make us famous."

"We're going to get a book deal after the acquittal." The image of walking out of jail, a free man looped in Jefferson's mind. He envisaged holding a press conference and raising his arms in victory on the courtroom steps.

Williams showed up at the Brig in El Paso as promised. However, he spent the morning in a one-on-one huddle with Cullen. After the meeting finished, Williams passed Jefferson's cell without saying a word. Jefferson asked the guard. "Hey, when is my appointment with my attorney?"

The guard glanced at his clipboard. "You don't have one, shitbird." And the first domino fell.

CHAPTER 25

Having skipped lunch with Uncle David, I spent the rest of the day packing up my office in preparation for my civilian life. Afterward, I worked out at the gym with a co-worker. By the time I arrived home, it was dark, no illumination on the porch, not a single light in the house. After fumbling with the lock for a minute, I opened the front door and stepped into the small foyer.

An edgy voice leaked from the darkness. "I cannot believe you left Uncle David in the middle of lunch."

"Actually, I left before lunch," I said.

Again, the voice. "You just walked out? You didn't even make an effort."

I weaved my way toward the sound. "Shit!" The pain in my right knee erupted about the same time I heard the vase shatter on the floor.

The voice remained flat. "You promised me you would try." Then came the litany of complaints I'd heard before:

"You never follow through."

"You always take the easy way out."

"You won't fight for yourself or your family."

She saved the best for last. "Daddy was right about you."

I dropped into the first armchair I managed to find in the dark. I heard movement.

The voice changed positions. Now, it was closer to the stairs. "Sleep on the couch, Max."

CHAPTER 26

O ver the weekend, I hung out at home, doing the dishes, playing with the kids, and completing my honey-do list. I was tired of being in the doghouse. I wanted out. So, I swallowed my pride, called David Kline, and apologized for having to run out on our lunch date. I told him it was a "military necessity," and he said he "completely understood." Both were lies, and we both knew it. Our feelings were mutual. He wanted nothing to do with me, and the lunch was a courtesy to Annabelle. By walking out, I did him a favor. Kline promised to get back in touch; to reschedule. I was more likely to believe he would attend an NAACP rally.

Annabelle must have gotten word of the call because dinner passed without incident, and at lights out, I was back in my own bed. I leaned over and kissed Annabelle's forehead. Half asleep, she smiled, patted my hand, and closed her eyes.

Then, my cell phone rang. "Hello," I said in a whisper.

"This is Colonel Paine calling. Is this Captain O'Donnell?"

I sat upright. "How can I help you, sir?"

"I'm following up on the plea deal," Paine said. "If there is no deal, then we need to discuss dates for the preliminary hearing."

"I'm off the case," I said as quietly as I could.

"The Army appointed someone else?" Paine sounded surprised.

"A civilian attorney, L. Edwards Williams, has taken Jefferson's case."

After a few seconds of silence, Paine started laughing.

"What's so funny?" I asked.

"Mr. Williams put in an entry of appearance on behalf of Sergeant Rodney Cullen," he said. "He does not represent Sergeant Jefferson. In fact, today, we discussed a plea deal in which Cullen would testify against your client."

What the fuck?

"There must be a misunderstanding," I said. "I have a lot going on here. My wife is about to give birth."

Covington Paine suddenly morphed into a human being. "Captain O'Donnell, I completely understand. My wife and I have five great blessings. Rest assured, if you are still on the case, I will work with you and set a convenient date for you and your family."

"I appreciate that."

"Well, God bless your wife and your family," he said. "We'll get this sorted out. Goodnight." He hung up the phone.

I peeked at Annabelle - her eyes were closed - I prayed she'd been asleep. I bent over to kiss her head. She snatched the sheets and turned her back to me. "You're such a liar, Max."

CHAPTER 27

The next morning, I made pancakes for Ethan and Eva and got ready for work. I left the kids on the couch, watching cartoons. Annabelle stayed in bed, brooding.

At the office, there were no calls from Jefferson. I figured something had been lost in translation, that Williams had contacted Jefferson, and that all was right with the world. I brewed a pot of coffee and spent the morning working on my resume. For lunch, I went to the Post Exchange and ate Popeye's spicy fried chicken with red beans and rice. After lunch, I planned on heading home early, surprising the kids, and making amends with Annabelle. Then, Jules called.

"Are you expecting someone in the office today?" she asked me.

"No. Why?"

"Sergeant Jefferson's family is here to see you. They seem a little desperate."

"I'm on my way," I said and hung up the phone.

Ten minutes later, I entered my office's waiting room. A man and a woman sat chatting. Each held a child. I approached the woman and extended my hand. "I'm Captain O'Donnell," I said. "We spoke on the phone the other night."

The woman stood and shook my hand with a firm grip. "Captain, I apologize for how I acted."

"It's okay, Mrs. Jefferson." I gave a dismissive wave of my hand. "It's nice to meet you in person."

"Please, call me Gabby."

I smiled and nodded.

"This is Aliyah, and this is Elijah." Gabby motioned to the children. "And this is Tyler's father, Reggie." She pointed to a giant black man who had been seated beside her.

Reggie stood and crushed my hand with a frying-pan-sized palm before I got a firm grip. Diamond studs the size of peas decorated his ears; a wooden toothpick hung from the corner of his mouth. "Reggie Jefferson," he said. "Twenty years with the Dallas PD."

"Nice to meet you," I said, wondering why that was relevant.

"I wish I could say likewise," he said through a clenched jaw. The pupils of Reggie's bloodshot eyes were obsidian. His weathered face bore a deep scar. He appeared to be a guy you didn't want to mess with. After an uncomfortable 10 seconds, he let go of my hand.

"We've been on the road forever," Gabby said. "We just got here."

"Gabby, I'm not sure how I can help. I'm no longer on the case."

Reggie stepped toward me. "Your office, now." He jerked his head toward the door. It was not a request. "This pretty young thing here can keep an eye on Aliyah and her brother," he said, pointing at Jules.

"Elijah, Aliyah." Gabby wagged her finger. "You behave for the nice lady, hear?"

This time, Jules reacted. "The nice Captain," Jules said, without any edge in her voice at all.

"Yes, ma'am," the children said in tandem, well-behaved and polite.

Inside my office, Gabby and Reggie sat in Vietnam-era imitation leather chairs. She was tense. He was angry. Reggie's voice was low and threatening. "What the fuck's going on, counselor?"

"Mr. Jefferson, calm down," I said.

"You quit fuckin' over my boy and lyin' to his wife. Then, I will calm the fuck down."

"Mr. Jefferson, I don't represent your son."

Reggie slammed his paw on my desk. "There's your first lie, motherfucker."

I pulled open a desk drawer and reached for a yellow legal pad.

"If you're thinking 'bout goin' for a piece," he said. "I'll drop you before you blink."

Was this guy for real?

"Mr. Jefferson." I raised my hands in surrender. "I'm getting a notepad."

Reggie leaned forward, like a cobra ready to strike.

Gabby put her hand on his massive forearm. "Enough, Reggie," she said. "If you can't behave yourself, then step outside."

Reggie crossed his arms and slouched in his chair like if his mother had put him in time out.

"Captain O'Donnell," Gabby said in a soft voice. "Tyler called me yesterday. He was frantic. Said something about getting screwed over, about being used. He said his 'friend' Cullen." She used air quotes. "And some scumbag lawyer were throwing him under the bus. He could barely talk he was so upset. After I hung up, I called Reggie, and we drove over here."

"You drove from Dallas?" I asked.

"All 16 hours." Gabby struggled to hold back her tears.

Reggie's face was impassive, but his eyes blazed. He'd rip me apart if I gave him a reason. Biceps strained against the cotton of what had to be an XXL tee shirt. His waist was thick, but not fat. He was 6 feet 4 inches, minimum. "We're flyin' blind here," Reggie said, unable to control his temper. "What the hell is going on?"

I started from the beginning and outlined the case as I knew it. I closed with the 10-year plea deal. I did not mention that the deadline had expired.

"So, you think Tyler should cut a deal?" Gabby asked, her voice wavering.

"It beats life in prison, and . . ." I hesitated. "There's a chance they could seek the death penalty."

I expected a meltdown. For Gabby to throw herself on my desk screaming, but her face registered nothing.

Suddenly, Reggie lunged forward and stuck an index finger the size of a sausage in my face. "Get this straight, Mr. (he read the nameplate on my desk) 'Senior Dee-fence Counsel.' Playtime is over. Like it or not, you're my son's attorney. Get your shit in a pile. Cause if you let this thing go to hell without a fight, I am going to grind your Irish ass into cornmeal. You got that?"

Reggie walked toward the door. Then, he turned to face me and said, "Don't bother asking me if that is a threat, Captain. It wasn't. It's a mother-fuckin' promise. Now, grow a pair and get to work. Here's my number. Call when you get more information on the case. I'm at your disposal." He tossed a card in my direction, and they were gone.

CHAPTER 28

After the Jeffersons left, I felt uneasy. I didn't really want this case. I didn't need the headache. My time in the Army was almost up, and I had to find a job. Quickly. Getting involved in a losing murder case, with an irrational client and his unstable father, did nothing to improve my situation.

I glanced at my bookshelf, and my eyes locked onto a photo of my mom that was taken days before she succumbed to cancer. She fought until the end and always had a smile on her face. She was a warrior. What would she think of me now? I thought of the Roberto Clemente jacket and the asshole who stole it. I remembered the emotion from that day - before I got my jacket back. It was the same as now. It was fear.

I was not sure exactly when or why, but I had lost my fighter spirit somewhere along the way. Four years ago, I would have jumped at the opportunity to defend Jefferson. Now, I was trying to duck out of the fight.

Then, I thought of my dad. What would he think? What would he say? I knew the answer.

As much as my inner voice said, "walk away," I couldn't turn my back on Jefferson. He needed my help, and I was his only chance at getting justice. I drove straight to Major Dill's office. His secretary waved me past. I went to his inbox, removed Jefferson's release memo, and shredded it.

On my way home, I called the Brig.

"This is Sergeant Jefferson."

"Sergeant, my boss won't let me quit," I said. "You're stuck with me."

Silence, for what seemed like a minute.

"Okay. Let's win this." His voice was confident.

"Going forward, do not talk to anyone - especially Cullen," I warned him. "He will screw you over in a heartbeat."

"Yes, sir. Thank you for staying on my case."

Quietly and secretly, I thanked my dad.

CHAPTER 29

In the following days, I felt a renewed sense of energy. Jefferson deserved the best defense possible, and I looked forward to the fight. I started getting to the office early, even beating Jules there. On a Thursday morning, I received an email from Colonel Michael Hackworth, the Investigating Officer presiding over Jefferson's preliminary hearing.

The communication was terse. "I am the IO for the U.S. v. Sergeant Tyler Jefferson preliminary hearing. The hearing will commence on Tuesday, 22 November 2005, at 0800 hours. I will conduct a conference call with counsel today at 1300 hours to discuss logistics." The hearing was in five days.

I wrote a quick reply. "The defense respectfully requests a delay. Unavoidable family issues. I have discussed with Colonel Paine, and he is agreeable."

This morning, Annabelle was scheduled for a follow-up appointment with her OBGYN. I planned on going with her to the check-up, grabbing lunch, and dropping her off at the house afterward. I'd talk to Paine and Hackworth on the way back to my office.

Turns out, the doctor was running late with a problematic delivery. At the exact moment, the nurse said, "The doctor will see you now," my phone rang. Annabelle stared daggers at me as she waddled behind the double doors.

I answered the call. Hackworth skipped introductions and got to the point. "Gentlemen, the preliminary hearing is set for this Tuesday. My understanding is that the defense wants a delay."

"That is correct, sir," I said. "The defense will be prepared to go after 10 December."

"Government, what's your position?" Hackworth asked.

I was halfway listening until Paine said, "We vigorously oppose a delay. We're ready to go on 22 November."

"Colonel Paine, we discussed this the other night," I said, barely avoiding calling him a liar. "My wife is due with our third child - eminently due. I thought we had reached an understanding."

Paine was ready. "I did not agree to a continuance," he said. "Justice delayed is justice denied."

"Colonel Hackworth," I said, "you know I am stationed at Fort Arnold. I have not met with my client yet. I was recently assigned to this case. So, I need a little extra time."

Paine's voice greased through the phone. "Actually, according to my notes, headquarters officially assigned this case to Captain O'Donnell on 1 November. I was told that he did not pick up the file until 5 November. Regardless, he has had this case for over 10 days. Even though he blew off a meeting with me in El Paso last week, he has had adequate time to consider a plea agreement, one he apparently has decided not to take."

"That true, Captain O'Donnell?" Hackworth asked.

"Sir, until two days ago, I thought a civilian attorney had assumed Sergeant Jefferson's defense," I said.

Hackworth recognized the dodge. "Don't quibble with me." His tone was aggressive. "It sounds like you have frittered away nearly two weeks and still want a postponement." Hackworth continued with a voice like Moses descending from the Mountain, "Captain O'Donnell, in life, nothing is certain. The doctors virtually guaranteed the due date when my wife was pregnant with our third child. We thought we had plenty of time. I put off painting the nursery. Well, you can guess what happened. The baby came two weeks early. For all we know, your wife could go into labor this afternoon, and you will be a proud papa handing out cigars at Fort Custer when you report here next Tuesday morning."

I thought about throwing out something about the impending Thanksgiving holiday, but I knew I was beaten. I signed off, hung up, and went to find my wife. A nurse guided me down a hallway and opened the door to an examination room. Annabelle was in tears.

"Placenta Previa is when the placenta lies low in the uterus and covers the cervix," the doctor explained. "During delivery, it may lead to severe bleeding. It can be dangerous for the mother and her baby."

The doctor's emotionless voice could have been describing the intricacies of the internal combustion engine. I barely heard her. She talked a lot. I remembered bed rest, I remembered "the baby is fine," I remembered something about reducing Annabelle's stress.

✕

Certain natural laws are immutable. What goes up must come down. All objects fall at a rate of 32 feet per second, squared. Dick Vitale will use the word "awesome" at least 70 times during any given basketball game. Every creature will eventually die. And, when Annabelle is angry, I go back to the couch. I should have pushed harder for a sleeper sofa.

That weekend before I left for Texas, I tried to make amends with Annabelle, but she pretended to be asleep. I headed downstairs and checked the flight schedule. The Monday before Thanksgiving is one of the busiest times of the year. I had a seat on a morning flight with a connection in Atlanta. Scheduled arrival in El Paso: 4 p.m. local time.

I pulled a blanket and pillow out of the closet and tried to sleep. Three hours later, I was awake and on my way to the airport. I scribbled a schedule for Annabelle on my way out the door.

"Monday afternoon: Arrive in El Paso/meet with Jefferson. Tuesday: hearing. Wednesday: Flight home. Give the kids kisses from me."

No need for a love note. She'd made her feelings clear as I left the bedroom.

"Don't hurry back," she'd said. "We'll do fine without you."

CHAPTER 30

In Washington DC, little had changed in The Olde Ebbitt Grill since it opened in 1856. Sure, décor and menu and even the location had been altered. Still, the atmosphere, the *gravitas* of a place frequented by politicians, lobbyists, and general governmental dirt mongers had remained virtually untouched for over 150 years.

Two men occupied a booth at the back of the establishment. They were not speaking. Robert Walters alternated between fidgeting with his double Johnnie Walker Blue Label and buttering the dinner roll on his plate. He wore the District's uniform - dark, pinstriped suit, Brooks Brothers tie, and matching pocket square.

Walters landed the position as the Secretary of the Army despite having never served. He had worked as an anti-green lobbyist for over a decade, stashing favors and spreading the wealth from industries more concerned with profits than the environment. He was a small, unassuming man, but those who underestimated Walters did so at their own peril. He was legendary for his relentless fund-raising efforts and ruthless political acumen.

The other man stared at his menu.

A hostess approached the table with a uniformed Army officer in tow. Walters stood and said, "Colonel, thanks for flying in on such short notice."

The men shook hands.

Paine offered his hand to the booth's other occupant and said, "Colonel Covington Paine, Army JAG Corps, it's a pleasure to meet you."

"Sit down," the third man said. "Don't fucking announce your presence."

Paine blushed and slid into the booth next to Walters.

"Colonel, this is Mr. Johnston," Walters said. "He can be an asshole when he's hungry."

Paine nodded. "Sir, your first name again?"

"Mister," Johnston responded and resumed his perusal of the dinner selections. Paine had been around the block enough times to recognize a CIA guy. Johnston was a muscular, middle-aged man with blond hair, a handsome face, and a high forehead. His gray eyes were intense, his face rugged thanks to years in hot, arid climates. With a constant smirk, he resembled a cocky Ivy League frat boy. In his time at the CIA, Johnston was notorious for sexually exploiting young female recruits.

Johnston had entered the CIA straight out of Princeton and slithered his way up the ranks, carefully crafting political alliances. During his tour as Deputy Station Chief in Kabul, Afghanistan, after 9/11, he took credit for the rapid collapse of the Taliban and the quick pacification of the country. Even with an IQ well into the MENSA stratosphere, he was more ruthless than brilliant.

An upbeat waiter approached the table and poured bottled water for the group. "My name is Marcos. It's my pleasure to serve you this evening."

"Listen, amigo," Johnston said, "can't you see we're in the middle of something?"

Marcos did not take the hint. "Can I start you gentlemen off with a cocktail?"

Walters intervened. "Marcos, give us a minute, please."

"Of course!" Marcos said, wandering off with a smile still plastered on his face.

"Damn, Johnston, you are a Grade-A asshole," Walters said.

"Fuck you, Bobby," Johnston replied. Then, he snapped his head toward Paine. "Colonel, let's cut the bullshit." Johnston rapped his knuckles on the table, causing the silverware to bounce. "What's going on with your cases?"

"Which ones?" Paine asked. "I have a lot on my plate."

Johnston scoffed. "Colonel, even an idiot private can figure out that the Secretary of the Army and the fucking CIA aren't here to discuss a case of grab-ass in the chow hall."

"You mean the Sangar cases?" Paine asked, trying to maintain composure. No one had spoken to him like that in, well, maybe ever.

"Yes, Colonel, the Sangar cases," Johnston said in a mocking tone. "The cases that should have gone away the day before our Lord was born."

"They've been on my desk for less than three months," Paine said.

"That's three months too long," Johnston replied. "Make them go away. Now."

"Why?" Paine said.

Their eyes locked.

"Why?" Johnston asked incredulously. "Because there are people involved in this that you don't want to fuck with."

Paine assessed the situation. Something told him pissing Johnston off could mean finishing his military career burning shit barrels at an airbase in Uzbekistan. Still, Paine was a tried-and-true Army Prosecutor. "Mr. Johnston," he said, "I'm going to hammer these defendants. We have rock-solid cases. They're scared and desperate. They'll plead out, or we'll crush them at trial." Paine was staring at Johnston, but he failed to see the warning signs.

"Good God, Colonel," Johnston said. "Did your momma drop you on your head repeatedly as a child, or did you have a lobotomy?" Johnston took a long, loud gulp of water. "I don't care how strong you think your cases are. These things go away. I mean away. They never see the light of day. Here's how this reads to the public. Some soldiers got frisky; they slapped some camel jockeys. They do some time, and everyone is happy."

"Sir, there were grave human rights violations at Sangar," Paine said. "Some of the prisoners were murdered in cold blood. The Army cannot allow its honor to be sullied by a few bad apples."

Johnston sighed. "Hell, you guys already look like shit because of Abu, but Sangar is different."

"How are they different, and how is the CIA mixed up in this?" Paine asked.

"You're catching on, Colonel." Johnston grinned. "Two beats behind, but you'll eventually get up to speed."

"Answer my question," Paine said.

"Are you fucking kidding me?"

"No, I'm not kidding. I need to be read-in on this."

Johnston didn't say anything for 10 seconds, then 20. Finally, after a full minute, he spoke in a quiet whisper. "Colonel," he said, "let me be direct. I will use simple words, so you don't miss the point." He held up one finger. "There's nothing to read, nothing to know, and nothing to say." Second finger. "I don't care if these soldiers only get 45 minutes in time-out because . . ." He held up a third. "No one is ever going to know anything about the Agency's involvement. If they do, two of the people at this table will be wearing paper hats and serving French fries. And, Colonel - to be clear - I never wear a fuckin' hat."

Both Walters and Paine wanted to speak. Neither one dared.

Johnston finally broke the silence in a voice that could have been heard in the Oval Office a half-mile away. "Hey,

Marcos! Are we ever going to get some fucking service over here?"

CHAPTER 31

Elsewhere in the nation's capital, Rose rolled onto her side. She'd waited long enough.

"Baby," she said, "I need something big."

"I thought I just gave you that," the man said, smiling.

"You know what I mean. I need whatever you have on the Sangar thing."

He cut his eyes at her and left the bed. At least he shut the door when he peed. He reopened it as he was brushing his teeth, then wandered back to bed. She could tell he was ready for Round Two. "Dammit, Rose. I've given you all you're going to get. Enough is enough. We shouldn't ruin tonight with a lot of shop talk. I'm leaving tomorrow."

She tried to sound disappointed. "Where you going, baby?"

"It's classified," he said. It wasn't, but he knew the words made her hot.

Rose could always get information - and she knew precisely how. Her hand slid across the sheet.

"Rose, I'm serious. I can't tell you anything else about the Sangar business. You have been waiting to put out the story; you want it to be spectacular. Even if I never tell you anything else, once you post it, everyone will know it came from me."

Rose laughed. Nothing dainty, a full-throated guffaw. "No, they won't, babe," she said. "Do you think for one minute that you're the only Congressman in the world who thinks I'm cute?"

He started to protest but was cut short as her head disappeared under the sheet.

Chapter 32

E ven at Fort Custer, in the U.S. military justice system, the accused is entitled to due process. Before a case can go to a General Court-Martial, an Article 32 Investigation, a preliminary hearing of sorts, must be conducted. Military law experts often compare the hearing to a civilian grand jury, a process designed to stop cases from going to trial when there is insufficient evidence. In the military, grand juries do not exist. Instead, a single officer sits in judgment. This officer is called the Investigating Officer, the IO for short. In high-profile cases, like the Jefferson case, the IO is often a military judge.

Some Investigating Officers conduct thorough investigations and draft comprehensive reports with well-reasoned recommendations. Most merely sign off on the paperwork and move the case along toward trial. This is why JAGs call Article 32s, "the rubber stamp."

Two days before the hearing, as required, Paine had sent out a witness list. The file in my lap listed 15 names. That meant that in the next 36 hours, I would have to meet my client, get a copy of the entire case file, read it, and interview those 15 witnesses. I needed some help. So, I picked up my phone and called Reggie Jefferson in Dallas.

"Who is this?" Reggie asked.

"This is Captain O'Donnell."

"'Bout damn time," he said. "What's going on with the case?"

"They set the preliminary hearing for this Tuesday."

"I figured the Army would move fast. How can I help?"

"The prosecution has 15 witnesses. I just got the list," I said. "I have no investigative resources. All I have are their names and phone numbers. Can you look into them for me?"

"Send me what you have."

"Thanks, Mr. Jefferson."

"Call me Reggie. What else do you need?"

"Can you make it to the hearing? I could use the backup."

"You got it. In the meantime, let me dig up some dirt on these motherfuckers."

CHAPTER 33

That same day at noon, Reggie strolled into the Dallas Police Department dressed in a black suit and red tie. He was on his way to visit an old friend, Assistant Chief Charles Davenport. Reggie and Davenport went way back. They attended the Police Academy together and worked their first assignment as partners.

After his first tour as a beat cop, Reggie went to the operations side; SWAT and then counter-narcotics. He loved taking out narco-traffickers. Davenport was drawn to the administrative side, where he quickly climbed the ranks. The two were bound by a dark history. Their first job as rookies was patrolling the projects in the Ross-Bennett Grid, rousting street dealers, and responding to domestic violence calls.

One rainy December evening, they found a 20-year-old woman screaming on the sidewalk. "He's gonna kill my babies," she said.

The officers ran into the two-bedroom walkup, with their guns drawn. They found the man, Deshawn Ward, standing in the kitchen wearing a white tank top, boxers, and Adidas flip-flops. His back was turned to the officers.

Davenport issued the command. "Police! Put your hands up."

The man, startled, spun around. He had a small paring knife in his hand. Davenport fired, spraying the white laminate cabinets with blood. Ward flew back, mortally wounded. Davenport stared at the sliced lime and unopened beer on the counter, as Reggie sprang into action. "Protect and serve" is a great motto, but the first rule on the streets is, "Cover your partner's ass." Reggie ground the lime in the disposal and put the beer in the fridge.

The woman from outside ran into the kitchen and screamed, "What did you do? You killed him."

She swung at Davenport and missed. He grabbed the woman and pushed her out of the kitchen. Reggie took a rag from the counter, opened a drawer, dug out a large kitchen knife, and carefully placed it in the dead man's hand. The subsequent investigation ruled it a "clean shoot," and Davenport was cited for bravery. Time to return the favor.

The oak door to the Assistant Chief's office swung open as soon as the secretary announced Reggie's presence. Davenport had not aged gracefully. Too much Texas BBQ and the mini-keg of Shiner Bock he kept in his garage undoubtedly contributed to his protruding gut. Gaining five pounds a year adds up, especially over a quarter of a century. Davenport still sported a buzz cut; once a Marine always a Marine.

"Hey, Reg." Davenport extended his hand. "How's life been treatin' ya?"

Reggie shrugged. "Ya know, same ole shit, different day."

Davenport gestured to a chair, and Reggie sat. The Chief opened a cabinet and poured two fingers of Scotch into a crystal glass.

Reggie sniffed, then tasted. "A little better than the shit we used to drink," he said. "You on the wagon?"

"No," Davenport said, "I am on the job. Enjoy it for me. It's 20-years old."

Davenport watched Reggie savor a sip from across his expansive desk. "What's on your mind, Reg? You didn't just drop by for a drink."

"I'm here about my boy, Tyler. You remember him?"

"Of course." Davenport nodded and flashed a crooked smile. "Tyler played Little League with my son, he was a helluva athlete."

"Yeah, sure was."

"So, what's up? He looking for work?"

"Nah. He's in some trouble."

Davenport crossed his arms. "What kind of trouble?"

"The Army locked him up." Reggie's eyes darkened. "Been accused of killing some terrorist in Afghanistan."

"Whoa. Ain't that what we send them boys over there to do? To kill terrorists?"

"Fucking PC politicians." Reggie's voice quaked.

"So, what you want, a letter or something?"

"No. I need background checks on some witnesses."

Davenport leaned forward and whispered, "Come on, man. I can lose my job doing shit like that. This job is high profile. People watch me every damn day."

"Then, don't get caught."

"Reggie, I retire in a few months. The last thing I need is IA up my ass."

"Fuck Internal Affairs and fuck your job," Reggie said. "I have never said this to you before, but you owe me, and I need your help."

The career cop thought for a moment and then nodded slowly. "How many names and when do you need it?"

Reggie pulled a folded piece of paper from his pocket and handed it to Davenport. "Fifteen in all - and I needed it yesterday."

CHAPTER 34

Covington Paine loved his job. He always loved his job. When Paine hazed plebes at West Point, he loved his job. When he prosecuted slackers, he loved his job. When he kissed the General's ass at staff meetings, he loved his job. Paine's passion arose from his devotion to God, country, and the United States Army. Anyone who had ever spent more than 10 minutes with him knew his core values - and recognized his fanaticism.

Once the War Crimes Prosecution Team was assembled in the conference room, Paine dimmed the lights, turned on the projector, and started his PowerPoint presentation. Paine's team were top-notch litigators: Major Hanna Weiss, Captain Steven Nelson, and CID Special Agent Adam Bronson. They were loyal and as hell-bent on winning convictions as their boss.

Before she joined the Sangar Team, Major Weiss spent six years prosecuting felonies at Fort Hood, Texas, the Army's busiest jurisdiction. There, she earned the nickname, "The Pitbull in Heels," due to her tenacity in court. Weiss styled her hair in a severe bun and shunned make-up like children avoid vegetables. She took the Abu Ghraib and Sangar cases personally. The granddaughter of Abraham Weiss, a Polish Jew who'd survived the horrors of the Treblinka extermination camp, Hanna saw the recent Army atrocities as an abhorrent descendant of the Nazi mindset.

Captain Nelson had the most trial experience. A life-long federal prosecutor in D.C., Nelson spent over 19 years chasing everyone from gang members to white-collar criminals. Frail and pasty, Nelson was more computer geek than Army soldier. At 44, Nelson joined the Army National Guard as a JAG lawyer. Eighteen-months later, he was mobilized to active duty to work on Paine's team.

Special Agent Bronson spent over 20 years investigating military crimes. To him, the end, which was a conviction, always justified the means, even if the ethics got a little blurry. He specialized in 14-hour interrogations, falsifying polygraph results, and getting witnesses to change their testimonies to suit his narrative. He believed he could tell whether a person was guilty just by looking into their eyes.

With orders to win at all costs, Paine's team was empowered to level whatever charges they deemed appropriate, whatever they thought would stick. "This is our next opponent. Captain Max O'Donnell." Paine clicked to the first slide. A photo of Max appeared on the screen. "He's defended a total of 22 felony cases in his career. Thirteen were guilty pleas, the other nine went to a jury. All resulted in convictions of some sort."

"He's never won a case," Bronson noted.

Weiss cracked her knuckles. "Piece of cake."

"Is he really going to fight this?" Nelson asked in disbelief.

"No way," Paine said. "He has three months left in the Army, and his wife's about to give birth. I'll bet you a steak dinner he'll fold before we carve the turkey on Thursday."

※

Later in the day, after receiving his briefing on the case, the famous L. Edward Williams had called Paine and tried to cut a deal for Sergeant Cullen. Williams demanded full immunity and no jail time for his client. The bold offer offended Paine's ego. So, he told Williams to go to hell.

Despite Johnston's comment about "45 minutes in time out," Paine was not about to let Cullen off easy. Cullen, after all, was charged with murder. Paine stepped out of his office and hollered down the hallway, "Everybody in the conference room. Now." After his team filed in and settled into their chairs, Paine thought out loud as he paced around the room. "Williams overplayed his hand, and I don't like having my balls busted by a media whore lawyer," he said. "He went for a home run when he should have been happy with a sacrifice fly."

The group grumbled their agreement.

"So." Paine rubbed his hands together. "We're going to play a little game of legal chicken."

"What's your idea, boss?" Bronson asked, keen on messing with people's minds.

"I want to up the ante and ask for the death penalty for Cullen and Jefferson," Paine said. "Once we put the screws to them, they'll beg for mercy. The first one to cave gets a sweetheart deal."

"What about the other one?" Weiss asked.

"Once we flip one of them," Paine said, "the other will have no choice but to take a dive."

"An experienced defense lawyer, like Williams, will dig in his heels and call bullshit," Nelson said.

Paine wagged his finger. "I think the possibility of lethal injection will bring him to his senses."

Major Weiss jumped in, "Agreed. We've been too lenient. War criminals, at a minimum, should get life in prison. Dozens of Germans and Japanese were executed after World War II."

Nelson shook his head in disagreement. "These are American soldiers. They aren't Nazis killing Jews. Besides, we won the war; the Nazis didn't."

"Does it matter?" Weiss snapped back.

"You're damn right, it matters," Nelson said. "You're looking at it from the wrong angle. How many American soldiers were executed for war crimes against the Nazis? None that I know of."

"So what?" Weiss huffed.

Then, Bronson spoke, "In a recent poll, the majority of Americans don't believe a U.S. soldier should face court-martial for abusing terrorists. Lots of bloggers are calling Jefferson and Cullen heroes."

"Bloggers?" Paine's face registered disgust. "More like rumor mongers. We need to change the public's perspective; dirty these soldiers up."

"How, exactly?" Nelson asked.

"That's the easy part," Paine said. "First, we smear them in the media. Release as much dirt on them as possible. Second, we stack every charge we can think of."

"Sir." Weiss sat up and passed a document to Paine. "I took the liberty of drafting additional charges." Nelson and Bronson rolled their eyes. Hanna was a great attorney - and a world-class brownnoser. "I think we should include maltreatment, conspiracy, aiding and abetting, failure to follow Army regulations, dereliction of duty, and obstruction of justice. Maybe even throw in a drunk and disorderly on Jefferson."

"We couldn't prove half of those charges," Nelson replied.

"It doesn't matter what we can prove," Paine said with an ominous grin. "All that matters is that they think we can prove it."

CHAPTER 35

My flight to El Paso was uneventful. After landing, I collected my bags and walked out of the airport. A black Escalade was waiting for me at the curb. I knew it was Reggie even before he rolled down the excessively tinted window.

"Get in," he said, motioning with his head.

I tossed my luggage in the back and climbed into the front seat. The Little Tree air fresheners tied to the dashboard, bombarded my nostrils with the scent of synthetic strawberries. An unfamiliar funk tune blared from the speakers, pulsating the cluster of Mardi Gras beads hanging from the rear-view mirror.

"How was the trip?" Reggie asked.

"Not bad," I said. "You have any luck with the witnesses?"

He rubbed his chin and laughed. "I got more shit than a chili truck. Takes a lot to surprise me, brother, but some of those witnesses are doozies." His toothpick twitched as he talked.

"What do you mean?" I asked.

"Counselor, I thought the Army had standards, but some of these cats are as nasty as a syphilitic whore. I got the reports in the back. Show 'em to you when we get to the motel," he said.

"Highlights?"

"We got check fraud, a deadbeat dad, some druggies, and a guy who went to jail for lying to a judge, and I'm just getting started."

"Not bad," I said and changed the subject. "Can we swing by Fort Custer? I need to stop by the prosecutor's office and pick up the evidence. Then, I need to meet with your son."

"Sure thing." Reggie checked the side mirror, then floored it. The big Cadillac jumped like a cat with a stepped-on tail.

This time I did not have to wait. I found Paine sitting behind a large wooden desk, decorated with military memorabilia. He introduced Captain Steven Nelson and Major Hanna Weiss, who sat perched on the couch, like vultures.

"O'Donnell," Paine said, "the minute we step into the preliminary hearing, all bets are off."

"Meaning?" I said.

Paine leaned back in his chair with his fingers laced behind his head. "You don't want this case to go capital, do you?" he asked.

I raised my eyebrows. "You're threatening Jefferson with the death penalty?"

Paine nodded. Weiss clucked in agreement. Nelson smirked.

"Maybe," Paine said, "if you make us go through with the hearing."

"That a threat, Colonel?"

"Interpret it any way you want." Paine sneered. "We've been discussing the case. Given its gory details, the death penalty is warranted."

"Think about how you'd feel if someone did this to an American POW," Weiss said.

"First, no court has established that my client did anything. Second, Nassar was a bad guy, a platinum-level terrorist. And, not to put too fine a point on it, I believe the current term is 'enemy combatant,' not 'POW.'"

"He was a human being," Weiss said, with the quivering voice of rage.

"Call him whatever you want," I said. "To me, and the rest of America, he's a terrorist."

"Do you want to cut a deal, or not?" Paine asked.

"What's the current offer?"

"We think 20 is fair. Plead him quickly and help us convict Cullen, and we'll knock it down to six."

With a six-year sentence, he'd be eligible for parole in two years. *Not bad*, I thought.

"I'll take it to Jefferson, but I have to see the evidence first," I said.

"Tick-tock." Paine tapped his watch. "Cullen is getting a similar deal later today."

"I'm sure he's already gotten it." I stood and picked up my briefcase. "No evidence, no deal."

"Fine," Paine said. "Wait in the spare office while we get the file."

The "spare office" was a tiny room with a broken swivel chair. It was heated to about 85 degrees. After half an hour, I started to nod off. Unexpectedly, the door slammed open, jolting me awake.

A stocky man sporting a Wilford Brimley handlebar mustache stalked into the room. He was 50-ish but trying to look younger. The lousy dye job on his ink-black hair fooled no one. His Wrangler jeans were too tight. He bulged so conspicuously, I suspected he had shoved a roll of quarters down the front of his pants. A nickel-plated revolver and rodeo belt buckle the size of a license plate hung from his western-style belt.

"Howdy, Marshal," I said. "You looking for the O.K. Corral?"

"Name's Bronson, Special Agent Bronson." He glared at me through deep-set eyes. "They told me you were Mr. Hilarious." He pulled in a hand cart and unloaded an oversized banker's box. "Here's the evidence on your shitbag client." I could tell it was full by the effort he put into hoisting it onto the desk. "Enjoy, asshole," he said and slammed the door behind him.

CHAPTER 36

"Motherfuckers!"

I'd read enough legal thrillers to understand what I was seeing. An evidence dump. Paine must have chained his paralegal to a copier for 72 hours straight. The box was stuffed to the rim, and not neatly. Pages were crammed, wedged, shoved, and mangled. Many of them were copies of copies in various states of illegibility. Half of the pages were heavily redacted.

I found an Army Field Manual, a massive CID Report of Investigation, *Human Rights Watch* articles, and many black-and-white headshots of what appeared to be soldiers. There was no index. I bet Paine had one.

The strategy was obvious:

Me: "Your Honor, I have never seen this evidence."

Judge: "Colonel Paine, have you provided this discovery to the defense?"

Paine: "Your Honor, esteemed counsel was furnished said evidence on 21 November. It was in Box A. We have the number of the exhibit as 2,454."

Then, I'd look either lazy or incompetent. It was a brilliant scheme.

"Motherfuckers," I said again.

I went through the box for two hours. The evidence did not paint a rosy picture of Sangar Prison. Numerous senior officers and American politicians had toured the facility, yet no military officers seemed to be in charge. The prison had a commander, but he had limited authority. Since the military can be almost comical with its specificity, the slipshod governance at Sangar was odd, to say the least.

Before deploying to Afghanistan, the Army took them to visit Ground Zero, where the remains of the Twin Towers were still being cleared. Decked out in their uniforms, they received hugs, kisses, and grateful tears from civilians visiting the site. The park service gave them an American flag that had flown for a day over the site. They took the sacred symbol to Afghanistan and hung it in the center of Sangar Prison. It was a reminder of what they were fighting for.

Equally alarming, no one ever trained the "guards" on how to guard prisoners. Jefferson and his buddies were Army Reservists. A road patrol MP unit, traffic cops who ended up guarding some of the top prisoners in the War on Terror. Guards were ordered to carry out "prescriptions" for the prisoners: sleep deprivation, exercise, whatever the interrogators posted on the board next to the Ground Zero flag.

Most of the stuff in the box was worthless unless I was going to start a fire. I couldn't tell what was relevant. I couldn't connect the dots. I was on information overload. There were too many names. Too many unanswered questions. I assumed all this would take on some meaning as the case progressed.

It was getting late, and I still had to meet with Jefferson. Reviewing the entire file before the hearing would have been impossible. *He needs to plead this out* was all I could think. I did some quick math. Talk to Jefferson. Convince him to take the deal. Go to Paine and announce our intentions to plead out. Hump it to the airport and miraculously transform my military service into a first-place spot in the standby line.

I closed the bulky box and lugged it out of the building. Reggie waited outside with the engine running. I heaved the box into the trunk and climbed inside. "Here you go." I handed Reggie a stack of papers.

"What am I lookin' at?" he said as he flipped through them.

"Sworn statements. You mind reading them while I meet with Tyler?"

"I'm comin' with you."

"You can't." I shook my head. "Family can only visit on weekends."

"Alright." Reggie nodded. "I'll take a look at 'em." He wedged the documents into his center console, and we drove across Fort Custer toward the Brig.

CHAPTER 37

Reggie dropped me off at the Brig and went to get a cup of coffee. Inside the Brig, a guard led me to the "Attorney-Client Meeting Area," a small, whitewashed room with a round stainless steel picnic table in the center. The electric buzz of fluorescent lights and the smell of Pine-sol overwhelmed my senses.

I sat and waited for my client. After a few minutes, a metal door creaked open, and Jefferson ambled into the room. His eyes darted from side to side.

"Please sit." I motioned to bench across from me.

Jefferson let out a long sigh as he plopped down and crossed his arms. "I've been waiting all day," he said. "Where've you been?" His gratitude from last week had apparently worn off.

"Trying to save your ass," I replied.

"How so?"

"I just came from the prosecutor's office. He gave me a stack of new evidence."

"How much?"

"Six thousand pages, give or take."

"Can you get through that by tomorrow?" He wasn't kidding.

"Sergeant, if I had my entire law school class helping, we would not make a dent by tomorrow - maybe not by next week."

He stared at me with his mouth open. Then he said, "Anything good in there?"

"Not really. There are many sworn statements from people who don't like you. Did you spend your entire tour pissing people off?"

"I guess I come on a little strong sometimes."

"Well, there is a big difference between being unpopular and being a murderer."

"Sir, I didn't kill nobody."

"If you didn't kill Nassar, then who did?"

Jefferson crossed his arms. "Don't know."

"You have no idea who beat the shit out of him?"

"Nope?"

"Was it Cullen?"

"No way."

"How do you know that?"

"I know him. He'd never do that."

"Could it have been someone else in your unit?" I asked.

"Don't know nothin' about it, except I had nothin' to do with it."

"Then why are so many people pointing the finger at you?"

"Some people just don't like me?"

"Why?"

"Because." He shrugged.

"Sergeant, throw me a bone," I said. "I'm trying to help you."

"Sir, I don't know nothin'."

"If you don't know nothin', then I'm wasting my time here." I slid a two-inch stack of papers across the table. "Read these sworn statements before you go to bed."

Jefferson flipped through the documents. "That's a lot of reading," he said.

"You got something better to do?"

He shook his head.

"Good. Your dad dug up dirt on some of these witnesses. I should be able to discredit them at tomorrow's hearing."

"My dad?" Jefferson's face soured.

"Yeah."

"Reggie's a piece of shit. I don't want him involved."

"Too late. He's here, and he's been helping me."

"Fuck him. He was never around. Now he shows up?"

I nodded and changed the subject. "By the way, the prosecution came back with another offer - 20 years - they'll drop it to six if you help convict Cullen. You'll be eligible for parole in two years."

Jefferson shot to his feet. "What the fuck, Captain? First 10, now 20? And, I ain't no buddy fucker."

I stood slowly and spoke in an even tone, "Sergeant, sit down, and do not raise your voice like that again."

He sat. "I ain't no rat," he said.

"Well, Cullen might be. They offered him the same deal."

"I don't want *any* jail time. I want to go home." Jefferson did not get it.

"Sergeant, after the mess at Abu Ghraib, if a U.S. detainee gets a bloody nose, someone is going to pay. You've been around the Army long enough to know that shit rolls downhill. In this case, we're not talking about a bloody nose. We're talking about a dead body - one to which you are directly connected. I'm trying to get you out of prison in time for you to see your children graduate from high school." I thought I was making progress. I thought wrong.

"Captain." Jefferson's eyes glazed over. "Tell them I'll plead to dereliction of duty. No jail time. No dishonorable discharge."

"That won't fly. Our counteroffer must be reasonable. It-"

"But I'm not a violent person," he said, interrupting me.

"Sergeant," I said with more edge than I wanted. "Do not interrupt me. No jail time, in a murder case, is not reasonable."

Jefferson huffed. "This is fuckin' ridiculous."

I slammed my hand on the table. "Stop talking and start listening. Your mouth is one of the reasons you're in this situation."

Jefferson could not contain himself. "Why would I kill someone? Why would I risk everything? I have two-"

"Shut. The. Fuck. Up! If you don't get anything else out of this meeting, get this: Stop talking!"

"Fuck - you - sir."

I walked out of the room with the same tired refrain playing behind me.

"I didn't kill nobody."

CHAPTER 38

O utside of the Brig, Reggie waited in his Escalade, and I climbed in. Rick James' "Give It To Me Baby," blared on the radio.

"How'd it go?" Reggie asked as I buckled up.

"Your son rejected the prosecutor's deal."

Reggie nodded and sucked on his teeth. "That's my boy."

We cruised north on U.S. Route 54. As the El Paso city lights faded behind us, I asked Reggie, "Where are we going?"

"A buddy of mine owns a motel on the East Side; he's gonna hook us up." I wasn't sure what he meant by "hook us up." The Army would pay for my room, so long as it was at the government rate. Before the trip, Reggie agreed to be my driver and arrange the travel details. I did not specify which hotel. Now, I wished I had.

"I read those statements you gave me," Reggie said.

"What do you think?"

"None of their stories add up. Trust me, I've seen trumped-up shit before. They're lyin' about my boy."

"How can you tell?"

"Easy," he said. "When a witness gives too many details and points the finger at someone else too hard, it's a red flag. They're tryin' to shift the blame."

It made sense to me.

"You know what else?" he said. "The cops wrote some of those statements."

"Why do you say that?"

"The statements made in Afghanistan, back in 2002, were all handwritten. They don't say shit about Tyler. But in 2005, those same 15 witnesses were re-interviewed by Special Agent Bronson. All 15 statements were typed. They all point the finger at Tyler, and every last one of those assholes refers to Tyler as 'The Perpetrator.'"

"Maybe they didn't have a computer," I said.

"Son, they had multi-million-dollar weapons systems. You don't think they had a fuckin' laptop?"

I wasn't so sure. To me, the statements seemed pretty straightforward. Multiple soldiers described Jefferson abusing prisoners. They gave times, dates, and described acts of violence that matched the physical evidence. Gory photographs corroborated their accounts. The autopsy conducted by the Army concluded that Hamza Nassar's death was a homicide caused by blunt force trauma.

"Here we go," Reggie said as he took a hard right into a motel parking lot. The Rodeo Inn was a one-story building. A glowing neon sign on the roof featured a cowboy riding a bronco. A few letters were burned out. It flashed: "Welcome to th Rode In." The place reminded me of a set from a low-budget horror picture.

"Seriously?" I said.

"It ain't the Ritz, but it's clean, and it's free."

"Good point," I said. Though I wasn't that confident.

Next to the motel was a large metal building with a well-lit sign that said, "Kitty Kat Lounge: All Nude Exotic Ladies & Gourmet Buffet. Open 24/7." Twin searchlights crisscrossed the night sky telling the world the Kitty Kat was open for business.

Reggie parked and hopped out of the SUV. "I'll get the room keys. You stay here," he said and slammed the door. A few minutes later, he returned. "You're in 15, next to the vending machines. I'm in seven, the deluxe suite." He tossed me a key and winked. I followed Reggie to the trunk, and we grabbed our bags. "Meet me in 10. We'll grab a bite and discuss strategy," he said, and we headed to our rooms.

A few minutes later, when we met, I started walking toward the Escalade. "Where you going, counselor?" Reggie lowered his sunglasses and raised an eyebrow.

"There's a Mexican restaurant a few miles back." I motioned toward the highway.

"Nah." Reggie shook his head in disapproval. "Kitty Kat's got some good wings. Some nice eye candy too."

I must not have hidden my skepticism well.

"Seriously," he said. "Trust me." I followed Reggie across the 100-yard stretch between the motel and the club. We passed a dude getting a blowjob underneath a big rig and a rat-faced woman who offered full-service sex for $40, or a threesome for $60. This was insanity. I was in the middle of nowhere fighting a losing murder case, my wife was about to go into labor, and my client's father was taking me to a strip club for dinner.

Outside the club, Mani, a thick-necked Mexican wearing a black leather vest, manned the entrance. Tattoos covered every inch of visible skin below his chin line. "Sup Reg? Long time no see." He and Reggie exchanged fist bumps and bro hugs. "You out here on business?"

Reggie shrugged.

"Enjoy." Mani unhooked a velvet rope and opened the door. Bass and cigarette smoke spewed from inside. As I passed him, Mani leaned toward me and shouted into my ear, "We got some fine ass tonight." I nodded and kept walking.

Inside, girls of all shapes and colors strutted the catwalk and swung from brass poles. Lights flashed, and the woofers made my insides vibrate. A tall Hispanic woman led us to a booth near the stage. A sign on the table said, "VIP." A painted-on mini-skirt began at her trim waist and ended just under her full hips. She wore a silk halter. Long black hair cloaked her tattooed back.

"Welcome to the Kitty Kat," she said with a Spanish accent, by way of Jersey City. "I'm Esmeralda." She placed her hand on her exposed chest and chomped her gum as she spoke. "I'm going to be taking care of you guys tonight. I heard you're close with Rico."

"We go a ways back," Reggie said with a lopsided grin.

I was intrigued. *Who was Rico, and how does he know Reggie?*

"Rico's out of town on business," she said as she caressed Reggie's shoulder. "He asked me to take care of you guys." Reggie eyeballed Esmeralda from head to toe, paying careful attention to her large breasts. Nodding his approval, he bit his lower lip and grunted.

Then, Esmeralda slid into the booth next to me. "Hey baby, whatcha drinkin' tonight?" Her skin felt like velvet against mine; she smelled of floral shampoo.

"Water, please," I said.

Reggie howled. "What the fuck kind of lawyer doesn't drink?"

My eyes darted to Reggie. "I have court tomorrow," I said.

Esmeralda moved to Reggie and sat on his lap. "And what can I get for you, big boy?" She slid her hand inside his red silk shirt, unbuttoned to mid-chest.

"I'll take a double Crown on the rocks." His mouth twitched. "And get that man a real drink."

Esmeralda batted her eyes at me.

"Whatever you have on tap," I said.

"Is Modelo all right?" she asked.

"Yeah, sure."

One beer turned into a second, then a third. Somewhere around the time we started doing shots, the night turned into a blur. I only remembered two things: Esmeralda bringing drinks and the feeling that I was - for the first time in a while - genuinely having a good time. I have a vague memory of my cell phone vibrating. I didn't answer.

CHAPTER 39

I woke naked in a pool of sweat. I never slept naked. The room was dark and stifling, like the inside of a coffin. As I felt my way to the bathroom, I stubbed my big toe on a table. Only then, I realized I was not at home. I flicked on a light and yanked open the curtains. Sunlight streamed through the window and split my throbbing head like a laser. My eyes searched for a trash can, just in case.

Dread overcame my hangover. A quick reconnoiter of the room relieved me a little. I was alone. My screw up had been limited to excess alcohol. I willed my watch into focus. It was almost seven o'clock in the morning.

Shit. The hearing started in an hour and 15 minutes. After I showered and shaved, I threw on my Army uniform and sprinted out the door. *Where is my rental car?* Then, I remembered I didn't have a car.

Reggie's suite was at the end of the building. His Escalade stood guard outside. I must have been walking east - the rising sun drilled into the back of my brain. Reggie didn't answer my knock, so I called his cell. The call went to voicemail after three rings. I walked to the Escalade and tried to open the front passenger door, hoping he left a spare key inside. The car alarm screamed.

Then, I heard Reggie's voice. "What the fuck are you doing with my ride, counselor?"

I turned. Reggie stood outside of his room shirtless, and wearing a G-string. "We're late for the hearing," I said.

Reggie moved to his room with all the urgency of a lumbering bear. He reappeared wearing jeans. He dug into his pocket and tossed me his keys. "You better haul ass," he said.

"You coming?" I asked.

A tall, bleached blonde walked up behind Reggie and wrapped her arms around him. Though hidden by Reggie's bulk, it was apparent she had not bothered to dress. "What's going on, baby?" she said in a childish voice.

Reggie ignored her. "Go. I'll get there. I have some unfinished business." Reggie leered at the woman behind him. If she was 18, she hadn't been for long.

I peeled out of the parking lot and hit the highway. The speedometer tipped 95 mph as I barreled toward Fort Custer. My cell phone beeped, and I stole a glance - five missed calls. All from Annabelle. All from last night. Calling now would only mean a fight. I didn't have time. I realized that my association with Reggie wasn't shaping up to be a good idea.

CHAPTER 40

At the Fort Custer gate, I popped three pieces of spearmint gum into my mouth, and lowered the windows, hoping it would disguise the alcohol emanating from my pores. I passed through the gate without a problem and drove to the JAG office. Inside, I found Jefferson shackled and flanked by two guards.

"Glad you could make it," he said. The sarcasm was evident.

"Follow me." Jefferson's shackles dragged across the wooden floor as he hobbled toward me. We ducked inside an empty, windowless room and closed the door. His guards stood watch outside. "Did you read the statements I gave you?" I asked him.

"Some of them," he said.

"Why didn't you read all of them?"

"They brought back too many bad memories."

"What about Nassar?" I prompted him. "What happened to Nassar?"

"He was a bad dude," Jefferson said, dodging the question.

"That is not what I asked. How did he die?"

"I don't know," he said. "I rarely worked in the VIP rooms."

"What VIP rooms?" My face scrunched. "There's no mention of that in the case file."

"That's where the OGAs did their dirty work."

"What the hell is an OGA?"

"Other Government Agency. Bad mother fuckers, probably CIA." I realized I was woefully unprepared for this hearing. I had a basic grasp of the case, but I knew nothing about VIP rooms or the OGA. If Jefferson was telling the truth, perhaps the OGA had something to do with Nassar's death.

A knock interrupted our conversation. Colonel Paine opened the door a few inches and said, "Judge Hackworth wants to see us."

I stood and followed Paine to the judge's chambers. I called to him as we walked, "Sir, when can I see the classified evidence?"

Paine stopped and faced me. "Never," he said. "We gave you what's relevant."

"I want everything, whether you think it's relevant or not, or I'll ask for a continuance."

"Do as you please." Paine pivoted and continued down the hallway.

Colonel Hackworth was finishing up a story when we entered his office. "I said, 'guilty of all charges,' and the dumb SOB took off like a jackrabbit, jumped out the third-story window, and broke his back. All he was going to do was six months in the Brig." Everybody in the room hooted. Hackworth stopped laughing when he saw me. "Take a seat," Hackworth said, motioning to a small brown couch in front of his desk. On the couch were Weiss and Nelson.

"Thank you, but I prefer to stand, sir," I said.

Hackworth stared at me. "Captain O'Donnell, sit down." Paine remained standing as I squeezed in between Weiss and Nelson and tried not to grunt.

"Good morning, everyone," Hackworth said. "I want to go over a few ground rules before we get started. First off, are there any outstanding issues?"

"All witnesses are present or on standby," Paine said, in his usual condescending tone. "However, I am worried that the defense may attempt to elicit classified evidence."

"Is that true, O'Donnell?" Hackworth said.

"Colonel, I-"

"It's 'Your Honor.'" Hackworth interrupted.

"Your Honor," I said, "I have no idea what information is classified and what isn't. The prosecution has not given me any classified evidence and-"

Now, Paine interrupted me. "Mike, (I noticed that Hackworth did not correct him) Captain O'Donnell cannot feign ignorance. According to National Security laws, whether he knows it's classified or not, releasing classified information is a felony."

Hackworth turned to me. "Is that understood, O'Donnell?"

"Sir, I mean, Your Honor. To do my job, I need to see all the evidence, including the classified evidence."

The judge removed his glasses and said, "Can you cite a rule that requires the prosecution to hand over classified material before a preliminary hearing?"

"Not off the top of my head," I said.

"Me neither," Hackworth replied. "We'll start the hearing at eight o'clock sharp. That should give everybody time to make final preparations and use the latrine."

CHAPTER 41

Judge Hackworth shook his head in disapproval when Jefferson and I walked into the hearing at 7:55 a.m. In the Army, if you aren't 15 minutes early, then you're late. The prosecution team preened at their table, obviously pleased with their punctuality.

There was no courtroom for the hearing, merely a conference room with three long tables arranged in the shape of a horseshoe. One for the judge and court reporter, one for the defense, and one for the prosecution. A folding metal chair for the witness sat in the middle of the horseshoe.

The room was 20 feet wide by 30 feet long. It felt crowded. It felt cramped. It felt claustrophobic.

The walls were covered with unpainted drywall. Old fluorescent lights buzzed overhead. A despotic Judge Hackworth lorded over the room. He had an array of multi-colored folders organized in front of him. The court reporter hurriedly adjusted his recording equipment.

Jefferson and I sat in chairs jacked up against the wall. I struggled to stand up straight because my chair could not push back far enough. The prosecution team was positioned directly across from us.

Two dozen cheap metal chairs were packed with the usual courtroom spectators: Army flunkies, paralegals, busybodies looking for some drama, and some disheveled news reporters. Most were there for a show, for entertainment, like people in centuries past who attended public executions. The only thing missing was popcorn.

Judge Hackworth shuffled through his papers, squirmed in his rickety chair, and glanced at his watch every 10 seconds. The hearing began promptly at 8 a.m. "This Article 32 hearing will come to order," Hackworth said, and the room fell silent. "Are you Sergeant Tyler B. Jefferson, the accused in this case?"

We hadn't had too much time to go over stuff, but Jefferson remembered at least one thing I told him. He stood at attention and said, "Sir, yes, sir."

"Thank you for the courtesy, Sergeant Jefferson." Hackworth motioned with his hand. "Please remain seated."

Jefferson sat, and Hackworth kept reading. "You have the right to be represented by your military defense counsel, Captain - (he looked down, raised an eyebrow) Maximillian Alejandro O'Donnell. You may also be represented by a military attorney of your choosing if such counsel is reasonably available. You also have the right to be represented by a civilian counsel provided by you at your own expense. Do you understand these rights?"

Jefferson leaned over and whispered to me, "What does he mean I can choose my military lawyer?" All eyes were on us.

"You can request a different Army lawyer, by name, if you know one," I said.

"Should I do that?" Jefferson asked.

"Do you know any military lawyers, aside from me?"

"No."

"Okay. Then answer the judge."

Hackworth's face contorted like he smelled a rancid piece of meat. Jefferson stared at the legal pad in front of him. After 20 seconds, Hackworth spoke. "Is there a problem?"

"No, Your Honor," I said.

"When you or your client are asked a question, answer the question," Hackworth said through clenched teeth.

I turned to Jefferson. "Answer him," I said under my breath.

Jefferson snapped to attention. His chair slammed back, punching a hole in the drywall. Someone in the audience snickered. "Out!" Hackworth pointed to the spectators. "Whoever laughed, get out." A young JAG lawyer in the front row stood, his face flushed with embarrassment. He grabbed his coat and dashed out of the room. Hackworth pointed at Jefferson with two fingers. "I'm not going to repeat this. Stay seated unless I tell you to stand."

Jefferson froze, like an opossum in the middle of the road, watching a life-ending pick-up coming around the curve. I pulled Jefferson back into his chair.

"By whom do you wish to be represented?" Hackworth repeated, his tone bordered on shouting.

This time I hooked two fingers over Jefferson's belt to keep him from standing. A bead of sweat formed on his brow. I pointed to the nametag on my chest. "By O'Donnell," Jefferson said.

"You mean *Captain* O'Donnell?" Hackworth asked.

"Yes, sir. Sorry, sir." Jefferson displayed a look of relief that made me wonder if he thought he'd survived the hard part.

Hackworth kept grinding. "I would like counsel to introduce themselves and state their qualifications." I sat directly across from Paine. He stood and droned away, ad nauseam, about his education, experience, and Army career. Then, he briefly introduced his squad of associates. I noticed Reggie had managed to make it and was now seated in the second row.

Somewhere along the way, I stood and introduced myself. Then, Hackworth headed into the Article 31 rights of the accused, the Army's version of Miranda - only no one can say them from memory. For the next 10 minutes, Judge Hackworth rambled on about the rules and procedures and listed the evidence he would consider. When he finished, he turned to me.

"Defense, do you have any objection to my consideration of this evidence?"

I found my first opening to launch a counterattack. "You only mentioned some of the evidence," I said. "Please order the Government to hand over all the evidence in their possession. You have to ensure a fair hearing. I cannot defend this case without having all the evidence."

Hackworth was flustered, but he tried to appear calm in front of the audience. "Captain O'Donnell, can you point to a specific document that you don't have?"

"Your Honor, how can I point to a specific document that I don't have if I don't know what I don't have?"

"Denied." Hackwork gave an exaggerated head shake. "You're asking me to go on a wild goose chase. I hope your defense strategy is more solid than that." A few of Paine's paralegals giggled.

I did not remove my eyes from Hackworth. I had him where I wanted him. "Your Honor, I demand all the classified documents in this case. I want the complete investigative file, with no redactions. I want a list of every person that entered Sangar Prison from June 2002 through December 2002. That includes military, civilian, CIA, OGA, everyone. I want Nassar's medical records. I want the duty rosters, so I can determine if Jefferson was even working in the facility on the dates charged. This evidence is relevant and may be useful in defending Sergeant Jefferson."

Hackworth was unfazed. "O'Donnell, unless you can show me some case law that requires them to hand over this *supposed* evidence, and I use that word loosely, then I again deny your request."

As we bickered back and forth, terror overtook Jefferson, who visualized the prison bars closing on him. He'd been understandably nervous going into the hearing, but I assured him that he would get a fair shake. I was wrong. Jefferson was screwed. We hadn't even begun to hear testimony, and he was already being railroaded.

By this point, the hearing room was standing room only. Onlookers filled the seats and lined the walls. In the corner of the room, I saw a striking young woman with black hair. Our eyes met, and she smiled softly. I was intrigued. She seemed out of place in a courtroom packed with soldiers and frumpy reporters. I wondered who she was.

"This is unacceptable," Hackworth said, bringing me back to reality. "I don't want anyone standing during this proceeding. It's distracting. We're in recess until someone finds more chairs."

During the break, Reggie approached me. Without acknowledging his father, Jefferson walked out of the room, flanked by his two guards. Reggie wore the same red silk shirt as the night before, and he reeked of cheap perfume and sex.

"How's it looking so far?" he asked.

"Terrible," I said. "A bunch of people are about to testify that your son is a murderer."

CHAPTER 42

After I talked to Reggie, I ran to the restroom. I was last in a long line at the only functioning urinal. When I reentered the hearing, Hackworth loudly cleared his throat and lit into me. "O'Donnell, this is the last time you'll delay this proceeding." Before I could answer, Hackworth ordered the prosecution to call their first witness.

Paine stood and spoke like he was announcing a prizefight. "The United States of America - calls Sergeant - Gary - Trott - to the stand."

A dumpy, 28-year-old man with a chipped front tooth and deep acne scars entered the room. Paine directed him to the witness chair.

"I hate this guy," Jefferson whispered, as Trott raised his right hand and swore to tell the truth.

When I read the case file, my initial impression was that Trott was a liar. In his first interview with CID, he claimed to know nothing about detainee abuse at Sangar. Three years later, Trott signed a 15-page sworn statement, accusing half of his platoon, including Jefferson, of abusing prisoners. Trott's allegations were light on detail and heavy on hearsay, gossip, and speculation, but the Army took them as Gospel.

Paine smiled at Trott and asked his first question. "Sergeant Trott, are you still on active duty?"

"Not for long," Trott responded.

"Why is that?"

"I am getting medically discharged. I have PTSD."

"Bullshit." Jefferson coughed into the crook of his arm.

Paine spun around and pointed at Jefferson. "Your Honor, did you hear that?"

"Huh?" Hackworth glanced from side to side. Thankfully, no one else had heard it.

Paine stared at Jefferson through squinted eyes. After a long pause, he continued in a soft voice, "I am sorry to hear about your PTSD. Is that a result of your deployment to Sangar, Afghanistan?"

"Yeah." Trott nodded. "After what I saw over there, I have nightmares. My wife, she, she left me." Trott's eyes moistened.

"Objection," I said, rising to my feet. "Sergeant Trott's marital problems and supposed PTSD, while lamentable, are irrelevant."

Paine gave me a dirty look and said to Hackworth, "His PTSD was caused by what he witnessed at the prison, including actions taken by Sergeant Jefferson."

"Overruled," Hackworth said. "Captain O'Donnell, you will refrain from impugning this soldier's service to our country or degrading his war wounds. God knows he's seen a lot more action than you. Colonel Paine, please continue, but don't get into the details of his psychiatric diagnosis. That would be an invasion of his privacy, and we don't want to re-traumatize him."

I sat down and asked Jefferson, "What's Trott's story?"

"He's a damn malingerer," Jefferson replied. "He tried to get out of the Afghanistan deployment, claimed his mother was dying. Turned out, she died six months earlier. At Sangar, he had light-duty because he 'hurt his back,' climbing an abandoned guard tower. We all knew he'd go up there to whack off. He hid in his tent and played cards the whole deployment - except for when he was taking out his own shit on the prisoners."

"What do you mean, taking out his own shit?"

"Whooping their motherfuckin' asses," Jefferson said as if I was stupid.

I made a mental note to get more details from Jefferson during a break. Meanwhile, I focused on Trott's testimony.

"Sergeant Trott, why did you have the courage to come forward in this case?" Paine asked.

"My momma always told me to do the right thing." Tears welled up in Trott's eyes. "I couldn't sit by and let Army soldiers mistreat prisoners. It's wrong."

In his testimony, Trott described Nassar as docile, terrified, and weak. On one occasion, Trott said he overheard Jefferson brag about beating prisoners and getting away with it because "It's my word against the word of a terrorist."

"Tell us," Paine said to Trott. "Did you ever witness Sergeant Jefferson strike a detainee?"

"Yes, unfortunately, I did," Trott replied.

"Tell us about that?"

"Well, I was on duty one night. It was pretty late. I heard a ruckus, and I went to check it out."

"What did you see?"

"I saw a prisoner tangled in a six-foot wall of concertina wire."

"What is he talking about?" I said to Jefferson.

Jefferson shrugged.

"Then what happened?" Paine asked Trott.

"Jefferson started hitting the detainee. Poor guy kept thrashing around. Blood sprayed everywhere."

"Did Jefferson provide the prisoner with medical care?"

"No." Trott shook his head. "He tore him from the wire and hogtied him."

"Why didn't you report this abuse earlier?"

Trott lowered his head. "I was afraid of what Sergeant Jefferson and his friends would do to me if they thought I was a snitch. They were called the 'Meathead Platoon' for a reason. I can fend for myself, but I'm not as big as them."

Everyone in the room looked at Jefferson. Some nodded. "What was the 'Meathead Platoon?'" Paine asked.

"The Crash Team guys. Jefferson's friends. We called them the 'Meatheads.' They were all jocks. All they did was lift. They always hung out together, at the gym, at chow. They wouldn't let anyone into their circle, and they made fun of anyone that wasn't part of their squad. I heard they were all juiced up on 'roids, and I believe it. They were aggressive. Ya know, 'roid rage."

"Objection. This is absurd," I said. "Now, this hearing is about steroids? Are you kidding me?"

"Sustained. Move on," Hackworth said, granting us a rare victory.

As Trott told his tale, Jefferson scribbled "he's lying" on a yellow legal pad and slid it to me. I pushed the notepad back and continued to listen to Trott's version of events. His in-court testimony varied widely from his original statement to CID. Then again, he had a couple of years to fabricate new details. Throughout his testimony, Judge Hackworth maintained eye contact with Trott and nodded as if he believed every word.

When Trott finished, the judge said, "Defense, it's almost chow time, how long will your cross-examination take?"

"Sir, it could take a while," I said. "It really depends on how forthcoming the witness is when answering my questions."

"Fine," Hackworth said and rolled his eyes. "We'll start at 1200 hours. Does everyone understand?"

Hackworth stared at me until I acknowledged, "Yes, Your Honor."

CHAPTER 43

During the lunch break, Reggie went to buy us some sandwiches at Subway. I stayed behind and met with Jefferson.

"That piece of shit, Trott, is lyin' his ass off," he blurted out as soon as I closed the door.

I held up my hand, telling him to stop. "We only have an hour," I said, "and name-calling is not going to help."

Jefferson crossed his arms and raised his chin. His macho man routine was getting old. "I don't know what to tell you, Captain. That concertina wire story never happened. I swear."

"Tell me everything you know about Trott and make it quick." After listening to Jefferson blather for five minutes, I cut him off. "Why would Trott lie about you? What's his motive?"

"The feud." Jefferson put his head in his hands. "It's all about that fuckin' feud."

"What the hell are you talking about?"

Jefferson stared at the floor. He must have thought it all sounded juvenile. He was wrong. It sounded idiotic. "At Sangar, we had our separate groups," he said. "They nicknamed me and my boys the 'Meatheads.' We were real soldiers. We wore our hair high and tight and spent our free time liftin'. Know what I'm sayin'?"

I nodded. "What about Trott?"

"Trott ran with the 'Outcasts.' They kept to themselves mostly. Piss-poor slackers. They hated the other guards, especially me and my friends. They were like vampires. They hid in their tents when their shifts were done and listened to some kind of weird, satanic music."

"You mean like Goth?"

"Yeah, somethin' like that."

"You guys push 'em around, Sergeant?" I asked. "A little like high school?"

"Yeah. We were pretty much assholes to 'em, but they deserved it."

"Now it's biting you in the ass, huh?"

"Seems that way."

"Go on," I said, barely disguising my disgust for professional soldiers who act like infants.

"The third group was the 'Cool Kids.' A bunch of entitled dickweeds. Most of these losers lived with their parents. They joined the Army Reserve for free college money. They played a lot of grab-ass and gossiped like a bunch of little bitches. They ruined a few good careers from what I heard."

"How did the groups get along?"

"Like shit," Jefferson said. "The Cool Kids manipulated the Outcasts; they were nice to their faces but talked trash about them behind their backs. All the witnesses against me are Cool Kids, except for Trott."

"Why is that?"

"We ran that prison and cracked down on the shitbags that didn't follow the rules. We were by-God soldiers, and they hated us for it. After the investigation started, they ganged up and decided to screw us."

What a coincidence, I thought.

After Jefferson finished telling me his conspiracy theory, I needed some fresh air. I headed outside and found Reggie in the hallway. He waved me toward him. "These motherfuckin' snitches are all talking and sharing stories," he said, pointing to a gaggle of witnesses standing near the water fountain. "They were promised sweet deals if they helped the prosecution."

"What do you mean?"

"Well, for starters, Sergeant Trott, that rat, won't get prosecuted if he testifies against Tyler."

"How do you know this?"

"During the break, I've been at the smoke pit bullshittin' with these cats. They don't know I'm Tyler's dad. They think I'm one of the good guys." Reggie grinned and flashed the badge in his wallet.

"They think you're a cop?"

He chuckled. "That's how the game is played, brother."

I felt a tap on my shoulder and turned. It was the court reporter. "Excuse me, sir. The judge wants to get started."

"Okay," I said, "I'll be right there."

I turned to face Reggie. "I gotta go."

"Sure thing." Reggie nodded. "I'll stay out here and keep my ear to the ground. You get in there and give 'em hell."

CHAPTER 44

After the break, Trott retook the witness stand. While waiting for Hackworth to restart the hearing, he fidgeted in his chair and picked at a scab on his arm. Trott was a loose cannon. There was no telling what he would do, especially if the prosecution put more pressure on him to embellish his story. I had to shut him down.

"Captain O'Donnell," Hackworth said, "proceed with your cross-examination."

I stood with a stack of papers in my hand and pretended to read from them. "Sergeant Trott, according to the investigation, you hit multiple detainees while working in Sangar Prison?"

"What? I duh-duh-don't understand," he said.

Paine rose. "Objection. Sergeant Trott is not on trial here, Sergeant Jefferson is."

Hackworth turned to me and said, "What does this have to do with Sergeant Jefferson?"

"Multiple guards saw Trott abusing prisoners. I believe he is lying to shift the blame away from himself."

Trott looked like he was about to have a panic attack.

"This is preposterous," Paine said as he jumped to his feet. "Sergeant Trott is not under investigation. He's a disabled veteran, about to medically retire. I find Captain O'Donnell's insinuations highly offensive."

"Alright. I'll give the defense a little leeway, but you better connect the dots, and quickly," Hackworth said.

I went back to questioning Trott. "Did you ever hit a detainee while working in Sangar Prison?"

"Well, uh, once or twice," he replied.

Game on.

Paine huffed loudly and threw his pen on the table in protest. I noticed Hackworth did not admonish him.

"Specifically, how many different detainees did you strike while at Sangar?" I asked Trott.

"I, I, I do-do don't remember," he said.

"You don't remember?" I paused while maintaining eye contact. "Was it more than 10 prisoners?"

"I do-do-do don't know," Trott stuttered.

"You don't know if you beat more than 10 different prisoners?"

"No."

"Could it have been 20 different prisoners?"

Paine threw up his arms and objected.

Hackworth overruled him.

"Let me repeat," I said, "could you have beaten 20 different prisoners?"

"No," Trott said.

"Then how many did you beat?"

"I don't remember?"

"Was it too many to count?" Trott went from looking nervous to psychotic. He stared at the microphone in front of him and didn't answer. "Did you understand my question?" I asked. No answer. Trott's breathing grew heavier like he was about to hyperventilate. "I think we need to read him his rights," I said to Paine.

"Why would we read him his rights?" Paine replied.

"He just confessed to prisoner abuse, a war crime the last I checked."

"You promised me this wouldn't happen." Trott pointed his finger at Paine. "You lied. Fuck you all! I want a lawyer."

Paine's jaw dropped as he waited for Hackworth to intervene, but the judge said nothing.

"I have no further questions," I said and sat down.

"Let's take a 20-minute recess," Hackworth said. "Prosecution, be prepared to call your next witness."

Paine, still fuming, snatched the file from his desk and stomped out of the room.

Getting Trott to plead the Fifth and demand a lawyer on the witness stand was a devastating blow to the prosecution. After he requested counsel, the only way to get him to testify was to officially offer him immunity, which immediately cast suspicion on everything he said.

CHAPTER 45

D uring the recess, I went back to our makeshift office with Jefferson. Ten minutes later, a loud knock on the door interrupted our conversation. Special Agent Bronson poked his head in and said, "Paine wants you in his office - now."

"We're busy," I said.

Bronson huffed and slammed the door. I resumed discussing strategy with Jefferson. Five minutes later, Paine pushed the door open. "Captain O'Donnell," he said in a docile tone. "May I please have a word with you?"

Well, he did say, "please." I left Jefferson with his guards and followed Paine down the hall. He whirled as soon as I cleared his office's door frame. "Captain O'Donnell, who is your supervisor?"

"Major Dill," I said. "Why?"

Paine scurried to his immaculate desk and started flipping through a directory of Army JAG lawyers stationed around the world like he was searching for a contact lens in tall grass. A cordless phone was tucked under his arm. "What's his first name?" Paine asked.

I smiled. "Dick."

"Dick?" Paine squinted.

"Yes, his name is 'Major Dick Dill.'" Paine thumbed through the directory - no success. "Here's his number," I said, holding up my Blackberry.

Paine snatched the phone from me and pounded it like he was tenderizing a steak. He glanced over at his couch, where Major Hanna Weiss sat scowling. "Make a note, Hanna," Paine said. "I want O'Donnell's supervisor to know how he's behaving at this hearing. His conduct is unethical and borderline criminal."

"You're tattle-telling on me? What is this, elementary school?" I said. Paine ignored me and stared at the phone in his hand. No answer. "You're not going to reach him," I said. "He's on a seven-day Caribbean cruise."

Weiss chimed in, "Yeah, right, smart ass."

Paine resumed his investigation of the directory and repeated the assault on the phone. He listened about a minute – 10 rings, I guessed. "Doesn't your commander have voicemail?" he asked.

"No, sir. He doesn't believe in it," I said.

Paine obviously thought I was joking or lying. I knew Dill never answered his phone, and I knew he refused to set up his voice mail. He always maintained plausible deniability. After two more attempts, Paine hung up.

"You reach him?" I asked.

"I know you think this is funny, O'Donnell," Paine said. "Just wait."

"You could try the bar at the O-Club," I said. "I have that number, too."

A vein in Paine's left temple throbbed. Even if Paine could have connected, wherever he was in the world, Dill was probably 60 percent through a 12-pack.

Paine waved his hand at me. "You're dismissed, O'Donnell."

"Sir? You cannot dismiss me. You can end the meeting, but you cannot dismiss me. I don't work for you."

Paine studied my face as he thought of a comeback. I wanted to stay a little longer to see if the vein in his temple would pop. "O'Donnell, get the hell out of my office."

"May I have my phone back, please?" If an NFL scout had seen my catch, I'd have gotten a try-out.

I walked down the hall with my head down. Not out of shame. I was trying to get a handle on the situation. A pair of shapely legs blocked my path. Judging from the length of the skirt, civilian legs.

"My name's Roselyn," the woman said. "My friends call me Rose." I must have jumped back a little because she laughed. "I don't bite," she said, followed by a grin. "Very often."

I noticed the "Press" badge around her neck. "I can't talk to the media," I said.

"We'll see about that." She touched my hand and glided away down the hall. When the tingling finally subsided, I realized I was holding her business card.

Back in the hearing, Paine called Special Agent Bronson as his next witness. Bronson breezed through his testimony, which was predominantly hearsay and speculation. He summarized what he thought the other witnesses would say and laid out his personal theory as to why Jefferson was guilty. Objecting was pointless because, in an Army Preliminary Hearing, the rules of evidence did not apply. Everything was admissible, hearsay included.

At the end of Bronson's testimony, Paine picked up a large box of documents and plopped it on the table in front of Colonel Hackworth. "The prosecution offers the entire Report of Investigation into evidence," Paine said.

"You really want me to read this?" Hackworth asked. "I'll be here all night."

"Yes, please," Paine said.

Hackworth rubbed his temples and turned to me. "Captain O'Donnell, do you object?"

"Yes, I do," I replied.

"On what basis?"

"I have not reviewed that box of papers." I nodded in the direction of the box. "So, I don't know what's in there."

"He's playing games," Paine said. "He has all these documents."

"I'm not taking his word for it," I gestured at Paine with my thumb.

Paine stood and pointed at me. "That is the last time you're going to attack my integrity, Captain O'Donnell."

Hackworth stepped in and said to me, "You can review these exhibits during the next break."

"How am I supposed to review thousands of pages during a 10-minute break?" I asked.

"Well, you better read fast," Hackworth said. "Government, call your next witness."

Paine faced Hackworth and put his hands on his hips. "After what happened with Sergeant Trott, our other witnesses don't want to testify. They don't want to be falsely accused by Captain O'Donnell."

"Are you saying they're unavailable?" Hackworth asked.

"Yes," Paine replied.

"Then I declare them officially unavailable, and I will consider their sworn statements."

"Sir, I object. They're not unavailable," I said. "They are sitting across the hall, in the witness waiting room."

"Not anymore," Paine said. "They departed after the lunch break."

"They're all staying at the Fort Custer Inn. They can be back here in 15 minutes," I said.

Hackworth squeezed his hands together and leaned toward me. He spoke in a low snarl, "These witnesses are no longer willing to testify, and they are not physically in this building. Therefore, I find them unavailable for the purposes of this hearing."

I held up the Manual for Courts-Martial and said, "According to Rule for Court Martial 405(g)(4)(B), you cannot consider the sworn statements of witnesses over defense objection."

"Unless they're unavailable," Hackworth responded. "Next time, read the rest of the rule. Now, does the defense have any witnesses?"

"Yes. I'd like to call the witnesses from the prosecution's list," I said, "the ones they didn't call."

"Denied," Hackworth said. "Do you have any other evidence to present?"

"No, sir."

"Then, you have until 2000 hours to review the prosecution's documents." Hackworth slid his chair back and stood. "We are finishing this case tonight," he said and walked out of the room.

I called Annabelle before I started reviewing the mountain of paperwork. She did not answer, so I left her a message letting her know I was working late.

CHAPTER 46

After sifting through the voluminous investigative report, my eyes were burning. I did, however, come across dozens of documents I had not seen before.

At 2000 hours, Hackworth reopened the hearing. To no one's surprise, he said, "I will consider the prosecution's evidence. Also, I recommend adding the following charges: maltreatment of prisoners, failure to follow Army regulations, dereliction of duty, false official statement, and obstruction of justice."

Jefferson's eyes were the size of coffee cups. "What does that mean?" he asked me.

"He wants to add more charges," I replied.

"How can they do that? They've already charged me."

"Under the UCMJ, they can."

"Such bullshit," Jefferson mumbled under his breath.

Hackworth's head swiveled toward us like the Terminator. "Accused and counsel, please rise." His voice quaked with rage.

Jefferson and I stood and faced Judge Hackworth.

"Captain O'Donnell, this is a formal proceeding, not a pool hall," Hackworth said. "Your client better control himself, or I will remove him, and we will continue in his absence. Am I clear?"

"Yes, sir," I said.

"Good. Now be seated," Hackworth continued. "Based on the credible evidence presented by the prosecution, I find there is probable cause, and I recommend forwarding this case to a general court-martial."

I was on my feet. "What credible evidence?" I said. I left out the "Your Honor" part on purpose. "There were only two witnesses. Trott was a lying criminal, and Special Agent Bronson's testimony was entirely hearsay. The defense has been denied every request-"

Hackworth cut me off. "Careful, Captain. Whether you like the decision or not, you are still an officer in the United States Army and will conduct yourself as one."

I realized how close I was to trouble, so I throttled back on the tone. "Your Honor," I said, "I object to your ruling. You have not even reviewed the stack of documents on your desk."

You could break rock on Hackworth's jaw. "Tread lightly here, O'Donnell," he said. "If the next words out of your mouth even remotely hint at collusion, I will have your bar license."

Jefferson slowly dug his elbow into my thigh. "I don't need a roommate, Captain," he whispered out of the side of his mouth.

"For the record, I will be filing a written objection," I said.

Hackworth smirked. "Do as you will, Captain O'Donnell. Just remember, people in Hell want ice water."

✗

After the hearing, I met with Reggie privately. "What the fuck happened in there?" Reggie wasn't loud, but his voice shook with fury. "They beat the shit out of you."

I had nothing to say. Reggie was right.

"Son," he said, suddenly more empathetic. "I asked around. You're not a bad lawyer. Everybody who knows you says you're a smartass, but no one says you suck as a shyster."

I ignored the age-old vocational insult. "Thanks," I said.

"You got the shit kicked out of you." Reggie moved his head closer to mine, his voice lowered to a conspiratorial whisper. "I can help you, counselor." I didn't respond. Somehow, I doubted Reggie had graduated from law school in the time since he'd left my Fort Arnold office. He moved closer. "I can level the field."

"How?" I said.

"Boy." The right side of Reggie's mouth twitched. "You must not remember my 20 years in the Dallas PD - most of it undercover." I acted confused, but I wasn't. I didn't want to hear what I knew was coming. "What do ya need?" he asked. "Someone to disappear? A witness to change his mind? A little nose candy to show up in someone's pocket?"

"I need you to back the fuck off and go home. So far, you've been nothing but a distraction, and I don't need any more distractions."

"I see how it is." Reggie crossed his arms and let out a grunt.

"Nice knowing you, Reggie." I hoisted the box of evidence and lugged it out of the room.

Before I hit the door, I heard Reggie's voice behind me. "Call me if you change your mind, counselor."

CHAPTER 47

After I left Reggie's company, I took a cab to Mariana's, a Mexican restaurant a few miles from Fort Custer. I sat sipping a beer at a sticky tabletop. Just then, bells tied to the front door rang. I looked up. It was Rose, as expected. Rose was tall and lithe, she walked with the assurance of a woman who knew everyone in the room was, or soon would be, looking at her.

I was there against my better judgment. After Rose gave me her card, I checked out her blog. To say her early content was tripe was an insult to tripe. I read one bland, retreaded gossip story followed by another - TomKat and Scientology, Brangelina, Jessica Simpson, and Nick Somebody I didn't know. The occasional news story contained mostly innuendo. At least three times in each story, the line, "As this reporter has learned," appeared. Rose seemed to have studied at the Hedda Hopper School of Rumormongering.

Then, in the Summer of 2005, the content in her articles took on weight. Almost overnight, she had something interesting to say. She wrote about the war in Iraq and Sangar Prison - a place few people in America had ever heard of. She mentioned "government secrets" and promised her readers a "big story to break at any moment."

Rose approached me, smiling. "Hi there," she said and slipped into the chair next to me.

"Want one?" I pointed to my half-empty beer bottle. She nodded, and I signaled the waiter for two beers.

Rose pulled out a small note pad and pen and wasted no time. "Was the CIA in Sangar Prison?" she asked.

"You know I can't talk about the case."

Her smile faded. "Then why are you here?"

"I'm hungry."

Rose smiled again and said, "Me too." She placed her pen on the table and picked up a menu. "I haven't eaten all day." The beers came, and we sipped for a few seconds. Then, she reengaged, "Captain O'Donnell, may I call you Max?"

I nodded and took another sip.

"Max, I think this is a CIA coverup, and your client's the fall-guy."

"Why do you say that?"

"Just a hunch. That's why I need to talk to you. I need more information."

I held up my hands in mock surrender. "Okay, but I don't know much," I said.

"Tell me what you know, and I'll see what I can dig up on my end."

Mariachi music blared on the radio, which made talking easier. We didn't have to worry about eavesdroppers. I reached into my briefcase and pulled out a folder. I opened the folder and passed a blueprint of the prison to Rose. "According to Jefferson, this is where the OGAs kept the high-profile prisoners." I pointed at the diagram.

"What happened there?"

"I don't know for certain."

"Do you know who these OGA people were?"

"No. I only know nicknames and general descriptions. Not enough to track them down. Rumor is, they were CIA." Rose jotted some notes and slid the blueprint back to me. I took a long pull on my beer. "Something fishy was going on in that prison," I said. "The Army's claiming Jefferson was a rogue guard."

"You don't think that's true?" She raised her eyebrows.

"Not at all," I said. "Everything in the Army is done by the book. Literally. There's a manual for everything, from how to clean a rifle, to how to dig a field latrine. Every unit in the Army has a written SOP, a Standard Operating Procedure. Still, I can't find a single document like that for Sangar."

"How does that help Jefferson?"

"What if the guards were ordered to abuse prisoners, and those in charge destroyed the incriminating evidence?"

"So, Jefferson was obeying orders?"

"Yeah, maybe," I said.

"At Nuremberg, the Nazis used the 'obedience to orders' defense."

I knew that after World War II, thousands of Nazis were prosecuted for committing war crimes. In their defense, many claimed they were merely obeying orders. The "Nuremberg Defense," as it was called, was unsuccessful. "I'm not raising The Nuremberg Defense, but-" My phone rang. It was Annabelle. "I have to take this," I said. "It's my wife."

"Sure, go ahead."

I answered. "Hi, honey."

"Max, it's after 11 here. Why haven't you called?" Annabelle's voice was about 80 percent on the pissed off meter.

"I called a couple of times today. Didn't you get my messages?"

"No, I've been busy with the kids."

I said nothing. I learned long ago that the best way to win an argument with her was to avoid it.

"I started having contractions today," Annabelle continued. "The doctor said I could go into labor within the next 48 hours."

As she spoke, our waitress approached and asked, "You want another round of beers?"

I shushed her away.

"Max, are you out drinking?" The tension in Annabelle's voice rose.

"No." I stood and walked toward the bathroom, hoping for more privacy. "I'm having dinner with Jefferson's father." Annabelle let out a long, heavy sigh, and I changed the subject. "The Article 32 was a disaster, but I'll be home tomorrow. I'm on the first flight out of El Paso."

I heard the line hiccup - call waiting. "That's Mother," Annabelle said. "You know she doesn't sleep when I'm here by myself."

"I love you," I said. "Goodnight."

"Bye," she said and hung up.

I walked back to the table. Rose was waiting with a fresh round of beers. "Everything all right?" she asked.

"Yeah, that was my wife calling to say goodnight."

"How long have you been married?"

"Seven years."

"Happily?" she asked with a coy smile.

I hesitated for a few seconds. "I shouldn't be here," I said.

"Why? We're adults, just having a drink and talking business." Rose slid her chair closer to mine. I wasn't ready, and when I caught a whiff of her perfume, I could feel my body reacting. I slid my chair a few inches back. "Relax," she said, "I'm not rabid."

I gave her a wary smile and turned my chair at an angle, giving myself a little more space.

"Max, maybe we can work together."

"How?"

Over the next hour, we ate, drank, and discussed how we could cooperate for our mutual benefit. I would give Rose newsworthy information, and she would write stories that would portray Jefferson as a heroic scapegoat.

When it came time to go, Rose asked, "You need a ride?" Her hand brushed my leg - *probably an accident.*

I pointed at the beer bottles on the table. "We'd better take a cab."

"To my place, or yours?" I felt her hand slide across my knee, headed toward the sentry in my pants. My hand caught her wrist.

"No," I said.

"You sure?"

"Yes." I hoped I sounded more certain than I felt.

"A faithful husband." She smirked and tossed her hair over her shoulder. "You're the first I've met in a long time."

CHAPTER 48

I took a taxi to the Rodeo Inn, stuffed with dinner and beer, and fell asleep. In the middle of a dream, my phone rang. It was Rose. The alarm clock on the nightstand flashed 3:14 a.m.

"Max, I need you to verify something," she said.

"Yeah, what?" I said, rubbing my eyes.

"Can you confirm that Hamza Nassar is the same guy who bombed the Embassy in Kenya?"

"I'm pretty sure."

"I can't mess this up, Max." Rose had dropped the sultry act. She was all business. "This has to be right."

"Yeah. He's the same guy. He was Osama bin Laden's top lieutenant in the Horn of Africa. He blew up churches, schools for girls, an embassy, all sorts of stuff." I could almost hear Rose salivating. "Why are you asking?"

"I'm writing a piece that connects the dots between the Kenya bombing, Nassar, Sangar Prison, and the CIA."

"Don't quote me."

"Max, you never said this was off the record. I cannot write a story without a source."

"Okay. Please don't mention my name."

"That's not how this works," Rose said.

"When's the story coming out?"

"In an hour or so."

"Can I at least read the article before you publish it, to check the facts?"

"No. That violates journalistic ethics."

"Huh?"

"I have to go," she said and hung up.

The moment the call ended, I regretted talking to her, but it was too late. I didn't know what Rose would write or what the fallout would be. *It's a blog*, I thought. *Who the hell reads that crap anyway?* I was about to find out.

After tossing and turning in bed for a while, I opened my computer and did a Google search for "Sangar Prison." Rose's article appeared as the first result.

Top Al-Qaeda Operative Murdered in Captivity, Lawyer Blames CIA

By Rose Sanchez

FORT CUSTER, Texas - A man once considered a top al-Qaeda operative was killed while in U.S. captivity at Sangar Confinement Facility, Afghanistan. A U.S. Army Reservist is on trial for his murder.

Sgt. Tyler Jefferson stands accused of abusing and murdering Hamza Nassar, Osama bin Laden's top lieutenant in the Horn of Africa. Nassar has been linked to the 1998 bombing of the U.S. Embassy in Kenya. The attack employed a series of truck bombs and killed over 200 people.

Nassar also claimed responsibility for a series of bombings that targeted Christmas Eve church services across Ethiopia in 1999. He was a significant threat in the region until Eritrean forces captured him in the summer of 2001 during a border crossing. How Nassar ended up in Sangar is unknown.

Captain Max O'Donnell, Sgt. Tyler Jefferson's Army lawyer, contends the CIA, not his client, tortured and murdered Nassar. O'Donnell, repeatedly stymied by the presiding judge, was unable to call any of the witnesses he intended to use in Jefferson's defense. This reporter has learned that O'Donnell believes the Sangar Facility housed a secret torture program, established and operated by the Central Intelligence Agency, in which atrocities were committed. Before today's hearing, the grisly fate of Nassar was unknown to the public.

Sergeant Gary Trott, a member of Jefferson's unit, testified in court that Jefferson attacked a prisoner as he hung from a wall of razor wire in a shocking display of barbarism.

Sources confirm that before his capture, Nassar had plans to carry out attacks in Eastern Africa, including a plot to bomb U.S. Naval vessels in the Red Sea on the anniversary of 9/11. During the preliminary hearing, Jefferson's lawyer demanded to know who had access to Nassar inside the prison; his requests were denied by the presiding judge, Colonel Michael Hackworth. More on this story as it develops.

It was 6 a.m. on the East Coast, and the blog already had over 18,000 hits. The counter was spinning like a Tilt-a-Whirl. I kept hitting refresh on my browser and watched the story take on a life of its own, as other news agencies wrote follow-on articles.

I had kicked over a hornet's nest. The story was everywhere. Some articles called Jefferson a war criminal, others a hero. Most focused on the CIA angle. I flicked on the television and turned to CNN. The U.S. Secretary of State was holding a press conference where he disavowed any government involvement in the abuses at Sangar. "This story is a red herring, a desperate attempt by a defense lawyer trying to shift the blame away from his client," the Secretary of State said.

I clicked off the television and hopped into the shower. I had to be at the airport in an hour, and I was behind schedule. As I washed my hair, I heard the shower curtain slide open. Before I could react, I was slammed face-first into the wall, and my wrists were zip-tied behind my back. My head was stuffed into a pillowcase. I was pulled out of the shower and forced to my knees.

"You got a small dick for someone with such a big mouth," a man's voice said.

"His poor wife," a second man said. "I'll show her a real cock."

"Put this on him," the first man said. "I can't look at that pitiful excuse."

They wrapped me in a sheet and marched me outside. A van door opened, and they shoved me inside. Tires screeched, and we sped away. I bounced around on a cold metal floor as the van took fast curves, spiked the brakes, and hit an excessive number of potholes.

Eventually, the van stopped, and the pillowcase was yanked from my head. Two men wearing ski masks and sunglasses hovered over me. One of the men kneeled on my ribcage. I struggled to breathe. The other brute put his face inches from mine. "We got ourselves a tough guy?" he said. His breath reeked of stale coffee and chewing tobacco.

"We'll see about that," the man on my chest said in a raspy voice. He sounded like he'd spent the night singing in a smoke-filled karaoke bar.

Coffee breath leaned in and whispered in my ear. "We know you passed sensitive information to that little whore reporter. Does Annabelle know you've been fucking that hot piece of ass?"

"I want a lawyer," I said.

The men burst into laughter. "When you aid and abet terrorists, you don't get a lawyer, motherfucker. Read the Patriot Act. God bless the USA," raspy said.

"Fuck you," I said.

Coffee breath leaned hard on my sternum. Oxygen was suddenly a precious commodity.

"Listen, *abogado*," raspy said, "you crossed the line. We know you passed sensitive information to Sanchez. We can't have sensitive materials ending up in enemy hands." He paused to let the information sink in. "Espionage. You know what that carries?"

Silence.

"Death," coffee breath said.

Raspy leaned close. "Stop running your fucking mouth, or we'll ruin you."

"Don't even think about calling the police," coffee breath said, "or next time, you'll end up in the morgue."

I nodded.

The man removed his knee from my chest. I sucked in gulps of air, as the van door slid open. "Get the fuck out," raspy said, and he shoved me out of the van, naked.

They tossed the sheet on the ground. I picked it up and wrapped it around my waist. The vans' tires spun, kicking pebbles across the asphalt. I squinted hard in the bright sun. I realized that I was in the motel parking lot when I saw the sign for the Rodeo Inn. We had probably been driving around in circles the entire time. I scanned the lot. Reggie's SUV was gone.

I ran to my room. The door was ajar. I hurriedly shoved my clothes into a suitcase and called a cab. By the time I got to the airport, it was past noon. I had no chance of getting a seat on standby. All the remaining flights were overbooked, so I decided to spend the night in the terminal. It was my best option. I wouldn't make it home in time for Thanksgiving dinner if I wasn't on the first flight out in the morning.

CHAPTER 49

Every emotionally charged family drama about Thanksgiving that I had ever watched contained the obligatory, bad dinner scene. Dad gets drunk. Mom gets shrill. Grandpa waxes eloquently on how things used to be. Kids shriek. Grandma makes snarky comments while acting like no one can hear her. I had always hated those. I thought they were totally fictitious and overdone, until I arrived home for Thanksgiving dinner.

I came late. Twenty-four minutes late, to be exact. I wheeled the Malibu into the drive for the divinely ordained hour of "the feast." Given how my week had gone, I fully expected to find smoke billowing from the oven while the turkey burned. But the only smoke came from my mother-in-law Martha's ears. Fuming hardly covered her mood.

Annabelle wasn't angry.

Glaciers don't get angry.

My attempt at kissing her cheek met only air as she deftly dodged my lips while guiding a sweet potato casserole into the dining room. Ethan sat in a chair in the corner. Eva sniffled mightily and clung to Annabelle's skirt. When she saw me, Eva raced toward me. I picked her up and kissed her cheeks.

"What happened to your face, Max?" Martha asked, referring to my black eye.

Damn, I thought I had done a better job of applying the concealer.

"Someone hit you?" Sterling chimed in.

"How did you guess, Sterling?" I said, my sarcasm blatant.

"Probably got into a drunken bar fight," Annabelle said in a vicious mumble.

Martha squinted at me through cobra-like slits. I put Eva down and went into the den to fix a rum and Coke.

"Dinner's on its way out, Max," Sterling said. "The bar's closed, old boy."

My own damn den. What the fuck?

"How's that job hunt coming along, Max?" Martha asked.

I ignored her.

Sterling filled the silence. "I heard the Public Defender's office is looking for Spanish speakers. Maybe you could apply there."

"Good to know, Sterling," I said.

"I wish you would take these things more seriously, Max," Martha pursed her lips like she'd been chewing a lemon rind. "We're truly concerned about your family."

"Mind your own business, Martha," I said.

"My daughter and grandbabies are my business," she replied. After that, the only sounds at the table were the ping of silverware - Martha's family flatware she'd brought with her like it was the myrrh from Bethlehem - and the occasional request to "pass the rolls, please."

Halfway through the driest dinner atmosphere I'd ever experienced, while quietly choking down the driest turkey in the history of poultry, Annabelle suddenly burst into tears. "I can't take this," she cried and ran to our bedroom.

When I stood to follow, Martha spoke directly into her green bean casserole. "Maybe that would have been helpful three days ago, Max." She slid a delicate forkful into her tight mouth and chewed.

Sterling reached to one side, hoisted a bottle of Evan Williams Single Barrel, and filled his tumbler.

I thought the bar was closed

CHAPTER 50

After the long Thanksgiving weekend, I was back at work for the first time since I'd returned from Texas. I passed Jules in the hallway and said, "Hello." She nodded and ducked into her office without saying a word. *Odd.* I walked into my office. As I unpacked my briefcase, someone knocked on my office door. "Come in," I said without looking up.

The door swung open. It was Major Dill. Two men in suits stood behind him. "Captain O'Donnell," Dill said, stepping inside. "These men would like to have a word with you."

A middle-aged man with a comb-over moved forward. "I'm Special Agent Martin, and this is Special Agent Garza," he said, gesturing to the man next to him. "We're with Army CID."

Martin's bulbous nose, swollen from years of hard drinking, resembled a shriveled potato. His rumpled grey suit, purple polyester shirt, and red tie told me he was either colorblind or didn't give a damn about his appearance. One of the laces of his scuffed brown shoes was about to snap.

Garza was younger, with slicked-back black hair and orange skin, no doubt the result of a cheap fake tan. He smelled like he had bathed in Drakkar Noir cologne. Garza was better dressed than Martin but just as shady looking. He sported a tight-fitting, pin-striped black suit, a gray shirt, and a skinny black tie. He wore shiny black loafers with no socks.

Classy.

Garza pulled a small laminated card from his wallet, turned to me, and said, "You have the right to remain silent-"

I interrupted him, "You haven't memorized the rights advisement?"

Garza blushed and slid the card back into his wallet. "Okay, smartass, you want a lawyer or not?"

"No," I said without hesitation. "What's this about?"

"Sit down, and I'll explain," Martin said.

We all sat.

"Would you care for a cup of coffee?" I asked them.

They shook their heads no.

I turned to Dill. "Are you here as my lawyer?"

"No, I'm here to observe."

"In that case, sir, you can leave." I pointed to the door.

Major Dill's face contorted. I wasn't sure if he was embarrassed or in disbelief. He was sweating profusely in my 68-degree office.

"Otherwise," I said, "you can all leave."

Dill stood, slumped over, and walked out of the room like a kid who dropped his ice cream cone on the sidewalk.

"Now that we got that cleared up," I said to Martin. "I'll take you up on that lawyer. I don't want you twisting my words." I picked up my phone and dialed it. "Please come to my office," I said and hung up.

A few seconds later, Jules poked her head into the room and asked, "What's up?"

"Get a note pad and pull up a chair," I said. "These agents want to ask me a few questions.

Over the past three years, I had watched dozens of interrogations and read extensively on the subject. Agents Martin and Garza were using the infamous "Hanscom Interrogation Technique." Named for legendary FBI interrogator John Hanscom, the technique used lies, trickery, and deceit to score a confession. The problem is, it does not work if the person being interrogated knows the method better than the guys asking the questions. I saw it coming a mile away.

"We know you gave Rose Sanchez classified information," Martin said with conviction. "What exactly did you give-?"

"Max!" Jules interrupted. "We need to talk." She leaned in close to me and said, "Don't talk to these guys. They already made up their minds. They think you're guilty." Jules was right. It's never wise to talk to investigators. They don't investigate you unless they believe you did something wrong.

"I got this," I assured her.

She pinched my arm. "That's what all criminals say before they confess. Plead the Fifth and tell these pricks to fuck off." She spoke loud enough for the agents to hear.

I ignored her and turned back to Martin. "What was your question?"

Martin replied, "What classified documents did you give Rose Sanchez?"

"I didn't give her any classified documents."

"We know you did," Martin said. "Why did you do it? Was it for money? Sex? Or, is there something else we should know about?" Martin glanced at Garza, who seemed more interested in the photo of Annabelle on my bookshelf than the faltering interrogation.

"You guys suck," I said and stood up. "Next time, before you interrogate someone, get your shit together." I pointed at the door. "Get out." The agents hurried out of the room. Through the window, I saw them speaking with Major Dill in the parking lot. "You see that, Jules?" I motioned out the window. "Our fearless leader is out there throwing me under the bus."

"Not surprising," she said. We watched as Dill and the agents shook hands. Dill then turned and walked toward our office building. "He's coming back," Jules said. "Brace yourself."

A few seconds later, I heard a knock at my door. "I'm in a meeting," I said.

The door thrust open, and Major Dill walked in. "Dammit, O'Donnell," he said. "I'm gone for two weeks. Two weeks! And you lose your mind."

Dill pointed at Jules and said, "You. Out."

"I want her to stay." I held up my hand. "As a witness."

Dill's face turned bright pink. "I want to have a private conversation with you," he said. "Don't forget, I'm still your commanding officer."

Jules stepped in. "Major Dill, Captain O'Donnell is going to plead the Fifth."

"You're in a lot of trouble, mister." Dill stuck his finger inches from my face. I noticed his fingernail was chewed down to the cuticle. "You are officially under investigation. You may be facing criminal charges, not to mention a bar complaint."

"That's bullshit," I said.

"I don't know what's gotten into you," Dill said. "You were sent out there to do a simple plea. Instead, you've created an international incident."

"I did my job," I said.

"O'Donnell! You can't keep your mouth shut, can you? You've pissed off a lot of people. People who can ruin your life." I smiled and crossed my arms. Dill mumbled "moron," before turning and walking away. He slammed the door so hard it knocked my law school diploma off of the wall.

"That went well," Jules said with a smirk.

CHAPTER 51

B ack at Fort Custer, Colonel Paine had been plotting ways to get payback on me. On his way to work, while listening to NPR, the idea hit him. Paine called Captain Nelson to his office first thing in the morning.

"Good morning, Steve." Paine waved him in. "Take a seat."

Nelson put his briefcase on the floor and sat down.

"I've been thinking about the Jefferson case," Paine said.

Nelson leaned forward in rapt attention.

"I think we should hand over all the evidence," Paine continued. "Jefferson deserves a fighting chance."

If the comment surprised Nelson, he didn't show it. From the start of the case, he had been advocating for full disclosure. Withholding evidence was always grounds for appeal. "Even the classified evidence?" Nelson asked.

"Of course. Give him everything. Bury that prick O'Donnell with so much evidence he'll regret the day he filed a discovery request. Upload it to a new directory and name it 'Jefferson Evidence.'"

Nelson agreed and went to work.

By noon, the directory was created, and the files were uploaded. Then, Paine spent the rest of the day implementing his maniacal plan. He mixed evidence together, duplicated data, deleted files, and renamed hundreds of documents. He combined classified evidence with unclassified evidence. He even did some cutting and pasting. When he finished, the file was an indecipherable mess. Paine's eyes twinkled as he envisioned me trying to make sense of this mountain of garbage.

CHAPTER 52

I was suspicious when I received Captain Nelson's email. For no apparent reason, the prosecution decided to turn over the classified evidence, the same evidence they refused to give me at the preliminary hearing. I called Jules into my office and showed her the email.

"What do you think, Jules?"

"Probably a setup."

I nodded in agreement.

Nelson's email was straightforward. "Captain O'Donnell, The Government, in its continuing effort of full disclosure, and to ensure a fair trial for Sergeant Jefferson, is allowing the defense to review the classified evidence in a Sensitive Compartmented Information Facility (SCIF). For access, report to Doolittle Air Force Base at 1130 hours on 1 December 2005. See Major Andrea Cooper for assistance."

After reading the email, Jules said, "You better hurry, that's in two and a half hours."

I thought for a few seconds. "You want to come with me?" I asked her. "You can be co-counsel at Jefferson's trial."

Jules smiled. "Are you serious?"

"Of course," I said. "I could use your help."

"Hell yeah. Count me in."

Before heading to Doolittle Air Force Base, we visited Steve Glendon's office. Glendon was the Chief of Operational Security at Fort Arnold. He also lived in my neighborhood. Glendon was a retired Army Colonel who had spent 26 years in Military Intelligence. When Saddam Hussein invaded Kuwait in 1990, Glendon was an Army attaché in the U.S. Embassy in Kuwait City. He helped evacuate the embassy and received a Bronze Star for his efforts. After he retired from active duty, Glendon got a job at Fort Arnold to be near his grandkids.

Glendon was a tall, sinewy man with reddish-gray hair and freckles. He reminded me of my favorite college history professor. He ushered us into his office the moment we arrived. "Max, to what do I owe the pleasure?"

"I need help dealing with classified documents," I said. "I don't want to violate any rules."

"Well, you came to the right place. Take a seat."

Trinkets and war trophies adorned his walls. A photo of Glendon with General "Stormin'" Norman Schwarzkopf sat on his desk. A glass-encased Arabian scimitar hung on the wall. After we sat, Glendon cut to the chase. "Bottom line, if a document is not marked as Classified, then it's not Classified." He picked up a Christmas card and slid it across his desk. "For example." He pointed at the card. "If I tell you this card is Top Secret, is it?"

I shrugged. "I don't know."

"It's not marked Top Secret, is it?" he asked.

I picked up the card and examined it. "It not marked as anything," I said. "It's just a Christmas card."

"Correct. It's not marked, so it's not classified. It's that simple."

"What about documents on a classified computer network?" Jules asked.

"Same rule," he said. "If I scan and save a bunch of restaurant menus on a Secret network, does that make the menus Secret?"

"I guess it depends on whether the documents are marked as Secret," I said.

"Exactly. If they're not marked, they're not classified," Glendon said. "Even if a document is stored on the CIA's most secretive network, that *does not* mean it's classified."

"Why would a non-classified document be on a Secret network?" Jules asked.

"Laziness, pure and simple," Glendon said. "People are too lazy to separate classified documents from non-classified documents. They often dump them all on the Secret network."

At 10 o'clock, we thanked Glendon for his time and proceeded to Doolittle Air Force Base, just 30 miles north, near Chester, South Carolina. Our destination was Building #4125, a one-story brick building with no windows. Satellite dishes and odd metal antennas lined the flat roof. Ringed in concertina wire, the structure reminded me of a prison.

Inside the building, an uptight guard with a hand-held wand searched us for contraband. "I need those pens and notepads." The guard extended his hand. "They're not allowed."

"We're lawyers," I said. "How are we supposed to take notes?"

"You're not," the guard said with narrowed eyes. "Nothing goes in. Nothing comes out."

After we complied with his request, the guard handed us clip-on badges with the word "VISITOR" printed in bold red. A few minutes later, Major Andrea Cooper, an Air Force officer, appeared and led us down a narrow corridor to an office where a nerdy-looking sergeant sat behind a desk.

"This is Captain O'Donnell and Captain Myers," Cooper said to the sergeant. "They're here to use our SIPRNET. They have access until 1300 hours."

The sergeant nodded and scooted his swivel chair to a filing cabinet against the wall. He opened a drawer and pulled out a stack of papers. "Sign this," he said, handing me the papers.

"What is it?" I asked.

"It's a non-disclosure agreement," he said. "You have to sign it before you can access the classified network."

The 20-page document listed rules (too many to count) and penalties (decades in prison) for violating the rules. The font was so small, I had to squint to read it. I sped through the document and didn't understand half of it. Nowhere did it say, "If it's not marked, then it's not classified."

Jules and I signed and followed Major Cooper down two flights of stairs. At the bottom was a hallway with metal doors on both sides. She led us to a door with the number "4" painted on it and used her badge to unlock it.

Cooper motioned inside. "Here you go."

The tiny room resembled a bomb shelter. The lighting was dim, and the air conditioning was on full blast. The room contained two plastic chairs, a small desk, a computer, a printer, and a shredder.

"I'll be back at 1330 hours," Cooper said and closed the door behind her.

I flicked on the computer. It booted as slow as a two-legged turtle crossing a highway. Finally, a login screen appeared. I punched in my password, and dozens of folders filled the screen. They had names like 536248HT-1 and AF329-200206031. The first folder contained hundreds of documents, images, and scanned files. Some of the pages were sideways and upside down. Others were illegible. Many of the papers were in foreign languages, perhaps Arabic, Farsi, or Pashto. I was not sure. All I knew is I couldn't understand them.

We clicked and scrolled through the documents, but saw no mention of Nassar, at least not in English. Many of the documents were stamped SECRET. Many were not. One file was a scanned baseball box score with numbers scribbled at the top.

"This is complete bullshit," I said.

Jules nodded. "What did you expect? They dumped a bunch of worthless stuff in these folders, just to waste your time." We pressed on. After 45 minutes, we found nothing helpful. "Keep scrolling." Jules pointed at a clock on the wall. "We only have a few minutes before they kick us out."

Two minutes later, something caught my eye. It was sideways - a little hard to read. It was an Army prisoner of war custody receipt. It wasn't marked Secret or Top Secret. It wasn't marked at all. I turned my head and carefully studied the document on the computer screen.

"What is it?" Jules asked.

"It's a form the Army uses to keep track of POWs."

"Who is the prisoner?"

"Prisoner 324, Faud Halbousi," I said.

Jules shrugged. "Does he have anything to do with Sergeant Jefferson?"

"I don't know, but according to this document, someone named Gregory Johnston, the Agricultural Attaché at the American Embassy in Kabul, signed Prisoner 324 out of Sangar on 8 August 2002, at three in the morning."

"That makes no sense," she said. "Why would an Agricultural Attaché be in Sangar Prison?"

"Don't know." I clicked the mouse, and another unclassified document appeared. It was the backside of the POW receipt. "Look at this." I pointed at the screen. "Prisoner 324 was transferred wearing a jumpsuit and an adult diaper."

"Why?"

"Maybe he was going on a long trip, and they didn't want him soiling his pants," I said as I continued scrolling.

"Stop. Go back." Jules said, snatching the mouse from my hand and frantically clicking. "There." It was a preflight medical exam for Prisoner 324. At the bottom of the page, a box labeled "Aliases" listed four names. One of them was Hamza Nassar. "Prisoner 324 is Nassar," she said. Jules looked at me with wide eyes and smiled. "If Nassar left the prison on August 8th, then Jefferson couldn't have killed him in September."

I motioned toward the printer on the floor beneath the desk. "Let's see if that thing works."

"They warned us," Jules said. "We can't take anything out of here."

"I'll say you tried to stop me if we get busted."

Jules snorted.

"What's so funny?" I asked her.

"Why is there a printer in here if nothing can leave this room?"

"That's the military for you." I clicked print, and the papers crawled out of the printer.

"Give me those." Jules took the papers, folded them into a small square, and stuck it inside her shirt.

Just then, we heard a metallic click, and the door opened. It was Major Cooper. "Times up," the Major said.

We followed Cooper through the hallway and up the stairs. The front desk guard collected our visitor badges, and we walked out of the building. Halfway to the car, a voice yelled, "Halt." We froze.

"Shit," Jules whispered. "We're screwed."

I turned and saw the guard trotting down the sidewalk.

"You forgot your pens and notepads," he said.

I managed a weak smile. "You couldn't think of anything else to say besides 'Halt?'"

"Sorry, sir," he said. "Habit."

We double-timed it the rest of the way to the car. I had to remind myself not to floor it until we cleared the base gate.

CHAPTER 53

I went back to my office and spent the rest of the day looking for Gregory Johnston. I scoured the internet, combed through public databases, and searched online phonebooks from across the country. Johnston was a ghost.

When I locked up the office at the end of the day, I noticed Jules's light was still on. I knocked on her door. No one answered. So, I turned the knob and pushed it open. Inside, Jules was at her desk, filling a cardboard box with personal items.

"Jules, what's going on?" I asked.

She turned and faced me. Her eyes were moist like she had been crying. "Someone outed me?"

"What?"

"Someone reported me."

"Reported you for what?"

"For being a lesbian, Max. Dill told me to clean out my desk. He said my Army career's over."

Thoughts of driving to Dill's home and kicking his ass raced through my mind. This was a low blow, even for Dill. It was 2005, and homosexuality was still illegal in the U.S. military. Under the *Don't Ask Don't Tell* policy, the Army could discharge soldiers that "demonstrated a propensity or intent to engage in homosexual acts." This law was still on the books, though it was rarely enforced.

"Max, Dill said they're going to kick me out of the Army."

"You've got to fight this."

"I don't know," she said and hung her head.

"When I'm done with Jefferson, I'll help you take care of this." I helped Jules finish packing, and we walked out of the office together. My phone rang as I drove home. It was Annabelle's number. I answered, "Hi, honey."

"Max," a male voice said. Sterling always sounded like he had something permanently lodged in his sphincter. "We need to talk."

"Is Annabelle okay?"

"No. Well, yes."

"Which is it?"

"Max, she's fine physically. The children are well, but that's not why I called. Martha and I don't think you should come home tonight."

"What?"

"Listen," he said, "I know you're in trouble with the Army. Given Annabelle's delicate pregnancy, I don't think she needs to know about your unfortunate incident with the lady of the evening the other night."

"What are you talking about?"

"Max, I know about the Mexican woman." Sterling had obviously been sampling Speyside's finest Scotch.

"What Mexican woman?"

"The one you had dinner with the other night."

"You mean Rose Sanchez?" I said. "She's a reporter doing a story on my case."

"Well, she didn't look like Jimmy Breslin to me." He chuckled at his own joke. "I was young once. I know I don't look it now, but I piloted my way around some pretty, sassy fillies in my day. Yes, sir. Ole' Sterling had his share of fun. I quit all that when I met Martha. A man has to do what's right - even when he has urges. But enough about me."

"Sterling, you're full of shit."

"No, Max. *You're* full of shit. I saw the report."

"What report?"

"An Army investigative report, with lots of photos," he said. "I know everything you did out there in Texas. Your boss, Dick, a real nice guy, dropped it off this evening. As the head of the family, he wanted me to talk some sense into you before you ruin your career and lose your family. Honestly, fooling around is bad enough, but leaking classified evidence and hanging out at a strip club with that Negro - what were you thinking, son?"

"I am not your fucking son, Sterling, and the investigation you are referring to is bogus. Put Annabelle on the phone, now."

Sterling apparently liked long, awkward moments of total silence. "She's unavailable, Max. She had to be sedated."

"Sedated? What for? She can't be sedated. She's about to have a baby for God's sake. What are you people doing over there?" I realized I'd been screaming into a dead phone for the past 20 seconds. I called back, and it went straight to voice mail.

I was afraid that if I went home, the drama could harm Annabelle and the baby. This would have to wait. I decided to sleep at a hotel near the Columbia airport because I had an early flight to El Paso the next morning. Luckily, I had picked up my uniforms from the dry cleaner earlier in the day.

CHAPTER 54

W hen they hear the word "courtroom," most people envision a richly appointed marble hall with lustrous, hardwood furniture, a stately and expansive bench from where a judge issues rulings and a spacious jury box surrounded by a substantive and elegant rail. Or, they see the quaint, ceiling-fanned Alabama confines of Atticus Finch, as he holds forth in a vain attempt to save Tom Robinson in *To Kill a Mockingbird*.

Neither of those images held anything in common with the courtroom at Fort Custer. The courtroom occupied the upstairs of a building that had been formerly used as a cavalry barracks. The men of the Custer Cavalry Unit, who battled the Native Americans for dominance of the area, lived above the horses. Years later, when the need for military justice began to outweigh the need for skilled horsemen, the Army converted the top floor into a courtroom. The courtroom's windows overlooked the parade grounds. A pleasant enough sight when the troops were on parade, but no one in the room would have time for gazing out the window.

The last attempt at decorating the room had obviously taken place sometime in the 1970s. The appearance of the worn burgundy carpet was only made more forlorn by the egregiously cheap "paneling." About the same time disco balls, Donna Summer, and the Hustle submerged the country's good sense and musical tastes, middle-class homes all over America installed quarter-inch sheets of pressed wood foisted on owners by salesmen swearing, "No one will ever know it's not the real thing." Whether the panel shade selected for the Fort Custer courtroom was originally tan or was simply the washed-out result of years of West Texas heat and sun, no one could remember.

The judge's bench was neither imposing nor particularly sturdy. It gave the appearance of having been built at one-half of the suggested scale. Behind the bench and to the left, a small door led to the judge's chambers. Any second-year karate student incapable of kicking a hole through the flimsy portal would have been laughed out of class.

The jury was empaneled behind a wobbly rail 30 inches high. No lawyer arguing a case at Fort Custer ever leaned on it more than once. The jurors sat on bulky swivel chairs bolted to the floor. Six in front, and six on a twelve-inch riser, with barely any legroom and no area in which to rotate. No provision had been made for any juror to take notes on anything other than their laps.

The prosecution's table appeared for all the world as if Grandma had left her dining room suite to the court in her will. Thick-legged and bulky, the table sat on what would typically be considered the wrong side of the room - the side farther away from the jury. About three in the afternoon on the first day of any trial, every new defense lawyer finally understood the arrangement. As the day wore on and phones and laptops ran out of juice, the only electrical outlets available resided on the prosecutor's side.

On the defense side, sat a wooden card table. The small work surface created the appearance that the defense attorneys were disorganized and sloppy as stacks of papers piled up during a trial.

The room was outdated, cramped, and substandard - 100% Army.

I remembered the quotation from Dante's *Inferno* as I entered the room: "lasciate ogne speanze voi ch'intrate" - the inscription over the gates of Hell.

"Abandon every hope - you who enter."

CHAPTER 55

A week after the preliminary hearing, despite my written objection, which was no doubt now residing in some landfill, the Commanding General forwarded Jefferson's case to a court-martial. The Army moved quickly and appointed a trial judge the same day, Colonel Bradley Rake.

With over 20 years on the bench, Judge Rake was the most senior judge in the Army, and he had yet to mention retirement. Sixty years old, the judge had whitish hair combed to the side, and a plump, ruddy face. Outside of the courtroom, he was jovial and friendly with everyone, including defense lawyers. He and his wife of 30 years hosted an annual JAG Christmas party. They treated young Army lawyers to Glühwein, a favorite holiday drink at German Christmas Markets, and regaled the assembled with stories of their travels while stationed in Europe during the Cold War.

Rake seemed the perfect judge. On the bench, he exuded a calm demeanor. His docket was never backlogged. Most lawyers enjoyed practicing in front of him - until they rocked the boat. Judge Rake had one pet peeve: Soldiers who pled not guilty. "Integrity is everything," Rake said on more occasions than anyone could count. "Any guilty soldier who pleads not guilty shows a lack of integrity."

Rake responded with reasonably fair sentences, as long as defendants, "accepted full responsibility," and never, "wasted the Court's time." Rake took not guilty pleas as a personal offense - *and let slip the dogs of war*. Soldiers refusing to show penitence, and beg forgiveness endured a process as painful as an ascent up Mt. Everest without shoes. The lawyers representing the ungrateful and defiant soldiers felt the full wrath of Judge Rake as well. Jury trials transformed the congenial jurist into a merciless harpy - part prosecutor, part avenging angel. Rake labored to maintain a neutral appearance, while his passive-aggressive comments and rulings steadily tipped the scales of justice in the prosecution's favor.

Colonel Paine demanded an immediate arraignment when the news of Judge Rake's assignment broke. His request was granted, which meant I had to return to Fort Custer for the third time in a month.

At an arraignment, the judge sets the trial date. The defendant enters a plea of guilty or not guilty and elects to be tried by a judge or a jury. Military arraignments routinely last about the time it takes to boil an egg. Both the prosecution and defense can weigh in on a trial date. But, the decision usually comes down to the judge's availability.

This morning, Jefferson and his guards were the only people in the courtroom when I arrived. He raised his arm in greeting. The shackles restricted him to a weak wave. Fashion models would have killed for his cheekbones, high and chiseled, made more distinct due to his noticeable weight loss.

"Good morning, gentlemen," I said to the guards and pointed at Jefferson's leg irons. "Can you please remove his shackles."

A skinny, pimpled guard opened a canvas bag. He rooted for a while, like a pig nosing for truffles, then dumped the contents on the table. Chains, belts, and handcuffs clattered on our flimsy card table. After a minute of rummaging, he stopped. "Ain't got the keys, sir. Must have left them back at the Brig."

"Then go get them," I said.

Jefferson interrupted, "What's the point? I'm going back to lock up when we finish."

I ignored Jefferson and said to the hapless guard, "Army rules prohibit prisoners from being shackled in the courtroom. One of you better go get the key."

Pimple Face plodded out of the courtroom, lowered his head, and muttered into his tee-shirt, "Asshole." He jerked his head sideways, pale with the realization he'd spoken loud enough for me to hear. I let it go. Racking this guy wasn't worth it. He realized I wasn't going to respond and scampered out of the courtroom in search of the key.

Five minutes before noon, Paine and his entourage entered the room and took their seats at the prosecution table. Not one of them acknowledged my presence. At precisely 12 o'clock, Judge Rake entered the courtroom, followed by Becky Grice, a washed-out court reporter in her late 50s. The cloying odor of stale cigarette smoke wafted across the room as Grice hurried about setting up her recording equipment.

The moment Judge Rake entered, Paine jumped to his feet and shouted, "All rise."

The judge squinted and asked, "Where's the bailiff?"

"Your Honor," Paine said, "we didn't think we needed a bailiff. The arraignment is only going to take a few minutes."

"This is a court-martial," Rake said. "A bailiff is required at all proceedings."

"Would you like me to get one now?" Paine asked.

"No, but from now on, I expect a bailiff."

Then, Rake turned to me. "Captain O'Donnell, are you ready to proceed?"

I stood. "Yes, Your Honor."

"How does your client plead?"

"Not guilty."

Rake lifted his head in slow motion and lowered his glasses to the tip of his nose. He was making a point. "Counsel, what is the status of plea negotiations?"

"There are none," I said.

"Captain O'Donnell." His tone was condescending. "You do understand that Sergeant Jefferson is facing premeditated murder?"

"Yes, Your Honor."

"Does your client understand that the mandatory punishment for murder is life in prison?"

I nodded. "Yes, Your Honor."

Rake held his gaze. One Mississippi, two Mississippi, three Mississippi. I did not flinch. "Understood. Let the Court know if Sergeant Jefferson changes his mind."

"Will do, Your Honor."

"Would he like a trial by judge or jury?"

"A jury."

"Noted." Rake scribbled on his notepad. "Now, let's talk about trial dates. Government, when are you ready to try this case?"

Paine stood. "The prosecution won't be ready until after the New Year," he said. "Our first available date is 21 February."

"That pushes this case out for almost three months." Rake shook his head and swiveled toward me. "Defense, what is your position?"

Paine had taken me by surprise. I figured he'd demand a quick trial date. He knew that 30 January was my last day in the Army. I would be released from the case, and a new lawyer would be appointed if Rake set the trial for February. I turned to Jefferson and whispered, "What do you think?"

"I want to get this over with." Jefferson's breath quickened. "I can't stay in jail for three more months."

"You'll be in jail for a lot longer than three months if we lose."

"I'll take my chances. We're either ready, or we're not. I just want to go home."

I turned to the bench. "Your Honor, my client is sitting in jail, and he wants out. He demands a speedy trial. We will be ready on 9 January."

"So, Sergeant Jefferson." Judge Rake licked his index finger and flipped through a pocket calendar. "Your lawyer demanded a speedy trial. Is that your wish?"

"Yes, sir," Jefferson said.

"Then, I'm looking at a trial date." Rake paused for effect. "Sometime in December. 12 December, to be exact. Colonel Paine, do you have any cases scheduled that week?"

"No, I'm wide open," Paine said. His sinister grin told me I had walked into a trap.

"Defense, what about you?" Rake asked.

"I'm not available that week," I said. "My wife is pregnant. In fact, she's overdue. It's a high-risk-"

Rake cut me off. "Counsel, my question was, 'Do you have other cases scheduled that week?'"

"Cases, no, but I don't think I can be ready that soon considering-"

Rake interrupted me again. "Captain O'Donnell, you demanded a speedy trial. Are you withdrawing your request?"

"No, sir, but I will not be ready until January."

Rake rolled his eyes at me. "Your request for a speedy trial is granted. This court-martial will reconvene on Monday. Both sides have 24 hours to file motions and submit their witness lists." Judge Rake closed his pocket calendar and peered at Sergeant Jefferson's feet, which were visible under the table. "Trial counsel." Rake scratched his head. "Why is the accused wearing shackles in my courtroom?"

"I didn't know." Paine shrugged. "Captain O'Donnell did not inform-"

Rake held up his hand, stopping Paine mid-sentence. "Captain O'Donnell should have informed you, but it is ultimately your responsibility," Rake said. "Next time, I expect his leg irons to be removed before he appears in my courtroom."

Paine's eyes bore into me.

"I am awarding Sergeant Jefferson one day of sentence credit for the violation." Rake hammered his gavel. "This court is in recess until Monday morning."

Jefferson tapped me on the shoulder. "What does that mean?"

"That means we have a week to get ready for your murder trial, and if you're convicted, you get life minus one day."

CHAPTER 56

After the arraignment, I canceled my flight home and booked a room at the Motel 6 near the El Paso airport. Over the next 24 hours, I'd have to work non-stop to meet the judge's deadlines. I checked into my room and compiled a solid witness list. A few hours later, I took a break and called Annabelle.

"Hello," a voice whispered. It was Martha.

"Martha, it's Max," I said. "Can you please put Annabelle on?"

"Max, do you know what time it is?"

"It's 10 o'clock."

"We didn't hear from you all day. Now you call late at night. What is wrong with you, Mr. Max O'Donnell? You should be ashamed of yourself."

"Look, Martha. I just want to talk to my wife and-" She hung up the phone. I called back. It went straight to voice mail. So, I hung up and continued working.

An hour later, Rose called. "Max, can we meet up?" she said. "I have something for you."

"I don't think so, Rose. You screwed me over last time we spoke, and I found myself at the other end of an investigation because of it."

"You'll want to hear this. It's a gamechanger."

"What is it?"

"I can't say over the phone, in case someone is listening."

"Fine. I'm at the Motel 6 by the airport. Room 116."

"Motel 6? You went all out."

"Nothing but the best," I said.

"I'll see you in a few minutes," she said and hung up.

Meeting with a sexy, conniving reporter in a two-bit motel to discuss an ongoing case, wasn't the smartest move of my life, but what the hell. She had her agenda, and I had mine.

Thirty minutes later, Rose arrived at my room carrying a backpack and a six-pack of Corona. "You plan on spending the night?" I pointed at her backpack.

"In your dreams." She winked and smiled. For a moment, we stood in awkward silence. "You going to invite me in?" she asked, raising her eyebrows.

"Yeah, come in," I said, stepping aside. "Make yourself at home." My stomach tightened as she slid past me. The same feeling you get when you're about to do something you know is wrong.

Rose sat on the edge of the bed with her legs crisscrossed. She opened two beers, handed one to me, and pulled a thick folder from her bag.

"What's that?" I asked, pointing at the folder.

"Research," she said.

"Research on what?"

"Nassar." She paused. "He may be alive."

I jerked my head back and said, "Alive? I have his autopsy photos?"

"That may not be Nassar," she said. "Do they match his Red Cross photos."

"What Red Cross photos?"

"At Sangar Prison, the Red Cross photographed every prisoner."

"The only photos I have are from the autopsy."

"Then, you need to request the Red Cross photos."

"Will do," I said, and jotted down a reminder in my notepad.

We spent the night combing through Rose's documents. One that caught my attention was a story published by Amnesty International, a human rights organization. The article claimed the U.S. was running a top-secret torture program that made prisoners disappear. These prisoners were labeled "Ghost Detainees" and sent to secret prisons in countries like Egypt and Yemen, to be tortured. The White House dispelled these rumors and called the Ghost Detainee story "completely false."

Rose handed me a page from the Amnesty International website. "Check this out," she said. The page contained the names of suspected "Ghost Detainees."

I scanned through the names. Nothing jumped out. "What am I looking for?" I asked.

"Omar bin Mohammed. That's one of Nassar's aliases."

"How do you know that's our guy?"

She flipped through the file and handed me a profile of Nassar, from her source at *The Washington Post*. It listed when he was captured, in which prisons he was held, and when he disappeared. It also included his known aliases and a photo of Nassar in his 20s. One of them was, "Faud Halbousi," the name on the POW custody form.

"This makes no sense," I said to her. "Why would the Army charge Jefferson with killing Nassar if he's in a secret prison?"

"It's easier to scapegoat a reservist than to reveal the truth."

If Rose was correct, then Jefferson was innocent. Dread crept over me as I thought of Jefferson being locked up for a crime he didn't commit. The trial was a week away, and I was nowhere close to having a winning defense.

"Want some coffee?" I said. "It's going to be a long night." Rose shook her head no. I stood, emptied my beer into the sink, and turned on the coffee machine. I scanned Rose's documents while the pot brewed. What I read was intriguing, though I was not sure how it would help Jefferson's case.

I noticed a pattern with the ghost detainees. In every instance, they were listed as official prisoners of the United States. Then, for no apparent reason, their names vanished from the list. When reporters and international organizations asked questions, the official reply was, "The prisoner is no longer in U.S. custody." Beyond that, no information was released.

After hours of reading, I yawned and looked at my alarm clock. It was almost three o'clock in the morning. Rose was asleep on the bed, still surrounded by papers. I put a blanket over her, shut out the light, grabbed a pillow, and laid down on the floor.

CHAPTER 57

The next morning when I woke, Rose was gone, along with her documents. I spent the morning doing legal research and writing the motions. At noon, I decided to workout. I did a few sets of burpees in the motel parking and then ran toward the Franklin Mountains. It was 65 degrees and sunny. I got into a rhythm as my mp3 player blasted 50 Cent's "In Da Club." For a moment, I was in another world, one without Sergeant Jefferson and Sangar Prison. With each step, my mood improved.

A few miles later, my Blackberry buzzed three times. I kept running. After the fourth buzz in two minutes, I stopped, pulled the phone out of my pocket, and checked my e-mail. Bad idea.

Paine had unleashed a barrage of damning new evidence against Jefferson. He included arrest reports, gossip from past co-workers, and a statement from an ex-wife I didn't know he had. It was a brilliant study of character assassination. I couldn't catch a break. One step forward. Two steps back.

The next e-mail contained an order from the Commanding General granting Sergeant Cullen immunity in exchange for his testimony against Jefferson. This was not a surprise. I had expected Cullen to turn on Jefferson. I just wasn't sure when.

The next e-mail was titled "Specialist Aaron Strickland - Sworn Statement." *Who the hell is Aaron Strickland?* I thought.

A slight sense of panic set in. I was almost out of time and options, and it was too late to make a deal, at least not a good one. With each day, the prosecution's case was getting stronger. I cut my run short and took a $16 cab ride to the motel. After I showered and changed clothes, I was on my way to the Brig. Sergeant Jefferson had some explaining to do.

I walked into the Brig, flashed my military ID, and was led into the attorney meeting room. The ever-present hum of the fluorescent lights and the pungent odor of Pine-sol stood out more than ever. I was tired of this place. I reminded myself that, win or lose, I'd be going home in two weeks, in time for Christmas. Jefferson, however, could be spending the rest of his life behind bars.

A few minutes later, a guard led Jefferson into the room. "Nice to see you *early* for once, Captain," Jefferson said.

"Cut the sarcasm," I said. "It's getting old."

"What's *your* problem?"

"For starters, I just got a bunch of evidence dumped in my lap, and it makes you look guilty as fuck." He started to say "bullshit," but I cut him off. "I'm not here to debate you. I'm going to lay it on the line."

Jefferson crossed his arms and frowned.

I continued, "Our case is getting worse by the day. Every time I get new evidence, it's bad."

"What new evidence?"

"For starters, I got a list of witnesses that say you're a lying sack of shit," I said. "Got any idea what that means?"

"What?"

"It means you're going to get destroyed on cross-examination if you testify."

Jefferson finally cracked. He put his head into his hands and sobbed. I let him cry it out. For a moment, I felt sorry for him. "How is this fair?" he said in a whiny tone. "Weren't they supposed to hand this stuff over a long time ago?"

"Doesn't matter. The judge will let it in," I said. "My guess is, once they realized this was going to trial, they sent out investigators to uncover every dark secret from your past."

Jefferson hung his head and sagged in his chair.

"There's more," I said.

Jefferson shrugged as if to say, "What else?"

"Your buddy, Cullen, was granted immunity."

"Huh?" Jefferson furrowed his brow and squinted hard, trying to grasp what I had said.

"Cullen is going to testify against you. He's going to say you murdered Nassar. They also added a new witness. Specialist Strickland."

Jefferson's face turned to a scowl. "What's that asshole have to do with my case?"

"He's going to say you threatened to kill Nassar, right before he died."

"He's lying," Jefferson said.

"That's what you say about everyone," I said. "The jury is not going to believe that every single witness is lying. Discrediting one or two people is no problem. Discrediting 10 is another story."

"Well, they're lying."

"I can't just go around calling people liars. I need some evidence to back it up."

"I don't know what to tell you."

"For once, you can start by telling me the truth."

After I met with Jefferson, I grabbed an early dinner and returned to the Motel 6. I went through a ritual every criminal attorney knows by heart, identifying the strengths and weaknesses of the prosecution's case.

I pulled out a yellow legal pad and drew a line down the middle. I wrote "Strengths," over the left column, and "Weaknesses," over the right. There were so many strengths I had to flip to a fresh sheet of paper. The prosecution's strengths took up two pages. The list of weaknesses was much shorter. I just confirmed what I had been thinking all day: *We've got nothing.*

Turning the prosecution's strengths into liabilities was our only option. The first strength on the list was Judge Rake. Rake would steer this case in Paine's favor, and help guarantee Jefferson's conviction. I moved down the list to Strickland. This mystery witness had allegedly overheard Jefferson say he was going to kill Nassar, and I had no way to rebut his testimony.

Not helpful.

Then, I turned to the weaknesses. They all had to do with the CIA's involvement in the prison. If I could show that Nassar was in CIA custody at the time of his death, then I could create doubt about their entire case. The problem was, I had no solid proof to back up my theory, only speculation.

CHAPTER 58

O n Monday, I arrived early for court, ready to argue. A row of reporters gawked at their cell phones while the soldier designated as bailiff for the day nervously fidgeted, waiting to call "all rise." Rose sat behind me. Reggie was absent. I hadn't seen or heard from him since we parted ways after the Article 32 hearing.

Paine's team obnoxiously laughed and joked while we waited for the judge. Jefferson tapped my shoulder and pointed at the prosecution table. "What are they laughing about?" he said.

"I don't know, but we're going to give them hell today." I tried to sound confident.

Over the weekend, I had cranked out a few well-considered motions. One compelled the Government to disclose what CIA agents were at Sangar Prison from July through October 2002. I demanded the Red Cross photos that Rose had mentioned, and all other images of Nassar, dead and alive. I requested cleaning schedules for the cells, a list of the meals the prisoners received, and maintenance records. Everything.

I knew it was a long shot, but I asked for the flight manifests of all the aircraft in and out of Sangar. It was an airfield after all. I asked for the records showing when Nassar entered and exited the prison and a list of guards who had access to him. According to Jefferson, the guards kept detailed logbooks regarding the VIP prisoners. Yet, Paine never provided them.

Anticipating my strategy to paint Nassar as a bad guy, Paine filed a motion to prevent me from referring to him as a "terrorist," "al Qaeda," or anything else other than "the victim." Paine also sought to stop me from referring to Nassar's terrorist background. He argued that, even if Nassar was a terrorist, his past was irrelevant.

At precisely nine o'clock, Judge Rake took the bench. The courtroom was silent as he shuffled through a stack of papers and organized them on his desk. "I carefully reviewed the motions filed by both parties and the pertinent law," he said. Then, he cleared his throat. "The defense motions are denied."

"The CIA is not on trial," he reasoned. "The defense will not be permitted to grandstand and drag the Agency's sterling reputation through the mud." He denied our motion for the Red Cross photos, claiming that "for the sake of national security," they could not be released. He denied our request for the green logbook. "The defense is on a fishing expedition," he stated. Finally, he denied our request for the list of guards who had access to Nassar. His reason: "locating such records would be unduly burdensome to the Government, and unlikely to provide any tangentially relevant evidence."

Meanwhile, Judge Rake granted Paine's request to prohibit me from calling Nassar anything but "the victim." Rake also ruled that we couldn't mention Nassar's terrorist history, or why he was captured and held at Sangar. "The United States abides by the rule of law," Rake said. "We treat all prisoners of war humanely and with respect, regardless of their background. Therefore, the fact that the victim was a suspected terrorist is not relevant and is highly prejudicial to the prosecution."

After Judge Rake finished reading his rulings, I stood. "Your Honor, I respectfully request that you reconsider your rulings. It is highly prejudicial to the defense to allow Nassar, a murderous jihadist, to be portrayed as a choir boy."

"I made my rulings, counsel." Rake waved his hand dismissively. "You wanted a trial. Now you have one, but I'm not going to let you turn this into a circus."

"I don't know about a circus," I said. "More like a kangaroo court."

With a solid smack of his gavel, Rake held me in contempt and ordered me into his chambers, along with the entire prosecution team. Once inside, he made me stand at attention as he scolded me for 20 minutes. By the time he finished, it wasn't even 10 o'clock. We were done for the day.

The prosecution team filed out of the judge's chambers giddy, like children on the last day of school. Jefferson was gone, probably back at the Brig, enjoying the standard prison lunch, a baloney sandwich on white bread, and fruit punch. I packed my bag and made my way down the narrow staircase that led to the parking lot.

On the way to my car, someone shouted, "Captain O'Donnell."

I spun around and saw a young Army officer walking in my direction. His crisp camouflage uniform accentuated his tall, cut frame. "Who's asking?" I said.

The man didn't answer until he was a few feet away. "I'm Lieutenant Luken," he said. "We need to talk. Privately."

"About what, Lieutenant?"

"Meet me at the Fort Custer bowling alley in 30 minutes," he said. "It's important."

"The bowling alley?"

"Yeah. It's empty this time of day. We'll need privacy. Be there in 30 minutes."

I watched him turn and walk away. Though I was skeptical, I had nothing to lose, so I headed to the bowling alley.

Located adjacent to a weed-filled parking lot that hadn't been paved in decades, the Desert Strike Bowling Center was a windowless, one-story brick building. The single car in the parking lot, a faded 1992 Oldsmobile Cutlass, hinted that the building was empty, aside from an employee or two. Inside, the 24 lanes were lit up as if they were anticipating a full house. The place was like any typical American bowling alley. The 1980s-era booths and the smell of sweaty feet and stale pizza reminded me of my youth.

A few minutes later, Luken walked through the front entrance. "Let's take a seat." He pointed at a neon sign that said, "The Strike Lounge." Below the sign was a bar that served Miller Lite on tap and days-old popcorn by the bag.

I picked a booth, and we sat facing each other. A stick-like woman in her mid-thirties limped toward us, wiping her hands on a rag that looked like it had been used to clean a lawnmower engine. Her deflated face was riddled with pockmarks. Her hair resembled a raccoon pelt. "Can I get you boys somethin'?" she asked.

"Not at the moment," I replied with a smile.

"Okay, darlin', let me know if you change your mind," she said and started wiping down tables.

I locked eyes with Luken. "Now, what is this about?" I said.

To start, Lieutenant Luken gave me his back story. He was a newly commissioned Army lawyer, fresh out of the University of Florida Law School. Fort Custer was his first assignment. Like all new JAG lawyers, he started at the bottom of the food chain in Legal Assistance, the Army's legal aid clinic. He wasn't involved in the Sangar trials but followed them in the news.

After he explained his background, he said, "They're setting you up, sir."

"Who's setting me up?"

"Everyone."

My stomach turned. If this was a joke, then Luken was an excellent actor. If it wasn't, then he needed to get to the point and quickly. "What are you talking about?"

"I work in the Fort Custer JAG office, and I see and hear things." His eyes darted from side to side.

"Like what?"

"I need your word that you won't mention my name.

"Sure."

"The Military Judge has been meeting with the prosecution," he said. "They've been discussing your case."

"How do you know?"

"I've seen Judge Rake leaving Colonel Paine's office several times," he said. "I didn't think anything of it until this past Saturday."

"Go on."

"I came on post to run on the track. After my run, I showered in the locker room. That's when I overheard a conversation."

"While you were in the shower?" I asked.

"No, I was drying off, and some men came in. They were talking, using the urinals, normal stuff."

"Who was it?"

"It was Colonel Paine and Judge Rake. Someone else was there too, but I didn't recognize the voice."

"Did you see them?"

"Yes. Through a gap in the curtain."

"You're sure it was them?"

He nodded.

"Did they see you?" I asked him.

"No. I stayed behind the curtain. They never came back there."

"What were they talking about?"

"Colonel Paine was talking about you and how you are trying to get your 15 minutes of fame."

"And Judge Rake?"

"He called you an incompetent imbecile. He told Paine he would shut you down hard on Monday and send you back to where you came from with your tail between your legs."

"What else?"

"They joked about finishing the motions hearing in time for a noon tee time," he said.

I glanced at my watch. It was 11:15 a.m. I exchanged cell numbers with Luken, jumped in my rental car, and hauled ass out of the parking lot. I had a golf game to catch.

Chapter 59

After I left the bowling alley, I realized I had no idea where the golf course was. In all my time here, I had never noticed it. The only green grass I'd seen in El Paso was the parade field next to the courtroom. After I stopped and asked for directions, I continued toward the Army's Eisenhower Golf Complex, an island of green surrounded by a sea of brown dirt. I pulled into the course parking lot and parked in an empty spot near the driving range.

Inside the clubhouse, I asked the golf pro if he had seen Paine and his guests come through. "Oh, yeah. They're playing the front nine on the Sonora Course. They're only a threesome, so they'll probably squeeze you in. We're running a little behind today. Problem with one of the greens mowers. We're usually right on time-"

I left him mid-ramble and contemplated my next move. I fiddled around the shop until the guy at the desk wandered over to talk to someone. I slipped the tee sheet out from under the clip and stuffed it in my pocket.

I hustled out the back door and followed the signs toward the first hole. When I rounded the golf cart shack, I saw Paine, Rake, and some guy in a lime green shirt clearing the first tee, each man pushing a wheeled cart. I didn't know whether to be appalled or impressed. It took some guts for a judge and a prosecutor to openly fraternize in the middle of a high-profile murder trial.

On the way to my car, I read the tee sheet. It was in black and white: Colonel Bradley Rake, Colonel Ryan Beaver (the Commanding General's lawyer), and Colonel Covington Paine had a noon tee time. Luken wasn't lying. Now I had evidence of - at the least - judicially inappropriate behavior. With a little luck, I might be able to get Judge Rake off the case after all.

From the golf course, I drove to the Brig. I wanted to get Jefferson's feedback because my next move would impact his case, for better or worse. While I waited, I thought about my options. First, I could do nothing, and we would go forward to trial with Rake as the judge. This was a bad idea. I could also confront the judge privately and ask him to recuse himself because of a conflict of interest. Not a viable option. Rake would never step down.

My last option was to file a formal request demanding Rake's recusal, but as the saying goes, "When you shoot at a king, don't miss." I could expect significant blowback if I accused a military judge of colluding with the prosecution. None of the options were ideal. However, the last option was my best bet, even though it was going to upset a lot of people.

After waiting 20 minutes, I approached the Brig's reception booth. Behind two inches of bulletproof glass sat a guard, reading *Teen Vogue*. She was barely old enough to drive a car. Every time I visited the Brig, I had to deal with her charming personality. She always seemed stressed out, even though I never saw her do anything aside from picking up the phone and announcing my presence.

I knocked on the glass. "Specialist Simbach, I've been waiting for half an hour." I tapped my watch. "Are they getting Sergeant Jefferson or not?"

Simbach lifted her head in slow motion. "He's at chow," she said in a depressing tone. "We can't get prisoners while they're at chow. Safety, ya know."

"What time is chow done?"

"Today?"

"Yes, today," I said, trying to keep my cool.

"Hmmm." She picked up a small notepad and flipped through it, taking her time to scan each page. After a few minutes, she said, "Today, chow ends at 1300 hours. We had an inspection, so chow was later." She pointed to a clock on the wall behind me. "It's only 1250 hours. You gotta wait 10 more minutes."

I shook my head and walked to the vending machine next to the bathroom, inserted eight quarters, and pushed the button for a bottle of water. After a few sips, a voice called on the intercom, "Captain O'Donnell, Sergeant Jefferson is ready for you."

According to the clock, it had been two minutes. I screwed the plastic lid on the bottle and prepared to be searched. After some buzzes and greased metallic clicks, Simbach came out with a burly male sergeant with a lazy eye. I stepped through a metal detector as Simbach turned my bag inside out.

"Looky, looky." She held up the almost-full bottle of water, shook it, and flung it into the trash.

"I wanted to finish that," I said.

Simbach grinned. "It's contraband, sir. Sorry."

The sergeant tapped a metal sign on the wall with his knuckles. "No outside food or beverages. Them's the rules."

Assholes, I thought.

The sergeant keyed his radio. "All clear. Open the main door." The metal door clicked, and the sergeant pushed it open and waved me through.

I found Jefferson in the visitor's room, in high spirits. He beamed as I told him about Judge Rake and Paine. "I knew it," he said. "This is all a big setup."

I gave him a half-hearted nod.

"What's the next step, Captain?" he asked. Jefferson's nostrils flared as I explained our options. When I finished, he leaned forward and said, "Take those fuckers down. All of 'em."

"Done." I shook his hand and launched what seemed like a kamikaze mission to remove Judge Rake. I called Rose the moment I walked out of the Brig. "I have a story for you," I said.

"I'm listening."

"I'm filing a motion to recuse Judge Rake. He's been colluding with the prosecution."

"That doesn't surprise me."

"Once I file it, I'll send it to you."

"Thanks," she said and hung up the phone.

Now, I had to tie up some loose ends. I made a final call before I filed the request to disqualify Rake.

"Luken," the voice on the line said.

"This is Captain O'Donnell. From the Jefferson case."

"I know who you are. What's up?"

"I need you to write a statement describing what you saw and heard."

"Sir, I don't want to get involved."

"You're already involved," I said.

"I really don't-"

"Listen, Lieutenant. I tracked down some additional evidence. You're not the only witness."

"Really?" He sounded surprised.

"Yeah. They were golfing and drinking together at the golf club. Lots of people saw it," I said with conviction.

"Then, why do you need me?"

"Because you heard them discuss the case."

"I don't know-"

"Lieutenant, we can do it the easy way or the hard way," I said. "You can either write an affidavit, or you'll be subpoenaed to testify."

"I'm not testifying."

"Then, your only option is to write a statement."

"Fine. Meet me in my office in 30 minutes. If, for any reason, you don't need my statement, don't use it."

"I promise."

On my way to Luken's office, I wondered if he would follow through. Many people talk about truth, justice, and doing the right thing, but most people only do the right thing when it's easy. I hoped Luken was an exception.

When I arrived at his office, Luken was typing on his computer. I entered without knocking. "Almost finished," he said, without looking up. I took a seat and examined the plaques on his walls. From what I read, he'd served as an enlisted infantryman, including time with the 75th Ranger Regiment at Fort Benning, Georgia. In a photo on his desk, he posed with a brunette woman.

"Is that your wife?" I pointed at the picture.

"Yeah. Her name's Megan. We got married last year," he said as he typed.

He printed the statement when he finished, and I read it. "Perfect," I said. "Let's hope this doesn't backfire."

His face turned ashen. "What do you mean?"

"We're accusing two senior Army officers of misconduct," I said. "They'll deny it, and we'll get some backlash."

"I saw what I saw. Why would I make this up?" Luken had a point. Why would a brand-new lieutenant make up this story and risk his career? It made no sense. "Do what you need to do," he said. "I'll live with the consequences."

I didn't sense any hesitation in his voice. "Go ahead and sign right here, swearing that this statement is the truth," I said, handing him a pen. After he signed, I thanked him and said goodbye. As I walked to my car, I had a bad feeling about what was about to happen.

CHAPTER 60

B ack at my motel, I wrote the motion to recuse Judge Rake and filed it, via e-mail, with the Court. I then forwarded the motion to Rose, along with the attachments: Luken's sworn statement and the golf roster.

Rose wrote back, "Thanks! The story will hit the wire tonight."

I closed my computer and grabbed a beer from the mini-fridge. It had been a long day, and I needed a break. Four beers and four *Seinfeld* episodes later, my Blackberry vibrated. It was a message from Judge Rake: "We will reconvene tonight at 2100 hours to litigate the defense motion to recuse. Defense: It's your motion, you have the burden of proof. Be prepared to present witnesses and evidence."

It was a 20-minute drive to Fort Custer, and while I was not hammered, I wasn't ready for a dress parade either. I immediately called Rose. "The judge is pissed," I said. "He wants to litigate the motion tonight, in less than an hour. Can you hold off on the article?"

"Sorry. It's going live soon."

"Can you give me a lift to court?" I said. "I'll explain later."

"Sure. I'll be there in 15 minutes."

"Got it."

I brushed my teeth, scrambled into the shower, and dressed. Outside, Rose was waiting. I jumped into her car, and we sped off. On the way to Fort Custer, I called Luken.

"Lieutenant, there's been a slight change of plans," I said. "I need you in the courtroom. Now."

"I'm in bed."

"Then get out of bed. You need to appear in court. We start in 20 minutes."

"Sir, I told you I did not want to testify."

"You don't have a choice."

The call went dead. I tried back twice. Luken did not answer. At a stoplight, Rose checked her phone and handed it to me. A nervous smile spread across her face. "The article is live." It was titled, *"Army Lawyer Accuses Military Judge of Misconduct in Detainee Abuse Case."*

I read the article on her phone, confident that recusing Rake was the right thing to do. It wasn't until we pulled into the courtroom's parking lot that my confidence faded. The JAG Office, which took up the first two floors of the building, was lit up. From the outside, it seemed like the entire office was at work. The parking lot had two dozen cars. A few civilians, probably reporters, huddled on the concrete steps that led to the entrance.

"Drop me off on the corner," I said. "I don't want us to be seen together."

Rose made a hard U-turn and stopped a block away. "See you inside, and good luck."

I hopped out of her car, and she drove off. I took a deep breath and walked toward the courtroom. A holler came from my right as I approached the building. "Captain O'Donnell." I glanced over to see a shadowy figure clutching a note pad. I reached for the door handle. "Captain O'Donnell! Wes Steuben, from the *Times*," the man said, wedging himself between my body and the door.

"Excuse me," I said.

He did not move. "Did your client torture detainees?"

"No."

When I pulled the handle, the man jammed his foot into the bottom of the door, stopping it from opening. No doubt a Grateful Dead groupie, his breath reeked of cigarettes and turpentine, closer to dead than alive. "Did the judge conspire to frame your client?" he said.

I jerked the door open, knocking the reporter to the side. "Jesus Christ, man," he said.

"Get out of my way," I said as I pushed past him and entered the building. Inside, I ran up the stairs to the third-story courtroom. I entered, and all eyes were on me. It was 8:58 p.m., and the room was full. Jefferson sat at the defense table with his usual accompaniment of guards. The prosecution's brood lingered in the front row, notebooks in hand.

Paine sat in the middle of the prosecution table, flanked by Nelson and Weiss. The remainder of the gallery was packed with Army lawyers, members of the command, reporters, and a bunch of busybodies looking to fill their daily quota of gossip. Even Paine's wife was there, eager to watch the carnage.

I walked over to Jefferson. He appeared as nervous as I felt. "Sir, what's this about?" he asked me.

"You know that motion to recuse the judge that we discussed?"

He nodded.

"I filed it and gave it to the press."

"Maybe you shouldn't have done that. I think we fucked up."

"What was your first clue?"

As I scanned the audience's faces, I noticed Rose had slipped in after me. Aside from her, the crowd was hostile. Across the room, Paine made no effort to hide his contempt. "O'Donnell, you're in a world of hurt," he shouted. Some of the voyeurs in the room cackled. "I'm talking to you,

O'Donnell." Paine stood and pointed at me. "I can't wait to cross-examine your ass." I ignored him.

"What's he talking about?" Jefferson asked.

"He's trying to mess with me. Don't worry about it."

"I hate to say it, but you look a little frazzled."

"I'm fine." I lied. I picked up my Blackberry and called Luken. Again, it went to voicemail. I knew he wasn't coming.

Paine jumped to his feet as Judge Rake entered the courtroom and hollered, "All rise."

The rest of the audience stood as Judge Rake entered and took his seat. He was out of breath. "This hearing is called to order," Rake said. "I apologize for disrupting everyone's lives, but I saw no other option. It was brought to my attention this evening that the defense filed a motion to recuse me from this case-" Rake's voice cracked. "-for allegedly colluding and conspiring with the prosecution in an attempt to deprive Sergeant Jefferson, of his right to a fair trial." Rake's eyes locked on me. "Also, it appears these allegations have been leaked to the media, presumably by the defense." The air in the room felt like it was going to tear. Nobody spoke, nor coughed, nor breathed, for what felt like minutes. "Defense counsel, you filed this motion. Call your first witness."

I stood. "Your Honor, in support of our motion, we submit a sworn affidavit from First Lieutenant Luken, an Army lawyer. We also submit the golf rost-"

"I said, 'call your first witness.'" Rake's voice boomed.

"I don't have a live witness. Lieutenant Luken stands by his affidavit, and for this hearing, an affidavit is an acceptable form of evidence."

Rake slammed his gavel. "I don't think so." His right eye twitched like he was on the verge of a nervous breakdown. I remained standing but said nothing. "This is unacceptable. We're all here at 2100 hours, ready to litigate this matter, and you have no evidence. Explain yourself."

"First off, Your Honor, you're the one who scheduled this hearing at 2100 hours, not me. Second, I have evidence."

Rake's eyes nearly bulged out of his head. "Sit down, now." My heart pounded as I sat. Rake continued, "I'm ready to state under oath that I never conspired with Colonel Paine. I never interacted with him in any personal manner, on or off duty." He turned to Paine and said, "Is there anything you want to add to the record?"

Paine stood and adjusted his tie. "Your Honor, I have never discussed this case with you outside of the courtroom and have never interacted with you in a personal manner."

I sprang to my feet. "Do you both deny golfing together this afternoon?"

"I golf every now and then, time permitting," Paine said. "Considering I've been working 18-hour days, I think I'm entitled to a quick game once a week." Some of the audience murmured in agreement.

"That does not answer my question," I said.

Rake hammered his gavel. "Sit down, O'Donnell."

I sat, and Paine said, "I had a tee time this afternoon with a colleague, Colonel Ryan Beaver. I couldn't make it, so I mentioned the opening to Colonel Rake. He took my spot. I stayed behind at the office. I had a lot of work to do."

"That is accurate," Rake said. "Colonel Paine mentioned the golf opening in the hallway following the hearing, and I agreed to fill in for him."

"Sir," I said, somehow astounded by the blatant untruths. "Your names are listed on the golf roster. You both signed in to play. You even rented pushcarts. That document is in evidence."

"That proves nothing," Rake said.

Paine stood and pointed at me. "O'Donnell's motion is frivolous," he said. "It was filed with malicious intent. I'm taking this up with his bar association. He should be sanctioned."

"Agreed. For my part, I will make this misconduct known to Captain O'Donnell's commanding officer, as well as to the Army Trial Judiciary," Rake added. "Now, I want to discuss the news article that appeared an hour ago, in which large portions of your recusal motion are printed. This article is slanderous to me, Colonel Paine, and the Army." Rake scanned the audience and pointed at Rose. "Ms. Sanchez, who gave you this motion?" he said.

All eyes were on Rose as she stood. "Your Honor," she said, without an ounce of fear. "I am a journalist. I cannot reveal my sources."

"I'm ordering you to tell me where this information came from."

"No, I won't do that."

"I can lock you up for contempt."

"Then do it."

Judge Rake had overplayed his hand. Jailing a reporter for contempt was technically legal, but it was a public relations nightmare. It made the entire process look corrupt, and it made Judge Rake look bad. Rose remained standing as Judge Rake fumbled through the Manual for Courts-Martial. He was buying time as he figured out how to undo the mess he created. After a few minutes, he stopped searching and closed the book.

"Ms. Sanchez, you may sit down. At this point, I am going to admonish all parties to follow the military rules for media contact. Moving on," Rake continued. "This Court finds that the allegations made in the defense motion are false and unsupported by the facts. There is no credible evidence, whatsoever, to support the defense's claims. The motion is denied. Furthermore, it appears that the defense is using the media in an attempt to influence this court-martial. Therefore, I am issuing a gag order on all parties. No one will leak, or cause to be leaked, any matters related to this case, to any member of the press or any news agency. That includes." Rake cleared his throat for emphasis, "Bloggers. Is that understood?"

"Yes, Your Honor," I said.

"This court-martial is adjourned until 12 December when we will commence jury selection." Rake smacked his gavel.

Jefferson turned to me and whispered, "The judge is fired up."

"Don't worry about him," I said. "He's mad at me, not you."

"Nah, he hates both of us."

I laughed and slapped Jefferson on the back. "You're right, he hates us both. Now get some rest. I'll be in touch."

I left the courtroom, expecting to find Rose waiting for me outside. She wasn't. It was nearly midnight, and I didn't have a ride. I reached inside my bag and pulled out my phone. It wouldn't turn on. The battery was dead.

I slipped the phone into my pocket and walked along the unlit sidewalk toward the main gate, where I could hail a cab. A few blocks later, an SUV approached me from behind and flashed its headlights. I never thought I'd be happy to see Reggie.

"I heard we got a problem judge," he said.

I nodded.

"Get in."

Marvin Gaye's "Sexual Healing" pulsed through the sound system as we cruised past strip malls lined with liquor stores and Asian nail salons. "You hungry?" Reggie asked me, keeping his eye on the road.

"Yeah."

"Wings?"

"Sure."

Somehow, I knew the only place that served wings this time of night was the Kitty Kat. Oddly, I felt like it was a safe place, away from Army rules and lying prosecutors. Inside the club, degenerates congregated around the stage, sucking on cancer sticks. Warrant's "Cherry Pie" blared as a redhead in a thong, and six-inch platform heels fired up the crowd. She was already topless, which meant she was mid-performance. Desperate, attention-starved men waved crisply folded dollar bills, hoping to lure her in their direction.

"Over there," Reggie said, motioning to an empty booth. We sat, and Reggie ordered a bucket of wings with blue cheese and a pitcher of Modelo Extra. "What happened tonight?" Reggie said. He folded his hands in front of him, making a giant fist. His eyes were intense. Different than before. More focused.

"The judge refused to step down," I said, after giving him the abbreviated story. "Now, we're stuck with him, and he's going to screw us."

"How's that any different from what's been going on the whole time?" I thought for a moment. Reggie was right. We'd been getting jerked around from the start, and Judge Rake was just a different guy singing the same tune. "Son, when you gonna learn?" Reggie shook his head like I let him down. "You never beat a bully at his own game - especially in his own backyard."

The pitcher of beer arrived, and the waitress poured two tall glasses. Reggie drained his in three gulps. "You got to go after their weak points," he continued. "Make them fight where it's not expected. You don't beat Goliath with a sword, you beat him with a well-aimed stone."

I nodded in agreement, although I wasn't exactly sure if we even had a stone to throw.

"For starters. This judge has got to go," he said. "We knock him out, then we start going after other weak points, like the snitches."

"Reggie, I tried to get rid of the judge, and it backfired."

"It backfired because you played their game. Boy, you think an Army judge is going to admit to misconduct, and recuse himself in front of the national media? Did your momma know you were stupid when she raised you?"

"Yeah, you're right." I actually laughed. "That was pretty stupid."

"We hit them where they been hitting my boy all along - below the belt."

I pulled out my notepad. "Where do we start?"

"Put that shit away, counselor. I got this." Reggie pulled a cell phone from his pocket and stepped away from the table. "I'll be back," he said and walked out the door.

When he did not return after 15 minutes, I looked for him in the parking lot. He was gone, and so was his Escalade. I walked back into the Kitty Kat, finished the wings, and took a cab to my motel.

CHAPTER 61

I got back to my room at half-past midnight and charged my phone. I had 14 new voicemails. The first 12 were from Sterling. All about the same. "Max, Sterling Hillyard here (yes, he introduced himself the same way a dozen consecutive times). Annabelle started labor about nine o'clock (yes, he mentioned that every time, too). You should call."

Lucky number 13 was different. "Max, Sterling Hillyard here. Annabelle had a little problem, and they had to take her in for an emergency C-section. You are the proud papa of a six-pound, two-ounce boy - mother and child are doing fine."

The fourteenth call was like fingernails on a chalkboard. "Well, congratulations, Daddy," came the consonant-dropping syrup of Martha's voice, magnolia blossoms falling from her accent. "So sorry you were too busy to be here for the birth of your child, but number three must be old hat to you. Anyway, my Sterling and I held the fort, and our brave Annabelle was a champ. Whenever you do decide to come home, I know you will be proud of your new son." She paused for a few seconds. Martha obviously wanted to ensure I was paying attention. "A beautiful little fellow. Lovely, peach-colored skin, and a strong, proud name - Sterling Hillyard O'Donnell."

I flinched so hard, I hit my head on the headboard. The "lovely, peach-colored skin," didn't bother me - classic

Martha. She always referred to Ethan, our slightly tan child, as her "little chestnut." She conspicuously favored Eva, our blonde, blue-eyed offspring. I'd come to an uneasy peace about Martha's barely concealed bigotry, but how did Maximillian Alejandro, Jr. - the name Annabelle and I had selected - transform into Sterling Hillyard?

I knew what time it was, but I didn't care. I dialed Annabelle. Three rings ... four ... five ... then the voicemail recording. A new one, not Annabelle's voice. "This is Martha. Annabelle and little Sterling are well. Thank y'all so much for your call. Please leave a message, and we'll get back to y'all in two shakes of a lil' lamb's tail. God bless." I could hear fumbling, and the telltale tri-tones while someone hit buttons by mistake. Then, Martha's voice, "How do I turn this off, Hon?" Then, "beep."

I laid there, thinking about my newborn son. I couldn't wait to see him. One thing was for sure, we would change his name when I returned - to anything, but "Sterling." Soon, I was fast asleep.

My phone woke me as the morning sun peeked through the curtains. Reggie's voice was calm. "Counselor, thought you'd be interested in the latest news."

"What are you talking about?"

"Our problem judge is a thing of the past," he said.

I could hear myself speaking, but the words sounded like they originated elsewhere. "Reggie. What the hell have you done?"

I put my fingers to my carotid and checked my pulse. I didn't know what a stroke felt like, but I thought I might be a candidate. I remembered reading somewhere that stroke victims smell burnt toast right before the event. I sniffed the air. Only the reassuring aroma of stale coffee.

"I ain't done nothin', Captain. I'm just reporting what I heard a little bit ago. Seems a young girl staggered into the hospital this morning 'bout 4 a.m. Said she'd been assaulted. She got swabbed and scraped and talked to two very concerned Special Victims Unit detectives." I struggled to control my breathing, while Reggie continued like he was telling a story about a recent fishing trip, "Once she mentioned a U.S. Army Colonel, the local police officers rushed to the nearest phone to call Fort Custer. Last I heard, a couple of MPs had him all handcuffed and shit."

"Reggie, they'll break that girl's story."

"Don't think so. She's got his skin under her nails. Her skin under his nails and there was semen in just about every female receptacle. Best part is, she's 17."

"Reggie, what the fuck? You and I can go to jail for this."

"For what?" he asked.

Then it hit me. "Reggie, when did the alleged incident take place?"

"Last night, after the hearing, Rake visited his favorite watering hole. At the bar, he happened to meet a young lady."

"Go on," I said.

"This morning, he woke up in a hotel room. Claims he doesn't remember anything, but I guaran-dam-tee you that the DNA test will light him up like a pinball machine."

It was all becoming clear. "Reggie, you rigged this before you picked me up. You knew about my motion, and you knew it wasn't going to work. You framed the ju-."

He cut me off. "Be careful with accusations, counselor, but you can bet your ass you've seen the last of Judge Rake." The line went dead.

This was bad. Reggie could play innocent all he wanted, but if the Rake situation backfired, I would spend the rest of my life breaking rocks somewhere. There were too many loose ends, and one of them could fray at any moment. Even without Judge Rake assisting the prosecution, I faced an uphill battle. What if Rake was replaced by a worse judge? Then what? Would Reggie set him up too?

I brushed my teeth and booted up my Army issued laptop. I needed to know more about Rake's situation, and what damage Reggie had caused. As my computer churned to life, I brewed a pot of coffee and showered. I Googled Rake's name. Only one article appeared, a "breaking news story" in the *El Paso Star*.

The article had few details, mainly what was released by the local Sheriff's Office. Judge Rake was being held in the El Paso County jail, awaiting a bail hearing. The initial charges included rape, strangulation, and kidnapping.

For a moment, I felt complicit, but not for long. Rake was a corrupt judge, and he needed to go. Nobody forced him to have sex with a teenager he'd met in a bar. He created this situation, not me. Part of me was relieved because Jefferson's trial would have to be delayed until the Army replaced Judge Rake. With the trial on hold, I decided to take the morning off and go to Denny's for breakfast. I tried reaching Annabelle, but once again, it went to voicemail.

By noon, I was back in my room, preparing to fly home when I received an e-mail from Colonel Antonio Bertram Gianelli, a senior military judge. "I am now presiding over the U.S. v. Jefferson court-martial. The trial will proceed as scheduled."

CHAPTER 62

Two weeks after Aaron "Greaser" Strickland escaped from the transport van, he figured that the Army had stopped looking for him. After three weeks, he was sure of it. Of course, no one had ever accused Aaron Strickland of being a genius.

Strickland and Misty, the erstwhile clerk at the convenience store, had spent almost every minute together since she'd facilitated his escape by hoisting him into the trunk of her 1989 Mercury Cougar, and abruptly leaving the employ of the gas station. That morning, she hacked off his shackles with a pair of bolt cutters from her grandpappy's tool shed.

Misty had some money. Her dead mother "left her a bundle." What was left of her $30,000 "estate" evaporated quickly during their three weeks of screwin', druggin', and "fancy eatin'." About the time Misty said, "Hey babe, I only have a few hundie left, maybe you should go get a job," Aaron took her for one last roll in the hay, then walked out the door.

"I'll be back," he said, as he buttoned the shirt she'd bought him at an upscale western wear store. No, he wouldn't. Misty was fun, but she looked a lot better when he was high, and it appeared sobriety was being forced on him by way of economic depravity. He reasoned that if he had to work, he wanted to come home to a better-looking piece of ass.

When he crawled out of bed at noon, Strickland had a plan. He'd snag a job, charm another sweet young thing, and spend a few months flipping burgers during the day and doing the meth-aided mattress Mambo at night. While Misty slept, Strickland "borrowed" her car, and drove into town. On his way, he stopped at a bar for a little liquid refreshment. Then, he headed to McDonald's. He'd done fast food. He could cook burgers. Hell, a trained chimp could bag fries. Over the next couple of weeks, he figured he could take a few bucks from the till every day (not too many) and liberate a box of patties every once in a while.

What Strickland did not figure on was the Army's dogged persistence. The Military Police had circulated wanted posters around town in the aftermath of his escape. Catching him with a wanted poster was a long shot. The MPs assumed he would be hundreds of miles away by the time they handed out his likeness. Unfortunately for Strickland, he had never left Stanton, Texas.

Strickland was busy making up "facts" on his application and munching on a complimentary Big Mac when a quartet of military policemen sitting in the dining area compared his face to the clipboard likeness they all carried. After they finished their sodas, two of them approached Strickland while the other two covered the exits.

"Mr. Strickland?" one said.

"I'll be finished in a second, boss," Strickland said, without looking up.

"Come with us, please?"

"I need a minute." Strickland kept his face buried in the application.

"You don't have another minute." One of the MPs pushed Strickland's face squarely into the Big Mac and held it there, while the other cuffed him.

As they walked out, Strickland turned his special-sauce smeared face to the taller of his two escorts. "Hey man," he said. "Can you grab the rest of my fries?

CHAPTER 63

Throughout the day, Martha and Sterling had tag-teamed the phones with the expertise of professional goalies, blocking every one of the dozens of calls I attempted. I finally talked to Annabelle, but only after a brief and ugly confrontation with her father.

"Max, Annabelle still has not regained her strength," he said.

I lost it. "Sterling, you arrogant prick. Put my wife on the phone, now." My outburst did the trick.

"Max?" she said faintly. She sounded mouse-like. And, she seemed glad to hear from me.

"Hi, baby," I said.

I was wrong. Annabelle was not glad. "Maximillian O'Donnell." An icepick ran up my spine. "Max, why haven't you called? Our - *my* son is a day old, and I am just now hearing from you. Are you going to tell me your case is more important than the birth of your child?"

"Annabelle-" was all I got out of my mouth.

"I have asked every hour or so about you, and Mother and Daddy told me you haven't called. They said you never returned any of their calls since little Sterling was born."

"I've been calling," I said. "I couldn't get through."

Silence.

"About the name," I said.

"Isn't it wonderful? Daddy is so thrilled. He's already set up an account for college, and even applied for the social security number so everything will be official."

"Honey."

"No, Max, don't you honey me."

"What?"

"I hope you're having fun on your little trip to Tijuana or wherever you are."

Annabelle knew that Fort Custer was in El Paso. She was parroting back whatever mental cyanide Martha had poured into her brain. I searched for an avenue of retreat. "Annabelle, I called to tell you that I love you, and I'm happy the baby is okay. I can't wait to see him."

"Well, he's okay, but barely," she said. "The little guy is scrappy. A real fighter, just like-"

I stood tall, waiting for it.

"-just like my daddy."

The only fighting Sterling Hillyard had ever done was making sure he and his partner, "Big Bob" Dalton (*of the Dalton, Georgia Daltons*, as Martha would say), got enough strokes on the first tee before their weekly Saturday cheat-fest disguised as a golf game.

"From now on, I'll call every day," I said.

"Well, don't put yourself out too much, dear," Martha said, as she grabbed the phone from Annabelle. Another stab, this one lower in my anatomy. "I know you are so busy fixing the problems of low-life Army criminals you don't have a lot of time for family matters. Don't you worry. Sterling and I have everything under control." I stared at the phone as it went dead.

After the call, I rushed to the airport and caught a flight back to South Carolina. I tried to relax but couldn't. As soon as the pilot turned off the seatbelt sign, I stood and paced the aisle for the rest of the flight.

Seven hours later, at the hospital, I found Annabelle in bed, sobbing. Her mother and our neighbor, Janet Grigsby, were at her side. The room was decorated with flowers and balloons, congratulating Annabelle on the birth.

I ignored the other women in the room and went straight to Annabelle. "Honey. What happened?" I said. She did not respond. She was inconsolable. I took her hand. "Annabelle, are you okay?" She didn't reply. "Where's the baby?"

"You mean little Sterling?" Martha jumped in.

Who do you think I mean? I thought, but I bit my tongue. "How's my son?" I asked.

"Like you care," Annabelle blubbered.

"Do we have to do this now?" I said.

"He's in the NICU," Martha said.

"The what?"

"The neonatal intensive care unit," Martha said.

My heart sank. "What happened?" I asked.

"He has elevated bilirubin - some liver enzyme," Martha said. "He has to be under the lights for a few days."

"Is it serious?" I asked.

Annabelle wailed, "My baby. What's going to happen to my baby?"

Martha and Janet stared at me like this was my fault. After Annabelle calmed down, she turned to me and said, "I think we need some time apart. Daddy told me about what you've been doing in Texas. He swears all the stress complicated the birth."

"Nothing happened," I said.

Martha huffed under her breath.

Janet nodded in agreement.

"Things have been bad for a while," Annabelle continued. "What you did brought old wounds to the surface."

"What are you talking about?" I asked, honestly confused.

"The drinking, the lying, the way you treat my parents. I've had enough," Annabelle said.

"Your dad is an asshole," I said. Shouldn't have, but it felt strangely liberating.

"That's exactly what I mean," Annabelle said. "You're volatile. My parents are scared of you. They don't think the children and I are safe around you. You need help."

"Not safe? What are you talking about?"

"I'm moving in with my parents for a little while," Annabelle said. "That should give you enough time to get your stuff cleared out of the house."

"What? Where am I supposed to go?" I said, raising my voice.

"Not my problem, Max."

"Are you fucking crazy?"

"There you go again," Annabelle said. "Your temper is out of control. I never know what you're going to do."

"I haven't done anything."

"Please leave Max," Annabelle said. "I don't feel well."

I stood and headed for the door, as Martha called out, "She knows about your dalliances with that Mexican homewrecker."

I whirled, barely in control. "My what?"

"Now is not the time to play coy, Max O'Donnell," Martha said. "My husband and I have been on to you for a long time."

"Fuck you, and fuck Sterling," I said, and walked out the door.

CHAPTER 64

t the hospital, Martha had told me Ethan and Eva were "at home." She meant their home, a mammoth of a house, complete with a four-car garage and a putting green. It was located in the oldest and wealthiest section of South Carolina's capital city.

I planned on picking up my kids and bringing them home with me when I left the hospital. No one was going to take away my children. By the time I pulled into Sterling's circular drive, I could feel my pulse banging away in my ears. I'd been played, made to look like an uncaring - worse, a philandering - husband.

Sterling opened the door as I reached for the bell. He'd been warned. "Max, is there something I can help you with?"

"Nice of you to give the butler the night off," I said, and shoved past him into the marble foyer.

Sterling made that inane chuckling noise he liked so much, a cross between a hiccup and a croak. "Charles only works in the evenings when Martha and I host functions," he said. He stopped when he saw my face. "Max, are you perturbed about something?"

"Where are my kids?"

"They've gone to bed. Perhaps you should come by in the morning."

I climbed the stairs and found Ethan and Eva in the spare bedroom playing with toys. "Daddy!" I collapsed under an avalanche of hugs and kisses.

"Are we going home?" Eva asked.

"Is my new brother at home?" Ethan asked.

"He's *our* brother," Eva retorted.

"Nope," Ethan said. "He's a boy. He's mine."

I interrupted the property dispute. "He's still at the hospital," I said. "Let's go home."

Sterling met us at the bottom of the stairs with a cordless phone in his hand. "They need to stay," he said as he stepped in front of me. I dodged to his left. Then, Sterling screwed up. He put his hand on my shoulder, and not in a buddy-buddy way. It was an attempt at restraint. "Max, you're already in trouble with Annabelle, and with the Army. Let's not make this worse."

"Get your hands off me, Sterling."

His eyes narrowed, and his hand stayed put. I turned toward the door, but Sterling gripped harder and pulled. Instinct kicked in. Instinct propelled by anger. I grabbed Sterling's hand and put him in an Aikido wrist lock. Sterling went to one knee, agony etched on his face.

"Touch me again, and I'll break your arm," I said, my voice a whisper.

The kids were by the door, watching us. "Daddy, are you and Papa fighting?" Eva asked, looking concerned.

"No, honey." I kept smiling. "Papa slipped. I'm helping him up." I pulled Sterling to his feet, grabbed the children, and headed through the front door. Outside, I saw two Richland County Sheriff's Department cruisers in the driveway. A pair of uniformed deputies approached the house.

Sterling's voice came from behind me. "There he is, deputies. That's him."

The deputy on the left reached for his taser. I raised my hands.

"All good here, guys," I said. "Just picking up my kids." I glanced over my shoulder, careful not to turn my back to the deputies. "Kids, go back inside with Papa," I said. "We'll go home in a second."

Ethan and Eva ran toward the house, and I heard the door close.

"Are you Max O'Donnell?" the deputy on the left asked.

"I am Captain O'Donnell, JAG Corps, U.S. Army," I said, hoping I might get a little professional courtesy.

"Captain O'Donnell, you are served," the deputy said as he handed me a piece of paper. "You've been ordered by the Honorable John S. Tolliver to have no physical contact with the following individuals until a hearing can determine the scope and necessity of this order. Annabelle O'Donnell, Ethan O'Donnell, Eva O'Donnell, Sterling O'Donnell, Sterling Hillyard, and Martha Hillyard."

I read the paper. "A restraining order?" I said. "Seriously?"

The one on the right nodded. "Yes, sir."

"Guys-," I said. I couldn't finish.

"Captain." It was the one on the right again. "We know how these things go. This is obviously a family thing that's blown up in your face. Go home, read the order, comply, and things will work out. You wouldn't want to do anything that might upset the little ones, would you?" He pointed over my shoulder.

"It's okay," the one on the left said. "You can look."

I turned around, and Ethan snapped to attention and saluted me. I returned it and headed toward my car.

"Sir," I heard one of the deputies say as I climbed in. "You probably ought to get yourself an attorney."

After I got home, I sat on my sofa and studied the order. For the next 30 days, I could not be within 500 feet of my family. I also had to vacate our home within 24 hours. This had been planned. It takes a day - at a minimum - to get a restraining order from a county judge. I was sure Sterling had set this up with David Kline, probably over a couple of Scotches at the club.

༐

Before I went to bed, I made a call. The gruff voice sounded the same as always. "Who is calling this late?"

"Hi, Dad," I said.

"Max?"

"Yes, sir."

"You okay, son?" The old man was getting soft.

"No, sir. I need help."

"Are you in jail?"

"No, sir."

"You need some money?"

"No, sir."

"Then what is it?"

I laid it out. Getting forced into a losing murder trial with three months left in the Army, no job prospects, and my marriage was in the toilet. The phone went quiet for a while. "Dad?" I could hear his breathing.

"Son," he said, "For starters, stop feeling sorry for yourself. It's unbecoming. Second, quit your whining about the Army. It's nothing but a gigantic bureaucracy run by assholes and egomaniacs. They eat their own. You knew that when you joined. You want to come out on top? Get your head right. If your head's not right, nothing else will be."

"But-"

"Knock off the pity party." He interrupted. "Life's not fair. We both know it isn't. Nothing in the world is fair. Use it."

"Sir?"

"Use the unfairness. Let it fuel you to fight and win. That's what we do. That's how I raised you. Remember - Battlemind."

I was back on the hill watching Chris Tomassi charge at me on the stolen bike. "Battlemind." The same thing Dad said to me before I reclaimed my jacket. I sat for a while. My dad couldn't see me, but I was nodding.

He spoke again. "Son, take the fight to those sons-of-bitches. Take back what is yours." With that, he hung up.

Chapter 65

I took an early morning flight back to Texas and headed straight for the Brig. When I saw Jefferson, I could tell the stress had taken a toll on his body and mind. He'd lost at least 15 pounds while in jail, mostly muscle. His cheeks were sunken, and he was depressed.

"What are our chances of winning?" Jefferson asked me.

Always a tricky question, because nobody ever wants to hear the truth. Criminal defendants want to hear what makes them feel good, and that is almost always a lie. "We have a fighting chance," I said, a vast over assessment of the odds.

The prosecution had eyewitnesses, a motive and opportunity, and enough lousy character references to convict a nun. Sure, a lot of it was petty gossip and hearsay, but there is such a thing as "death by 1,000 cuts." Someone eventually bleeds out.

"So, what's the plan?" Jefferson asked in a flat tone.

"We're going to attack the prosecution's weaknesses. The more we focus on their weaknesses, the more the jury will focus on them. Each weakness helps build reasonable doubt. We only need one reasonable doubt to win."

"That's it?" Jefferson threw up his hands. "That sounds like legal mumbo-jumbo. How are you going to prove my innocence?"

"Sergeant, I've explained this a dozen times. We don't have to prove your innocence. We don't have to prove anything. The prosecution has to prove that you're guilty beyond a reasonable doubt."

Jefferson nodded, though I was confident he didn't understand.

"Listen," I continued. "We win by attacking the prosecution's witnesses. Their memories, their motives, their credibility. We win by pinning this on the CIA. We make a big deal out of the missing evidence. That is how we win. That is how we raise reasonable doubt."

"What about our case?" Jefferson slumped in his chair. "Who are we calling as witnesses?"

"Nobody," I said. "We win this case on cross-examination. We attack, attack, attack. We force them to defend. It's difficult to prove a case beyond a reasonable doubt, especially when you're on the defensive. The more we attack, the more Paine has to defend. The more he is forced to defend, the stronger we become." I was dangerously close to believing my own bullshit.

CHAPTER 66

Colonel Antonio Bertram Gianelli, "Tony" to his drinking buddies, was a stout man with hams for hands and a 50-terabyte computer for a brain. A West Point graduate with a crackling competitive streak, he continually defied stereotypes. Though built like a nose tackle, a position he played fiercely and well in high school, Gianelli opted to pursue more esoteric extracurricular activities at the Point, playing oboe in the Academy's Concert Band. While his classmates manned the howitzers for the cannonade during the "1812 Overture," Gianelli steered through the passages of Tchaikovsky's most recognizable work with a facility that brought looks of wonder from his fellow performers.

Perhaps it seemed odd that a master musician was best known in military circles for his proficiency with a pool cue. Many a young JAG lawyer, and more than a few senior officers had retreated from an evening of nine-ball with "Tony the Stick" Gianelli searching their wallets in a vain attempt to find enough scratch to catch a taxi home.

From the beginning of his time at West Point, Gianelli had designs on the law. He'd excelled in the classroom in every subject but was particularly adept at anything involving research, oratory, and writing. Upon graduation, Gianelli was commissioned as a Second Lieutenant in the Armor Corps, where he commanded an M1-A1 Abrams Tank. He'd served his six-year service obligation at the top of his peer group.

Half a dozen years after graduation, Gianelli left the world of combat arms and went to William & Mary Law School. Thirty-six months after that, he made the Army JAG Corps his lifelong home.

This morning, I would face Judge Gianelli for the first time. I hoped he was better than Judge Rake. I glanced around the room, and the scene was depressing. The preening paralegals sat behind the prosecution table, notebooks at the ready. On our side, Jefferson appeared gaunt and disinterested. Reggie occupied the last chair on the back row behind me, and Rose mirrored his position in the front row.

On cue, we all stood for the new judge. "This general court-martial is called to order." Gianelli's baritone voice carried absolute authority. No one questioned who was in control. "Counsel," Gianelli continued. "Please announce your qualifications for the record."

Paine slowly stood and straightened his tie before speaking. "Colonel Covington Spencer Paine for the prosecution, Your Honor." Paine acted so much like Neidermeyer from *Animal House,* I wanted to laugh. He started to introduce his team as if they were the Twelve Apostles at the Last Supper.

Gianelli interrupted him, "Colonel Paine."

"Yes, Your Honor?"

"Do you have the court-martial script in front of you?" Gianelli asked, peering over the bench.

"Ah, no. I don't need it."

"Yes, you do," Gianelli said, "This is not an improv class. Under the Uniformed Code of Military Justice, we follow a script for a reason, so that things run smoothly." Gianelli tapped his gavel. "This court is in recess until the Senior Prosecutor finds a script." Gianelli stood and exited the courtroom.

Paine turned to Major Weiss. "Where's my script? Find me a script. Now!" Embarrassment made his voice higher and faster. He sounded like a chipmunk on meth. Weiss,

Nelson, and Bronson pawed through binders and boxes of documents while Paine neurotically clicked his ballpoint pen.

"Hey, Colonel," I said. "I have a script you can borrow." A discernible giggle rolled across the gallery. I crossed the courtroom and dropped a stapled stack of papers on Paine's desk. "Here you go," I said. "But I'm going to need it back." I returned to my desk. No one but the bailiff could see me smile. Behind me, I heard papers flutter through the air.

"I don't need your help," Paine snarled. I left the papers on the floor in front of Paine's table. I sure as hell wasn't picking them up.

Then, the bailiff knocked twice on the door, and Gianelli reentered. "All rise."

"Please, be seated," the judge said. "Colonel Paine, put your qualifications on the record."

Paine and his team continued to excavate. The only sound was the flurry of shuffling documents. "Your Honor, I need another moment to find the script," Paine said.

Gianelli removed his glasses and squinted. "What is that?" he asked, pointing at the floor. No one answered. "Trial Counsel, why are those papers on my courtroom floor?"

"Those are Captain O'Donnell's," Paine said.

Gianelli shifted his gaze toward me. "Is that true, Captain O'Donnell?"

"Yes, sir."

"Pick them up, now," Gianelli said. I stepped from behind the table and walked toward the papers. I saw Paine smirking from the corner of my eye. As I bent over to retrieve them, the court reporter whispered into Gianelli's ear. The judge's head jerked up. "Captain O'Donnell." I froze. "Put those papers back on the floor and return to your seat." Gianelli slowly pivoted toward Paine, like a leopard preparing to pounce on its prey. "Colonel Paine, on your feet." Gianelli's voice sent a shiver down my spine. Paine snapped to attention, and the courtroom fell silent.

Gianelli continued, "You are an Army officer and a graduate of West Point. Yet, on the first day of trial, you came into my courtroom unprepared and trashed it. Then, you disrespected a fellow lawyer and officer. You should be ashamed of yourself. Now, apologize to Captain O'Donnell."

Paine turned to me and said, "I apologize."

"Apology accepted." I managed not to smirk.

"Now, pick up those papers and read them," Gianelli said in a commanding voice. Paine walked around his desk, picked up the script, and began reading. His voice cracked, whether from outrage or a bruised ego, I couldn't tell. Gianelli addressed me when Paine finished. "Captain O'Donnell, please announce your qualifications." I stuck to the script - read it verbatim. "Thank you, Captain," Gianelli said. "Now, is there anything else we need to take up before we call the panel?"

"Yes, Your Honor," I said. "The defense moves this Court to compel the production of a witness who goes by Mr. Johnston-"

"Objection," Paine interrupted. "This is classified. I suggest we close these proceedings and reopen them in a classified setting."

"Very well." Gianelli nodded. "This hearing is now closed to the public." No one in the gallery moved. Gianelli smiled and addressed the courtroom, "Members of the audience, please collect your belongings and step out of the courtroom. I have to conduct some classified business with the lawyers. I will reopen the Court when we finish discussing classified material, and you can come back in to watch."

After the onlookers departed, I outlined my request. Then, Judge Gianelli asked Paine, "Is this witness, Mr. Johnston, a Federal employee?"

"He's an OGA," Paine said.

"A what?"

"An OGA. He works for an Other Government Agency."

"What specific agency did he work for?"

"I'm not at liberty to say."

"Interesting," Gianelli said. "Because a CIA lawyer, Ms. Carolyn Reynolds, called my office this morning. She left a long message on behalf of the Central Intelligence Agency. Somehow, she knew all about what was going to happen in my courtroom this morning - even before I did. She requested that I block Mr. Johnston from testifying. I found her ex-parte interference with this case quite troubling and inappropriate. So, it appears that Mr. Johnston works for the CIA. Colonel Paine, do you dispute that?"

"I can neither confirm nor deny that," Paine said.

Gianelli removed his glasses and placed them on the table in front of him. "Don't play games with me. Mr. Johnston, sure as heck, does not work for the Environmental Protection Agency. The CIA wouldn't be calling me if he did."

Paine's shoulders slumped. "Yes, Your Honor."

I sat back in my chair, watching my opponent on the ropes.

"I'm taking judicial notice that Mr. Johnston works for the CIA," Gianelli said. "Now, why did you refuse to subpoena him?"

"He is not relevant," Paine said.

"He's not relevant?" Gianelli raised his eyebrows and leaned forward. "According to a motion filed by the defense, Mr. Johnston removed Hamza Nassar from Sangar Prison on 8 August 2002, and never returned him. Sergeant Jefferson allegedly killed Nassar on 20 September 2002, in the prison. I think Mr. Johnston has some explaining to do? Don't you?"

Paine picked up his notepad and read, "First, the charge sheet says, 'On or about 8 August 2002.' The jury may find that Nassar was murdered on a different date. Second, Mr. Johnston told me that he doesn't know Sergeant Jefferson, and he never issued any directives to any U.S. soldiers. He has no recollection of ever visiting the Sangar Prison." Paine flipped the page and continued reading, "Mr. Johnston never authorized, directed, or attempted to order any military personnel to behave in any manner toward any detainee at the Sangar Prison. Therefore, Mr. Johnston has no relevant testimony or evidence on the matters at hand. His production would only lead to testimony that is irrelevant, confusing to the panel, and a waste of government resources."

I knew Johnston had been present at Sangar Prison, and I had the documents to prove it. It would be game over if he took the witness stand and denied ever being in the prison. I could easily prove that he removed Nassar from the prison and lied about it.

Paine sat down, and the judge turned to me. "Defense, what is your position?"

"Mr. Johnston is an alibi witness. He had control of Nassar at the time of the alleged murder, and my client did not."

Judge Gianelli nodded at me and addressed Paine, "Anything else?"

Paine was caught off balance. "I strongly urge you to deny this witness. It's a matter of national security. Requiring Mr. Johnston to testify could cause irreparable harm to the United States."

"Now it's a matter of national security?" Gianelli said. "Before, you said Mr. Johnston was not relevant. Which is it?"

"Both," Paine replied.

"Captain O'Donnell," Gianelli said, "the burden of proof is on you. Do you have any evidence to support your proffer?"

"Yes, Your Honor." I pulled a manila folder from my briefcase, removed two sheets of paper, and walked to the court reporter. I'd like to have these marked as Defense Exhibits A and B."

"Please show a copy to the trial counsel," Gianelli said.

I walked to Paine, who was standing with his hands on his hips. "Here you go," I said, handing him the exhibits.

Paine snatched the papers from me and scanned them. He shook his head as he flipped back and forth between the pages. "This is outrageous." Paine tossed the papers on his desk like they were contagious. "I object. This is trial by ambush. I've never seen these documents before. How do we know they are authentic? These could be fabrications."

"Let me see them," Gianelli said, motioning me forward. I handed him a copy. His eyes widened as he studied the papers. "Captain O'Donnell, where did these come from?"

"The prosecution provided them in discovery. "

Gianelli nodded. "How do you plan on authenticating them?"

"By calling Mr. Johnston to the stand," I said.

"For the record, what's your theory of relevancy?"

"These documents prove that Mr. Johnston removed Nassar from Sangar Prison on 8 August 2002. According to the charge sheet, Sergeant Jefferson killed Nassar on 20 September 2002. This is proof that Nassar wasn't in the prison on the date of his murder. It's exculpatory and highly relevant."

Gianelli smiled. "I would agree."

Paine was like a puppy with a slipper; he wouldn't give up, even though everyone in the room knew he was wrong. He rambled for a few minutes before sitting down in a huff.

Judge Gianelli made his ruling, "I hereby order the production of Mr. Johnston. His testimony is material and relevant to this case. If portions of his testimony are classified, we will cross that bridge when we get there." Finally, a win for us.

The joy was premature and short-lived. Within an hour, the President of the United States signed an Executive Order declaring Johnston indefinitely unavailable because his testimony "would cause irreparable harm to national security."

CHAPTER 67

After a lightning-fast jury selection, we had a panel, the Army word for a jury. Five officers, four enlisted. Seven men, two women. A blend of ages, ranks, and backgrounds. They were all experienced soldiers and combat veterans, each one looking progressively more grizzled than the last. The panel president was a crusty Special Forces Colonel with more ribbons than I could count. They all had something else in common: None of them wanted to be here.

As they entered the room, each one of them eyeballed Jefferson from head to toe, no doubt inspecting everything from his medals to the shine on his shoes. In front of Jefferson, a nameplate read, "The Accused." I was sure they were all wondering, "What did this poor guilty bastard do?" After all, innocent men usually don't find themselves in a court-martial.

Jefferson leaned over and whispered, "What a bunch of hardasses."

He was spot on. After the jury settled into their chairs, Judge Gianelli advised them that the prosecution had to prove their case beyond a reasonable doubt and that the burden never shifted to the defense. Then, Gianelli gestured to Paine. "Trial counsel, you may present an opening statement."

Paine oiled his way over to the jury and commenced reciting his opening. "On a dark night, in Sangar Prison, the defendant, Sergeant Tyler Jefferson, beat, tortured, and murdered a detainee in the custody of the United States, Mr. Hamza Nassar-"

In the 1964 movie, *Robin and the 7 Hoods*, a chagrined, outmanned, and outgunned criminal, played by Frank Sinatra, listens to a suave Dean Martin's plan for revenge. With his fedora rakishly tilted to one side, Martin offers his own brand of Chicago-style wisdom: "When your opponent's sittin' there holdin' all the aces, there's only one thing left to do - kick over the table."

I took a deep breath - and stood. "Objection, Your Honor. Hamza Nassar is not dead." The jurors perked up. Some seemed confused, others surprised, the rest shot me ice-cold stares.

Paine's cheeks reddened, and his eyes bulged like he'd been kicked in the groin. He sputtered for a moment. "Your Honor," Paine said, almost a whine. "He interrupted my opening."

Gianelli remained stoic. "The basis of your objection, Captain O'Donnell?"

"But-" Paine continued.

Gianelli held up his hand and peered over the reading glasses that sat at the tip of his nose. "Colonel," he said, "someone objects. I listen. You respond. I rule. Got it?" Paine nodded. In the first 10 minutes, Judge Gianelli was already better than Judge Rake. "Captain O'Donnell," Gianelli said, "what is the basis of your objection?"

"Your Honor, the Government has charged murder, but there is no *corpus delicti* - no dead body," I said. "Other than a highly questionable autopsy report, the Government has made no offer of proof that Hamza Nassar is, in fact, dead. We have a good faith basis to believe that Nassar is still alive, or he was when he departed Sangar Prison."

"Your Honor, this is unprofessional and inappropriate," Paine said.

Judge Gianelli calmly addressed the jury. "Members," he said, "opening statements are not evidence. It is what the attorneys expect the evidence to be." Then, he addressed me. "Captain O'Donnell, you'll have your chance to address the jury soon. Objection overruled."

Whether I gained or lost any points with the jury was anybody's guess. I hoped, at a minimum, I had planted a seed in the back of their minds. One thing was for sure: Paine had lost momentum. He limped through the remainder of his opening and took his seat.

I kept my opening statement short and focused. "Sergeant Jefferson is not guilty. He did not abuse, torture, or kill anyone. These are serious accusations, and they must be proven beyond a reasonable doubt. The prosecution's case is based on speculation, on assumptions. Their case rises and falls on the testimony of known liars. Witnesses who have been promised immunity in exchange for their testimony. Witnesses that cannot be trusted."

I paused for a moment and made eye contact with each juror. "The alleged victim, Hamza Nassar, is a violent man. At Sangar Prison, he attacked American soldiers and seriously disfigured two of them during an escape attempt. All the guards despised him. All of the guards had access to him. Many of the guards had a motive to beat him. Nassar was kept in a special section of the prison designed for the most dangerous terrorists."

"Objection," Paine said.

"Sustained," Gianelli ruled. Some of the jurors appeared confused.

I continued unfazed, "This alleged victim was housed in a section of the prison designed for the most dangerous inmates, where he was repeatedly interrogated by civilian intelligence agencies, behind closed doors. On 8 August 2002, Hamza Nassar was removed from Sangar Prison by a civilian intelligence agency, a month before Sergeant Jefferson allegedly killed him."

"According to the charges." I held up a thin stack of papers. "Sergeant Jefferson allegedly beat and killed Nassar on 20 September 2002." I slowed down for effect, "Nassar wasn't in Sangar Prison on that day. He was long gone. Where was he? Who knows? But we do know that he was never in Sangar Prison after 8 August 2002."

I placed the papers on the podium in front of me and delivered my final lines in a slow, methodical rhythm. "If someone beat him, it was not Sergeant Jefferson. If he is, in fact, dead, Sergeant Jefferson didn't kill him."

"Members of the jury, Sergeant Jefferson did not beat, torture, or kill Hamza Nassar. They cannot prove it because it did not happen. Before jumping to conclusions, wait until you've heard all the evidence." I turned, took my seat, and waited for the prosecution's first witness.

CHAPTER 68

Judge Gianelli's voice bellowed, "Government, call your first witness."

Paine stood and stepped to the podium. "The government calls Sergeant Rodney Cullen."

A side door swung open, and Cullen entered the room.

Jefferson leaned into me and whispered, "He's my boy."

"We'll see," I responded, a hint of skepticism in my voice.

Jefferson was foolish to think that Cullen, or any of his buddies, were going to help him. They had too much to lose. In criminal cases, when freedom is on the line, friends often turn on each other to save themselves. In this case, Cullen was a cooperating witness. He was testifying under a grant of immunity in exchange for a lighter sentence. He wasn't on Jefferson's team.

Sergeant Rodney Cullen was a lifelong snitch. Back in high school, he routinely ratted out his classmates for underage drinking to kiss up to the principal and the local police. Meanwhile, he would steal hooch from his grandpa's stash and sell it to his friends. According to Reggie, Cullen was a deadbeat dad with three kids to three different baby mamas scattered throughout the Big D.

His Army personnel file showed a man with thick, Coke bottle glasses and a thin mustache. Today, he was clean-shaven and wearing contact lenses. Pants creased, blouse starched, brass gleaming, what few ribbons he'd earned displayed and arranged in close order on his chest. His tie disappeared into his shirt as per regs, and his shoes glistened.

His lawyer, L. Edward Williams, had worked out a sweet deal on Cullen's behalf. In exchange for his testimony against Jefferson, the Army reduced Cullen's murder charge to simple assault - an arrangement too good to pass up.

Based on the case file, I wasn't exactly sure why Paine called Cullen as a witness; Cullen hadn't made any statements implicating Jefferson. Paine was calling him first, so he had something up his sleeve. At trial, prosecutors usually front-load their most persuasive witnesses.

"Good morning, Sergeant Cullen," Paine said, smiling.

"Good morning, sir." Cullen smiled and nodded back. "Nice to see you again."

Jefferson shot me a glance that screamed, *What the hell?*

After Cullen swore, to tell the truth, the whole truth, and nothing but the truth, Paine asked his first question. "You served at Sangar Prison from January 2002 through December 2002, correct?"

"Yes, I did," Cullen replied.

"He's leading the witness," Jefferson mumbled.

"I know that. Pay attention and take notes," I said, shifting my attention back to the witness.

Paine extended his arm and pointed at Jefferson. "Do you know the accused?"

"Yeah. We're great friends." Cullen nodded his head vigorously. "We played ball together from the time we wuz five or six. He was always thunder. I was lightnin'."

"In total, how long have you known him?"

"Nearly 20 years, I figure. He's like family to me."

"And there is no tighter bond than family, isn't that right?"

"That's the way my mama raised me," Cullen said, looking proud.

"Why are you willing to testify against your friend?" Paine's tone was compassionate.

"What he did wasn't right. No, sir. Tyler whupped that A-rab... I mean, enemy combatant, that Nassar guy - real bad. Real bad."

"Let's back up a little," Paine said. "How do you know Hamza Nassar?"

"He was a detainee at Sangar while we wuz there."

"Did you ever guard Hamza Nassar?"

"Not that I recall," Cullen said. "But I was there when the actions in question occurred."

"What actions are you referring to, Sergeant?"

"When Tyler beat the shit out of him. I mean, (and here Cullen's memorization was perfect) when Sergeant Jefferson repeatedly struck Hamza Nassar about the head, shoulders, and legs with his fists and knees causing... (memory faltered for a second) ah... grave... bodily... harm. Once in the VIP cell and once when he was being transported to the latrine."

"You personally witnessed the beatings?" Paine asked him.

Cullen paused. "Beg your pardon."

"Did you see Sergeant Jefferson hit Hamza Nassar with your own two eyes?"

"Yeah. I saw it," Cullen replied.

"Tell us about the first time."

"Hmm." Cullen stroked his chin and thought for a moment. "The first time, Jefferson was escorting Nassar to the latrine, and he kneed him right here." Cullen pointed to his outer thigh, an inch above the knee. "He struck him so hard I winced."

"Ouch." Paine grimaced at the jury. "Then what happened?"

"The detainee fell to the floor and screamed in pain."

"Was Sergeant Jefferson in danger? Was he perhaps acting in self-defense?"

"No way." Cullen shook his head. "Nassar was shackled at the wrists and ankles."

"Let's talk about the second assault. What happened that time?"

"One night, I was Sergeant of the Guard," Cullen said, "and for no reason, Jefferson showed up and went into his cell."

"That's a lie," Jefferson said in a loud whisper. "Nassar was out of control."

Judge Gianelli darted his eyes at our table. I put my hand on Jefferson's knee and squeezed - a warning to be quiet.

"Please continue, Sergeant," Paine said.

"Well, I heard chains shaking, and what sounded like flesh striking flesh."

"What did you do next?"

"I heard moaning, so I walked to the cell and called his name. Jefferson turned and faced me." Cullen's voice quivered. "Then he said, 'I didn't do nothin', Sarge.' He had this look on his face. I'll never forget it. It haunts me to this day."

"Can you describe the look?"

"Like, you know, a guilty look."

"Objection." I jumped from my seat. "This witness cannot comment on whether or not my client looked guilty."

"Sustained," Gianelli said.

Paine marched on. "Aside from the look on Jefferson's face, did you notice anything out of the ordinary?"

"Yeah. Nassar looked like he had been beaten."

Paine stepped closer to Cullen and lowered his voice. "Why did it look like he'd been beaten?"

"Nassar was winded, and his face was sweaty and red."

Jefferson never expected those words to come out of his friend's mouth, either because of naivety or foolishness. Jefferson leaned toward me. The rickety metal chair squeaked under his 200-pound body. "Why is he telling these lies?" his whisper more of a shout. All eyes in the room were on us. I ignored him and kept my gaze on Cullen.

Paine continued, "How was the victim positioned when you entered the room?"

"He was chained to the ceiling by his wrists, hands over his head."

"So, Nassar had no way of striking Jefferson?" Paine asked.

"Heck no. The man was hanging like a piñata."

"What happened next?"

"I never saw that poor man again. I guess he died or something."

I stood. "Objection."

"Sustained."

Paine cleared his throat and spoke dramatically. "Sergeant, based on what you saw, did this detainee, who was chained to the ceiling, dangling like a piñata, pose a threat to Sergeant Jefferson at that time?"

"No. He was as harmless as a baby."

"Thank you. I have no further questions." Paine returned to his chair as the jury stared at Jefferson with cold, hard eyes.

Some friend, I thought.

On the witness stand, Cullen sat with his hands between his knees, palms together, subconsciously protecting his groin. He rotated his high school class ring around his thick finger. I stood and collected my papers. Cullen rocked from side to side like a metronome. "Sergeant Cullen," I said in a commanding voice. "You saw Jefferson hit Nassar, is that correct?"

"Which time?" Cullen cocked his head and smirked at me. "It happened more than once."

"How many times did he supposedly hit him?"

"He didn't supposedly hit him. It happened. Twice to be exact." The prosecution team chuckled and whispered amongst themselves. Cullen was feisty. I had to tighten up my questions and fast. "On both occasions, you were in charge of the night watch?"

"Define 'in charge.'" Cullen grinned at Paine.

"You were the highest-ranking guard on duty?"

"I guess."

"I don't want you to guess. Were you the highest-ranking guard on duty or not?"

"Objection," Paine said. "He's badgering the witness."

"Overruled." Gianelli did not appear to appreciate Cullen's snark.

I repeated my question. "You were the highest-ranking guard on duty that night?"

"Is that a question or a statement?" Cullen said. Based on the jury's dour facial expressions, Cullen wasn't scoring any points.

I asked my question again, slowly enunciating each word and syllable as if I was talking to a fool. "You - Sergeant - Rodney - Cullen - were - the - highest - ranking - guard - on - duty - that - night? Correct?" Cullen knew I could drag this out all day.

"Yeah," he said.

"That night, your position was Sergeant of the Guard?"

"Yeah."

"The Sergeant of the Guard is in charge of the other guards on duty?"

"Yup."

"You were required to document all interactions between the guards and detainees?"

"Yup."

"You were required to document these interactions in a logbook?"

"Yeah."

"Sergeant Cullen," Judge Gianelli interjected. "You are speaking to an Army officer. Start showing proper military bearing."

Cullen swallowed hard. "Huh?"

"Captain O'Donnell is an officer," Gianelli said. "Refer to him as 'Sir' or 'Captain.' Is that understood?"

Cullen's face reddened. "Yes, sir, Judge, Your Honor."

Gianelli gave me a thumbs up. "Captain O'Donnell, please continue."

I moved on to my next question. "You never documented Sergeant Jefferson's abuses, did you?"

"Yes, sir. I did. In the logbook."

"Oh, really?" I paused. *Could I have overlooked this?* "You're telling us that in the logbook, you wrote down the dates and times that Sergeant Jefferson hit Nassar?"

"Yes. That's what I just said."

My next question was risky because I didn't know the answer. "What happened to this logbook?"

Cullen shrugged. "How should I know? I told CID about it."

"You're positive you told CID about this logbook?"

Paine rose. "I object! This is pointless. We don't have the logbooks."

"Captain O'Donnell," Gianelli said, "how is this relevant?"

"The logbook is relevant because it goes to Sergeant Cullen's credibility. Sergeant Cullen still faces charges for prisoner abuse and murder, and he's testifying under a grant of immunity. Now, for the first time, he claims that Sergeant Jefferson beat Nassar, that he documented the abuse in a logbook, and that CID knew about the logbook. The truth is, CID did not find any records, anywhere, that mention Sergeant Jefferson abusing prisoners. In his CID interview, Cullen said he never witnessed any abuse. Conveniently, years later, when he's facing his own charges, Cullen claims to have witnessed Sergeant Jefferson abuse prisoners. He's lying to save himself." I noticed some of the jurors were taking notes. I hope I had made my point.

"This witness doesn't know where the logbook is," Gianelli said. "Move on."

Next, I went after Cullen's bias and motive to lie. As I continued his cross-examination, Paine objected more, and Gianelli shut me down at every turn. I ran out of material, so I shifted to Cullen's ability to observe Jefferson hitting Nassar. "Where were you when Jefferson kneed Nassar?"

"In the prison," Cullen replied.

"The prison is a big place. Exactly where were you standing when you saw Jefferson hit Nassar, the first time?"

Cullen took a deep breath and slowly exhaled. The jurors leaned forward. The question was simple enough, but Paine either didn't prepare Cullen for it, or he never thought to ask. Cullen scanned the courtroom as if looking for someone to feed him an answer. After a minute, he said, "Can you repeat the question?"

"Where were you standing when you saw Jefferson hit Nassar the first time?"

"In the break room. We shared it with the Red Cross."

"Objection." Paine scoffed and put his hands on his hips. He reminded me of every frat boy in every movie I had ever seen. "The Red Cross's presence at Sangar is classified."

I turned to Gianelli. "Sir, how is the Red Cross classified?"

Gianelli held up his hand, stopping me, and said, "I need the jury and all spectators to depart the courtroom."

Once the room was cleared, I said, "The Red Cross is a well-known, international relief organization. They advertise on television for crying out loud."

Paine was ready for the argument. "If Your Honor will refer to the CID report, page 141, you will notice all references to the Red Cross at Sangar Prison are classified."

Gianelli picked up his reading glasses, perched them on his nose, and flipped through a stack of papers. A minute later, he looked up with a blank expression on his face. "I'm mystified. It seems all references to the Red Cross at Sangar are classified and cannot be discussed in open court."

I threw my hands in the air. "Your Honor. I have to be able to cross-examine the witness."

"I understand, but do so without asking about classified material. Is there anything else we need to take up before I reopen the Court?"

"Yes. I offer the prison floor plan into evidence," I said, holding up a document.

"Classified," Paine said. "Page 145."

More thumbing. "So it is," Gianelli said. "Captain O'Donnell, you are 0 for 2."

"Your Honor, I was given this floorplan in discovery. It's not classified."

"Let me see it." Gianelli beckoned me forward. I walked to the bench and handed the judge a copy. He reviewed it and gave it back to me. "Captain O'Donnell is holding what purports to be the prison's floor plan," Gianelli said. "It is not marked as classified." Paine stood to respond, but Gianelli cut him off. "Government, did you provide this floorplan to the defense?"

"Yes, but-"

Gianelli interrupted Paine again, "I'm admitting the floorplan into evidence. Bailiff, recall the jury and get Sergeant Cullen back in here."

Cullen retook the witness stand. I handed him the exhibit and asked him, "Is this what the Sangar Prison floorplan looked like back in 2002?"

Cullen squinted at the diagram. "One and the same."

"Do you see where you were standing when you saw Sergeant Jefferson hit Nassar the first time?"

"Yes, right here," Cullen pointed at the drawing.

"Are you sure?"

"I'm positive."

I stepped forward and handed him three Sharpie markers. "Using the red marker," I said, "write the letter C on the floorplan to show where you were standing when Jefferson hit Nassar the first time." Cullen marked the paper. "Now, use the green marker and write the letter J to show Jefferson's location." Cullen took the marker and followed my instructions. "Last one, Sergeant," I said, "take the blue marker and draw a straight line from the C to the J." Cullen complied. I turned to Judge Gianelli. "Your Honor, I'd like to show the jury the floorplan."

"Go ahead," Gianelli said.

Using an overhead projector, I displayed the floorplan on a pull-down screen that hung from the wall. The jury studied it. Some of them took notes. I pointed at the screen with a laser pointer and said, "Sergeant Cullen, what is that black line separating the C and the J?"

Cullen scratched the back of his head as his eyes darted around the room.

"Go on now," Gianelli said.

"It's a wall."

"A concrete wall?" I asked.

Cullen nodded. "I think so."

"Sergeant, are you Superman?"

"Huh?" Cullen glared at me sideways.

"Do you have x-ray vision?"

"Objection," Paine said.

"Sustained."

"Can you see through concrete walls?"

Before he answered, I glanced at the jury. "I have no further questions," I said and sat down. Back at the table, Jefferson was laughing, like he was at a comedy show. I tapped his leg. "Knock it off. The jury's looking at you."

I watched as Paine desperately tried to rehabilitate Cullen's testimony. It was too late. The jury had lost interest. Some smirked, as Cullen tried to explain how he "saw around the wall." Others stared out the window. Gianelli must have noticed the jury was daydreaming. After Paine finished questioning Cullen, he recessed for the evening.

Paine stormed out of the courtroom. His entire team, including the paralegals, secretaries, and possibly the janitor, were ordered into a conference room where Paine berated them for "blatant and inexcusable incompetence." After Paine ran out of insults, he and his prosecutors stayed until midnight, coaching their next witness.

※

After court, I met with Jefferson and Reggie, who had by now made amends, to discuss the day's testimony and the way forward. Inside our makeshift office, Jefferson wore a broad, confident grin. Reggie, on the other hand, wanted to rip someone's head off.

Once I closed the door, and we had some privacy, Jefferson blurted out, "That was tight. You think they'll drop the case?"

"Not a chance," I said.

"Why not. I mean, you completely exposed Cullen as a liar."

"They have two dozen other witnesses lined up behind him. We have to-"

Reggie interrupted me, "I'm gonna murder Cullen, that son-of-a-bitch."

"Reggie, you're not murdering anyone," I said.

"I don't take orders from you, counselor," he replied.

"Cut the macho bullshit, Reggie. It's not helpful. Tomorrow, they plan on calling the forensic pathologist. He's going to be a powerful witness. Have you found any dirt on him?"

"Not yet. He's pretty strait-laced."

"Then, you got some homework. Stay out of the strip club and find me something I can use."

Like a scolded child, Reggie crossed his arms and sighed.

"And Reggie," I said, "keep away from Cullen. The last thing we need is you in prison. We caught some lucky breaks today, but this is far from over."

CHAPTER 69

The following morning, the prosecution called Dr. Antoine Toure, a forensic pathologist. Dr. Toure was a tall, black man who walked like he was on stilts. He awkwardly adjusted his body in the cramped witness box, and neurotically dabbed sweat from his forehead with a white handkerchief. His three-piece suit, large maroon bowtie, and wire-rimmed glasses lent a professorial aura.

Paine began his direct examination by outlining Dr. Toure's education and experience. He encouraged the doctor to explain every tedious detail of his 35-year career, starting with his undergraduate degree. Finally, 40 minutes later, Paine got to the point. "Dr. Toure, what is your current duty position?"

"I serve as the Chief Medical Examiner at the Armed Forces Institute of Pathology," Toure explained in a crisp, clipped accent of a West African schooled in England.

"What are your duties as the Chief Medical Examiner?"

"I investigate sudden, unexpected, or unnatural deaths, and determine the cause and manner of said deaths?"

"Do you perform autopsies?"

"Yes. Routinely."

"How many autopsies have you conducted?"

"As the Chief Medical Examiner, or in total?"

"Both," Paine replied, with a smile.

Toure squinted and stared at the ceiling as if he was counting in his head. A moment later, he nodded at Paine.

"Over 1,500 as the Chief Examiner," Toure said. "In total, I have conducted over 7,500 autopsies."

I studied the jury. They were all taking notes.

"Your Honor," Paine said, "the government asks this Court to recognize Dr. Toure as an expert in the field of forensic pathology."

"He is so recognized."

Paine moved on. "Dr. Toure, did you review the autopsy report in this case?"

"I did."

"What exactly did you review?"

"I carefully reviewed the examiner's report, the photographs, and the lab results."

"In the photos, did you observe anything unusual on the victim's body?"

"Yes. Both the upper and lower torso were covered with hematomas of varying sizes."

"What is a hematoma?"

"A hematoma is when blood collects outside of the blood vessels, and pools inside the skin. It's like bruising, but it can be life-threatening. You can see it clearly in the photographs."

"What causes a hematoma?"

"Trauma." Toure cleared his throat and continued, "Trauma is the primary cause of hematomas."

"What causes trauma?"

"Trauma can be caused by various things. Such as a car accident, a fall, a gunshot wound, or blunt force injuries."

"Doctor, what was the likely cause of the hematomas in this case?" Paine asked in a melodramatic tone.

"In my opinion, blunt force trauma. This man was struck dozens of times. This was not a natural death."

"Dozens of times?" Paine squinted like he was shocked by Toure's answer. "Why do you say *dozens* of times?" Paine emphasized the word "dozens."

Dr. Toure faced the jury and removed his glasses. "During my review of the file," he said, "I noted multiple areas on the body that were consistent with blunt force trauma. In the photographs, you will see many purplish-blue circles that are surrounded by lighter colored bruising. To me, each circle indicates a specific injury site."

"What type of trauma could have caused these injuries?"

"Possibly a club, a bat, a fist, a knee, or some other blunt object."

"Were you able to determine how many individual injuries were on the body?"

"I counted 16 separate hematomas that were well defined," Toure said. "There were several bruise clusters that were morphed together. These were likely caused by repeated trauma to the same area. "

"So, hypothetically, if someone struck this victim dozens of times with fists and knees, would you expect to see these types of injuries?"

"Absolutely."

"Doctor, have you formed an expert opinion as to the likely cause of Mr. Nassar's death?"

"Yes."

"What is that opinion?"

"This man was killed by repeated massive blunt force trauma to the body."

"Could you please put that in layman's terms?"

Toure sat up, turned to the jury, and intoned his opinion. "The man was beaten - to death."

"Thank you. Those are all my questions." Paine slowly plucked his notebook from the lectern and slinked back to the prosecution's table.

Judge Gianelli said to me, "Cross, Captain O'Donnell?"

I stood and walked to the podium. Now, it was my turn. "Doctor, you never physically examined the victim's body, did you?"

"I was asked to review photos, and to render a decision based on the autopsy report I received."

"So, you never personally examined the corpse?"

"No." Toure shook his head. "I did not personally examine the corpse."

"But you are certain as to the cause of death?"

"Absolutely," Toure snapped back. "The autopsy I reviewed listed blunt force trauma as the cause of death, and I concur that Mr. Nassar was beaten to death."

"With fists?"

"Pardon?"

"Did someone beat him with their fists, or was it a bat or a hammer or a golf club?"

"Oh, certainly not the last two," Toure replied.

"Why do you say that?"

"There are no gouges or deep lacerations. Something with an edge like a golf club - a nine iron, for instance - would have left canyons in the skin. A hammer could have cut the skin deeper as well." The doctor pistoned his arm back and forth as if wielding a Stanley claw hammer.

"What if the victim had fallen?" I asked.

"Objection," Paine said. "Calls for speculation."

"Overruled. Dr. Toure is an expert in forensic pathology. The very nature of his training requires highly-informed speculation. Please continue Captain O'Donnell."

"Doctor, what if the victim had fallen?"

"Perhaps," Toure said. "But it would've had to have been a long fall with multiple points of impact."

"Like down a flight of stairs?"

"Yes. That is possible but highly unlikely."

"Because?"

"First, there is no indication of broken bones," Toure said, "and I have been assured there are no long staircases at the site of the death. It is my professional opinion that the deceased died from repeated physical abuse, not a fall."

I shuffled through some documents, trying to buy time. Toure was polished, too polished. So, I switched tactics. "Doctor, were you present when the autopsied man died?"

Toure laughed. "No, of course not."

"Were you in Afghanistan when he died?"

"No, sir."

"Have you ever been to Afghanistan?"

Toure's eyes narrowed. "No."

"You did not conduct the autopsy in this case, did you?"

"I think we've established that fact, more than once," Toure said, glancing at the judge.

"You did not witness anyone beat Mr. Nassar, did you?"

"Of course not. I have never laid eyes on the man."

"You don't know who, if anyone, beat Nassar?"

"Correct."

"You don't know if one person beat him?"

"Correct."

"You don't know if 30 people beat him?"

"As I said, I was not there."

"So, 30 different people may have beaten him?"

"That's correct." A drop of sweat dripped from Toure's brow.

"You do not know for certain *how* he was beaten?"

"I cannot determine that from the autopsy report."

"You have no first-hand knowledge of *when* he died?

"Correct."

"You have no first-hand knowledge of *where* he died?"

"Correct."

"The man in the autopsy photos could have been killed anywhere?"

"I presume."

"Doctor, how do you know that the man in the photos is Hamza Nassar?"

Toure scoffed. "That's what it says on the report, doesn't it?"

"I am not asking what it says on the report. I am asking if you are 100 percent certain that the man in the photos is Hamza Nassar?"

"I assume the prison keeps accurate records," Toure replied.

"Let's not assume anything, Doctor," I said. "You are not 100 percent certain that the man in the photos is Hamza Nassar, are you?"

"No."

"Doctor, if I died, there are ways you could positively identify me as Max O'Donnell?"

"Well, yes."

"One way to identify me is through my dental records?"

"Yes."

"In this case, nobody used dental records to identify this body?"

"Not to my knowledge."

"You could use DNA to identify a body?"

"Yes."

I could see Paine out of the corner of my eye, frantically scribbling notes. I pressed on. "You could also use fingerprints, tattoos, scars, or birthmarks to identify a body?"

Toure nodded. "Yes."

"In this case, nobody used DNA, fingerprints, tattoos, scars, or birthmarks to identify this body?"

"I don't believe so."

"You could also use family members to identify a body?"

"Yes," he replied.

"That was not done in this case?"

"No," Toure said. "Not that I am aware of."

"Are you willing to bet your life that the body in the report is Hamza Nassar?"

"Objection," Paine said.

"Rephrase the question," Gianelli responded.

I nodded at the judge. "Doctor Toure, can you testify with a medical degree of certainty that the body in question is Hamza Nassar?"

"I don't know Nassar," Toure replied. "So, I cannot say for certain."

"Is it possible that the dead man in the photos is not Nassar?"

"Anything is possible. I cannot confirm the identity, just the likely cause of death."

"Is it possible that the man was killed at a different location? By someone other than Sergeant Jefferson?"

"Objection," Paine shouted as he threw his pen across the table. "This is preposterous."

"Overruled, and watch your tone." The doctor wiped the sweat from his brow. "Dr. Toure, please answer the question," Gianelli said.

"I cannot say where this man died or who was involved with his death," Toure said. "All I can say is that his death was likely the result of blunt force trauma."

I turned to Judge Gianelli. "Your Honor, I have no further questions."

Chapter 70

Colonel Paine started with his two strongest witnesses - Cullen and Toure - and now he was building. From Tuesday afternoon on, for over two days, a parade of bad character witnesses took the stand and trashed Jefferson. I attempted to interview all these witnesses before trial. Every single one refused to speak with me. We did the same dance when Jefferson and I reviewed the final witness list.

Me, asking: "Who's this?"

Jefferson, blank expression: "A guy from my unit," "A dude at the grocery store," "A buddy of mine," "Someone I knew in high school." He never amplified or expanded his remarks. His confidence in his own likeability seemed unshakable, and way off base. I was flying by the seat of my pants as I cross-examined each witness.

Witness after witness spoke of the quiet terror Jefferson instilled in people, his willingness to intimidate, his occasional lack of judgment and self-control. They testified to his destroying a high school locker with a football helmet, his profanity-laced tirades at peewee football referees, his road rage. Another witness recalled how Jefferson had shot-putted a paper boy's bicycle across the street because the morning news consistently landed in the bushes - instead of on the front stoop.

I parried the charges and accusations as best I could. Still, Jefferson's complete lack of self-awareness (or his total lack of memory) made any aggressive defense almost impossible.

By far, the prosecution's most ridiculous witness was Maria Gutierrez. Paine affixed his most concerned face.

"Mrs. Gutierrez, how long have you known the defendant?"

Maria's thick accent made comprehension a little challenging, but I knew the jury was getting the drift. "Mr. Jefferson (it came out 'Yefferson'), nasty man."

I stood. "Objection."

"Sustained."

Paine continued, "Ma'am, how many years have you known Sergeant Jefferson?"

"Muchos años," she said. "Many years."

"How do you know him?"

"He beat my son, José."

Again, on my feet. "Objection. This is absolutely irrelevant."

I turned to Jefferson as Gianelli contemplated my objection. "What's her story?"

He shrugged. "Don't know."

As usual, Jefferson was holding out on me, and it was hurting his case. I squeezed Jefferson's forearm and whispered. "Listen, asshole, you told me this lady was a family friend. Now, she says you beat her son. What the fuck is going on here?"

"She's more of an old acquaintance. Me and her son had some dust-ups in the past, but that was 15 years ago when we were in middle school. Ya know, kid stuff."

"When was the last time you fought with her son, no bullshit?"

"In middle school. In high school, we hung out together. We played ball together. I swear to God."

"You don't have to swear to God. Just stop holding back information."

He nodded. "Yes, sir."

I stood and addressed the judge, but I wanted the jury to hear, "Your Honor, this testimony is irrelevant. Mrs. Gutierrez is referring to an incident that happened 15 years ago. Sergeant Jefferson and her son, José, got into a fight in middle school. They were both suspended. Eventually, they became friends. They played high school football together." I repeated for emphasis. "It was 15 years ago."

Gianelli turned to Paine. "How is this relevant?"

"It goes to Sergeant Jefferson's propensity to commit violent crimes. It's Jefferson's modus operandi to beat and abuse innocent victims."

"Well, we're talking about 12-year-old boys," Gianelli said, shaking his head. "They probably hadn't hit puberty yet. This is not relevant."

"But, Your Honor," Paine protested.

Gianelli held up his hand, instructing Paine to stop. He then turned to the jury. "You are to disregard the testimony of Mrs. Gutierrez as it relates to Sergeant Jefferson allegedly assaulting her son. That information is irrelevant. It shall be completely disregarded by you. Do you understand?" The members of the jury nodded. "Now, does Mrs. Gutierrez have anything relevant to add?" Paine returned to the prosecution table and whispered with Major Weiss for what seemed like five minutes. "Colonel Paine, do you have any more questions of Mrs. Gutierrez?" Gianelli asked, the frustration in his voice evident.

"I have one follow-up."

"Go ahead."

"Mrs. Gutierrez, in your opinion," Paine said, "is Tyler Jefferson, a violent or peaceful person?"

"Objection."

"Overruled," Gianelli said, "but she's limited to her personal opinion. Feel free to attack the foundation for her opinion on cross-examination." Gianelli turned to the witness. "Ma'am, please answer the question."

Mrs. Gutierrez nodded. "Tyler is a violent man. Very dangerous."

"No further questions," Paine said and took his seat.

"Captain O'Donnell," Gianelli said, "you may cross-examine the witness."

I considered questioning Mrs. Gutierrez about her son's supposed friendship with Jefferson. I went with my gut and got her off the witness stand as quickly as possible. "Your Honor, I have no questions."

CHAPTER 71

Gianelli was the featured speaker at an American Bar Association conference in San Francisco on Friday. We were done after Thursday's session with the understanding that we would reconvene on Monday morning. If the weather had been decent, I might have played golf, even though I feared running into Paine and being tempted to cave in his head with a sand wedge. The temperature dropped, and the wind howled. No way I was going out. Every night, Reggie dropped by my room to see if I wanted to "grab dinner and drinks." I told him I had a lot of work to do and ordered take-out.

On Monday, we were delayed for reasons no one ever bothered to explain. At noon, when court finally got underway, the prosecution called Brian Rickard as their first witness, with Major Hanna Weiss asking the questions. Rickard had worked at Sangar at the same time as Jefferson. He left the Army after his deployment and enrolled at the University of Texas.

Brian Rickard was a pretty boy, tall and lean, with light brown eyes. At Sangar, the Meatheads teased him when they learned he had been a high school cheerleader. Jefferson was the soldier who harassed him the most. Now, it was Rickard's turn for payback.

After Brian Rickard took the witness stand, Major Weiss got straight to the point. "Mr. Rickard, while you were deployed to Sangar Prison, did you ever witness Sergeant Jefferson strike a prisoner named Hamza Nassar?"

"Yes, I did," Rickard said, "on more than one occasion."

"Tell us what happened."

"On the first occasion, I was working the isolation cells. That's where we kept Nassar. My shift had ended, and Sergeant Jefferson was my replacement. After I briefed him on the status of the prisoners, I left for the evening."

"Then what happened?"

"I was turning in my gear, and I realized I left my canteen in isolation. So, I walked back over there."

"And?"

"Well, Jefferson wasn't at the desk where he was supposed to be."

"Did you find that odd?"

"Yeah," Rickard said. "Guards are supposed to stay at the desk. We're not allowed to go into the cells alone. For safety reasons."

"Interesting," Weiss said. "Where *was* Sergeant Jefferson?"

"I found him inside Nassar's cell. He was working him over like a speed bag."

Jefferson shifted nervously. Then, he leaned toward me and started mumbling gibberish. "Write it down," I said to him. Jefferson scribbled "Fucking Liar" on a scrap of paper and handed it to me. It was hard enough to focus without having to filter out Jefferson's babbling. I crumpled the note and caught up with Weiss.

"Where were you standing when Jefferson struck Nassar?" she asked Rickard.

"Outside Nassar's cell. Looking through the small window."

"What did you do next?"

"I pretended like I didn't see anything. I just took my canteen and left."

"Did you say anything to him?"

"No. I was afraid of what he would do to me if I reported him. We were in a combat zone. Everybody had access to weapons. That's why I waited until I got back to the States."

"What, if anything, did Nassar do to provoke a physical reaction from Jefferson?"

"Nothing I saw," Rickard said. "Nassar was sleeping when I left the area, and he was chained to the ceiling by his wrists."

"How did Nassar react when struck?"

"He groaned in pain." Rickard hung his head like he was ashamed. "I should have stopped him."

Weiss lowered her voice. "I have no further questions of this witness," she said and sat down.

I stood and walked to the podium. "Mr. Rickard, I want to talk about the isolation cells you mentioned," I said.

"Okay."

"The isolation block had six cells?"

Rickard counted on his fingers. "Yes, sir."

"These isolation cells were used for high-value prisoners - or VIPs?"

"Pretty much."

"What were the guards ordered to do to the high-value prisoners?"

Weiss sprang to her feet like a jack-in-a-box. "Objection. Hearsay."

"Overruled," Gianelli said. "Mr. Rickard, please answer the question."

"We were ordered to implement sleep deprivation and physical exercise."

"What is sleep deprivation?" I knew the answer but wanted to get this information in front of the jury.

"We let them sleep for 15 minutes. Then, they stayed awake for hours."

Weiss squirmed in her chair.

"How do you force someone to stay awake for hours?" I asked.

Rickard shrugged. "Don't know."

"You were ordered to hang prisoners from the ceiling using chains?"

"We had to keep them awake. They just happened to be chained." Forced exercise. Sleep deprivation. Rickard made it sound perfectly reasonable.

"You were also ordered to force prisoners to exercise to the point of exhaustion?" I said.

"At Sangar, PT was as regular as three-square meals a day. They did PT, like all Army soldiers do."

"Army soldiers are not shackled to the rafters for days on end, are they?" I asked.

"I didn't do anything that wasn't authorized by Army regulations." He was getting defensive.

"What Army regulation authorizes you to hang prisoners from the ceiling by their wrists?"

Rickard stared at Weiss, who conveniently avoided eye contact and flipped through some papers. "I don't recall," he said.

"Have you ever, in your military career, read an Army regulation that authorizes you to hang prisoners from the ceiling?"

"I don't recall."

"Would it surprise you that no Army regulation authorizes such behavior?"

Rickard shook his head. "I did what I was told."

"Told by whom?"

"By the interrogators."

"What interrogators?"

"I don't know their names."

"Were they civilians?"

"Yeah."

"Were they CIA?"

"I have no clue who they were."

"Were you specifically ordered to break Nassar?"

"Objection." Weiss was on her feet. "Asked and answered."

"Sustained. Move on, counsel."

I continued, "If prisoners didn't comply with your orders, you were instructed to strike them in the peroneal nerve in their leg, correct?"

"Objection."

Judge Gianelli turned to me and said, "My patience is wearing thin. Now move on to another topic."

"I have no further questions," I said and sat down.

After Rickard exited the courtroom, the prosecution called a handful of filler witnesses, none particularly relevant. The jury lost interest as the day wore on. When the president of the panel nodded off, Gianelli struck his gavel and recessed for the day. Jefferson wanted to stick around to critique Rickard's testimony, but I declined. The damage had been done. Jefferson's lying and complaining had wasted enough of my time. He was like an albatross around my neck, dragging me down. Tonight, I needed to rest.

CHAPTER 72

O n Tuesday morning, Paine strutted into the courtroom like a high school quarterback who'd just won the State Championship.

"Your Honor, the prosecution calls Major Walter Needham."

On cue, the door swung open, and Major "Doc" Needham, an Army physician, marched into the room. A damn recruiting poster. Needham's uniform had been custom-tailored, accenting his broad shoulders. After Needham was sworn in, Paine commenced his questioning. "Doctor, do you know the accused?" Paine pointed at Jefferson.

"Not personally, but I knew of him. He had quite the reputation."

"Did you ever have chow with him, play cards with him - anything like that?"

"No, sir." Needham shook his head. "I do not fraternize with the enlisted. Like I said, I knew who he was."

"How did you know who he was?"

"We all knew the Crash Team guys. They were bigger than the rest. They looked like the offensive line of the New England Patriots." Some of the audience snickered. Needham seemed credible. His demeanor radiated confidence - and emanated trust. To see him, to hear him, to be around him, was to believe him. Needham glanced at the jury and said with a sneer, "I heard some crazy stories about those guys."

"Objection. Hearsay," I said.

"Sustained."

Jefferson scribbled a note and passed it to me. It read: "This asshole never worked in the prison. He worked in the medical clinic." Finally, Jefferson was contributing. I crumpled the note and handed it back to Jefferson as Paine launched his attack.

"Doctor Needham, did you ever see Sergeant Jefferson subdue an unruly prisoner?"

Needham paused as if he was thinking. After a few seconds, he answered, "Well, not exactly."

Paine acted surprised by the answer. "What do you mean, 'not exactly?'"

"I saw him assault detainees, but they were never unruly."

"Interesting," Paine said as he leaned on the podium and stared at the jurors one by one. Some of the jurors avoided eye contact. "Doc, why were you in Sangar Prison?"

"I was in charge of the Sangar medical clinic. Every week, I went to the prison to treat prisoners with minor issues."

"When was the first time you witnessed the accused assault a prisoner?"

Needham turned to Judge Gianelli and asked, "Your Honor, may I refer to my notes?"

"Absolutely, if it will refresh your recollection."

Needham had the reference points marked with multi-colored tabs. After reviewing his notes, he slid them back into his pocket. "On 18 July 2002, at 2345 hours," Needham said, "I saw Sergeant Jefferson, and members of the Crash Team, escorting three prisoners inside the prison. I think they were going to the latrines, but I'm not sure."

Paine seemed positively giddy. "Please, tell the jury what you witnessed."

"Without provocation, Sergeant Jefferson slammed a prisoner into the wall. He acted like it was an accident. It wasn't."

I wanted to strangle Jefferson. We had gone over this sort of thing many times. "Did you ever hit a detainee?" "Did you ever push or berate a detainee?" - and the big one - "If you did, who saw it?" Jefferson had responded to every question in the negative. He wanted me to believe, next to him, Sunday School teachers were like streetwalkers.

"Doctor, please tell us about the other incident," Paine said, using air quotes around the word "incident."

"On 21 August 2002, at 0215 hours. I witnessed the perpetrator deliver a peroneal strike to a non-resisting detainee, again during the escort process."

"He struck a defenseless man, right here?" Paine struggled to look concerned as he pointed to a spot above his knee.

"Yes, sir. He struck the peroneal nerve. That will bring an elephant down. It hurts badly and can cause permanent damage."

"Objection," I said. I regretted it the moment the word left my mouth.

"Basis?"

I should have withdrawn the objection, but I didn't. "This witness has not been qualified as an expert witness."

"Your Honor, he is a licensed physician," Paine replied. "He is board-certified in internal medicine, more than qualified to describe the pain caused by a peroneal nerve strike."

"Overruled."

I sat. Paine had what he needed. But he wanted to push the knife in a little deeper. "Are you sure it was Sergeant Jefferson that did this?"

"Yes, sir." Needham nodded. "The second time, he did it in front of my entire medical team. I was shocked. I chewed him out and immediately reported it to my commander. I also sent an e-mail to his supervisor that evening. I figured they did something about it because I never saw him in the facility after that."

"No further questions," Paine said as he took his seat triumphantly.

I stood and approached the podium. "Doctor Needham," I said, "you have flown on Army helicopters before, haven't you?"

"Affirm-"

"Objection," Paine said, slowly rising to his feet.

"Basis?" Gianelli asked.

"Counsel is moving beyond the scope of the direct testimony."

Gianelli motioned for my response.

"Your Honor, I'm going to connect these questions with his direct testimony. They will become relevant soon."

"Objection overruled."

I continued, "You have flown on Chinooks and Blackhawks while in Afghanistan, correct?"

"Every soldier deployed to Afghanistan has flown in a helicopter," Needham said. "I know you JAGs don't leave the wire much, but that's how real soldiers move around. You would know that if you had been deployed."

I ignored his intended insult and pressed forward. Gianelli sat up in his chair, his face turned to a scowl. He didn't seem to care for Needham's cockiness, and I hoped the jury felt the same way. Needham wanted to draw me into a slap fight. All I had to do was poke a few holes in his testimony. So, I let his comment pass. "You didn't fly the helicopter, did you?" I asked.

"No."

"You were not part of the regular flight crew?"

"No."

"As part of your duties in Afghanistan, you flew at night?"

Needham leaned forward and spoke into the microphone. "Yes, Captain. We flew at night because it was safer. It's harder to hit a helicopter in the dark."

Members of the prosecution team laughed. I did not. "Some of your missions involved transporting detainees?" I asked.

"Objection. Classified."

"Overruled." Gianelli shook his head. "Colonel Paine, I'm growing weary of your 'Classified' objections. Unless you can site the classifying authority, do not make another 'Classified' objection. The witness will answer the question."

Paine blushed and slid into his chair.

I repeated my question, hoping to drive home the point. "Doctor Needham, did some of your missions involve transporting detainees?"

"I had a variety of missions."

"And, some of them involved transporting detainees?"

Needham's mouth was almost touching the microphone. "Yes."

"Doctor, you don't have to lean into the microphone," Gianelli said. "It does not amplify your voice. It only records it. And you don't need to be that close for it to record."

"Roger that," Needham said.

I continued, "In the summer of 2002, you were in charge of the Sangar medical clinic?"

"Correct."

"Did you go on combat missions?"

"No. I attended to my duties at the clinic. We sent combat medics on combat missions. We didn't have enough doctors to spare."

"If you did not go on combat missions, where a doctor might actually be needed," I said, "why did you go on prisoner transport missions?"

"I accompanied the detainees."

"You rode in the back of the helicopter with the prisoners?" I asked. "That's all you did?"

"Sometimes, I was asked to perform certain duties."

"Can you elaborate?"

"If a prisoner needed medication or special attention, I provided it."

Now we were getting somewhere. "How did you know if a prisoner needed medical attention?" I asked.

"I was told."

"Told by whom?"

"By the people running the operation."

I could almost hear Paine wincing behind my back. "On these prisoner transport missions. Were the people giving you orders in the military?"

Needham hesitated. I was blocking his view of the prosecution team - not by accident. The doctor desperately wanted to crane his neck.

Gianelli was running out of patience. "Let's go, Doctor. Answer the question."

"No," Needham said. "They were civilians."

"Were they Americans?"

"They appeared to be."

"What agency did they come from?"

"I don't know," Needham said.

"Since when does an Army doctor follow orders from random civilians?" I asked. "That seems like it violates your Hippocratic oath."

Needham shrugged. I glanced at the jury; some of them seemed confused. A Sergeant Major in the back row shook his head and wrote in his notepad.

"Let me get this straight, Doctor. Some unfamiliar American civilians got into a helicopter with you, in Afghanistan, with enemy prisoners on board, and told you, a medical doctor, what medical services to provide to the prisoners? And, you followed their orders? Do I have that right?"

"I follow orders," Needham said. "I am a soldier."

"Doctor, were all your flights logged?"

"Objection," Paine said.

I ignored him. So did Gianelli.

"Your Honor, I objected," Paine said.

"Oh, yeah," Gianelli said. "Overruled."

"Doctor Needham," I said, "were all your flights logged?"

"Every flight is logged. That's the standard operating procedure."

I expected Paine to object again. He didn't. He sat there with parted lips. He was breathing through his mouth, and his eyes were slightly glazed. "Your Honor," I said, "the defense requests copies of all helicopter flight logs to and from Sangar Air Base from 1 August 2002 to 30 September 2002."

Paine rose, spreading his arms like Charlton Heston parting the Red Sea. "Your Honor," he said, the tone condescending and overblown, "why don't we just give Captain O'Donnell the name of every American intelligence asset in the Middle East while we're at it?"

Gianelli was not amused. "Colonel Paine." You could grind an ax on the grit in his voice. "I'm not sure how you have conducted yourself in the past. Maybe all the judges were your golf buddies, but you better watch your tone. Either object in a decorous fashion or be quiet."

"Sorry, Your Honor. I object to the request by opposing counsel because all flight logs from Sangar are classified."

"Colonel Paine, you're telling me that *all* of the Sangar flight logs from 2002 are classified?" Gianelli asked. "I don't believe it."

Judge Gianelli turned to me. "Captain O'Donnell, what's your position?"

"Your Honor, these are not classified, and they never were. Besides, we're talking about flight logs from three years ago. Anyone who was going to be attacked in those flights has already been attacked. Any supplies or troops that were going to move have already been moved."

"It doesn't matter," Paine said. "They're still classified."

Gianelli stared out the window - for a while. Then, he spoke in a thunderous voice. "Colonel Paine, I warned you about throwing that word around, but here you go again. Tell me, who classified the flight logs? The Air Force? The Army? Her Majesty's Secret Service? What governing body determined that a bunch of flight numbers and flight times were secret?"

Paine apparently noticed a blemish on his shoes - one he examined for a long, long time. "I don't know," he said.

"I'm tired of these games. By tomorrow morning, I want a copy of the flight logs on my desk. That way, I can see for myself whether they are classified or not. We are adjourned until 0800 hours." Judge Gianelli tapped his gavel and disappeared into his chambers.

X

When I left court, I called Perry Elliot, a well-connected lawyer I golfed with back in South Carolina. I told him about the temporary restraining order.

"Sounds bad, buddy," he said.

"Anything you can do to make it go away?"

"Sorry, Max, even with my connections, I can't do anything. These situations are touchy, you know."

"Can you call Annabelle and see if you can smooth this thing out - sort of backchannel?"

Perry laughed. "I'll see what I can do."

"I appreciate your help," I said and hung up the phone.

CHAPTER 73

The next morning Paine's entry into the courtroom was more of a slink than a strut. He looked like he rolled out of an all-night bachelor party and into court. Dark puffy circles framed his bloodshot eyes. The faint odor of bourbon emanated from his pores.

I turned to Jefferson and said, "I can tell by the way he's walking Paine doesn't have the flight logs."

At eight o'clock, Judge Gianelli called the Court to order and immediately addressed Paine. "Where are the flight logs?" Paine fell all over himself, trying to convince Gianelli the flight logs possessed magical powers and had disappeared. Gianelli shook his head in disapproval and said, "The flight logs were, at some point, in the Government's possession, and they lost them. It appears these records could possibly exonerate Sergeant Jefferson."

"Judge," Paine said in a snarky tone, "we have no way of knowing for sure if these logs would exonerate the defendant." I had to hand it to Paine. He was going down like Rocky.

Gianelli raised his voice a notch. "Exactly. We *don't* know for sure. Why don't we know? Because the Government lost them. I will not let the defense suffer because of the Government's incompetence. I see three options here. I can dismiss the charges. I can abate the proceedings for as long as necessary until the flight logs turn up. If they appear, then we will continue the trial. Or, I can have Captain O'Donnell draft a stipulation outlining what he believes the flight logs will show. If the prosecution objects, then I will consider other remedies."

Paine put his hands on his hips. "Are you honestly considering dismissing these charges?" Paine acted like a kid who didn't get what he wanted for Christmas.

"I said I *might* dismiss the charges," Gianelli replied. "Defense, aside from a dismissal, what is your preference?"

"Your Honor," I said, "may I please discuss this with my client."

"Two minutes," he said.

I nodded. "Yes, sir." I spoke to Jefferson as quietly as I could. I might as well have used a PA system because the room was silent, and everyone was eavesdropping. "The judge is not going to dismiss the charges," I said. "He's trying to scare the prosecution, but he may stop the trial until they find the flight logs."

"For how long?" Jefferson asked.

"Weeks. Months. There is no time limit. The trial could be put on hold for a while."

"Screw that. I'm sitting in jail. I need to get this over with, one way or another."

"The other option is for me to write up a document called a 'stipulation of fact.' I'll describe what the flight logs say. The problem is, we don't know what they say."

"I don't care. So long as there's no delay."

I stood and addressed Gianelli, "My client wishes to conclude this case as quickly as possible. Therefore, we prefer a stipulation over an abatement."

"Understood." Gianelli nodded at the bailiff. "Bring in the jury and recall Doctor Needham."

After Needham returned to the witness stand, I continued my cross-examination, "Doctor Needham, did you fly on a mission the morning of 8 August 2002?"

"Yes," Needham said.

"Was that aboard an Army helicopter?"

"Yes."

"What time did the flight depart Sangar Air Base?"

"We lifted off after midnight?"

"What time did you return?"

"About 90 minutes later."

I glanced at Paine. His face contorted like his testicles were caught in a zipper. "On that mission," I said, "you were transporting a prisoner, correct?"

"I don't recall."

"Would it refresh your memory if I told you that you were transporting Hamza Nassar?"

Needham shook his head. "No. It wouldn't."

"What actions did you take during the flight?"

"Don't recall."

"You didn't record any of this in your notes?"

"No."

"Why not?"

"Don't know."

Doctor Needham went on to answer, "I don't recall" or "I don't know," to my next 50 questions. He was overly coached and hostile. It looked like the jury stopped paying attention to him a while back.

"Was an American prisoner on the return flight?" I asked him.

Needham stared out the window.

"Answer the question," Gianelli said.

"For the hundredth time, I - don't - recall." One of the jurors rolled his eyes and shook his head as if to say, "Give me a break."

"Did you provide medical treatment to an American POW on the return flight?"

"Don't recall."

"You cannot remember if you provided medical treatment to an American POW?" My tone was incredulous. "Isn't that something you would remember?"

"Maybe. Maybe not."

"No further questions," I said in disgust and sat down.

CHAPTER 74

After a brief recess, the prosecution called its next witness. As Specialist Aaron Strickland strolled into the courtroom, he waved at Jefferson and flashed his brown rotten teeth. Some of the jurors noticed.

"Friend of yours?" I said to Jefferson. "I wonder what he is going to say."

"Whatever it is, it'll be a lie."

Strickland raised his hand and immediately told his first lie - to tell "the truth, the whole truth, and nothing but the truth." Then, he told his second lie. "So help me God."

"He's a piece of shit," Jefferson mumbled into my ear.

"Got it. Now, pay attention."

Strickland's buzz cut was fresh, no more than a day old. His polyester, white button-down shirt still bore the fresh-from-the-wrapper creases, undoubtedly purchased by Paine the night before. His red clip-on tie was at least three inches too short - *bet they got it in the Juniors Department*. His plastic leather shoes gleamed.

The courtroom waited in anticipation while Paine made a great show of looking over his notes. He never took this long. The judge noticed. "Colonel, your witness." After another 30 seconds, Gianelli lost his patience. "Today, if you please."

Paine took a languorous stroll to the jury rail, quite an accomplishment given the tight space, opened his mouth, and began coughing.

Seriously?

He wandered back to his chair. Made a little motion to the judge begging his indulgence, then spent almost a minute quenching his thirst. Just as Gianelli prepared to launch a verbal Hellfire missile, Paine took a breath and started. "Aaron," he said, approaching the witness like they were old chums, "please introduce yourself to the panel."

"Hi there, I'm Specialist Aaron Strickland."

In unison, the jurors looked at the judge, then at Paine, then back at Strickland. Some of their expressions soured like they smelled fresh vomit on a hot day.

"Specialist Strickland," Gianelli stepped in, "are you currently serving in the United States Army?"

"Yeah?" He inflected "yeah" like he was asking a question.

Gianelli turned to Paine. Fuses blow with fewer hisses. "Why isn't this witness in the proper uniform?" Paine stuttered, trying to respond, but Gianelli cut him off. "Colonel Paine, it's your responsibility to ensure that all military witnesses are in the proper uniform."

"I can explain," Paine said. "He's only a Reservist."

Gianelli replied, "He's a U.S. Army soldier, and this is a general court-martial. Now, call a witness in the proper uniform."

"I don't have any other witnesses on standby."

The jurors watched the banter with amusement.

"We'll recess until 1400 hours. That should give you plenty of time to get this uniform situation squared away."

"I don't think it's possible to outfit this soldier in a new uniform and have it tailored in three hours," Paine said.

"Where's his old uniform? The one the Army issued him?" Gianelli asked.

Paine was quiet as he thought of a response.

"I pawned it," Strickland interjected. "I needed the cash."

The jury burst into laughter.

Even Gianelli cracked a slight smile. "Government, this is your problem. Fix it."

"That's going to be difficult," Paine said.

"Colonel Paine, we are all soldiers here. Soldiers work, rain or shine, night or day until the mission is accomplished. You've been dragging this case out, and I am sure this jury would prefer to finish this trial before Christmas." Gianelli addressed the jury. "Am I right?" Every juror nodded. "Alright. This Court is adjourned until 1400 hours. Counsel and the accused, stay behind." After the jury exited, Gianelli said, "Colonel Paine, do you know anyone at Clothing Sales?"

"Probably," Paine replied.

"Good. I hope to God you have not irritated anyone over there with your sparkling personality. Because they need to help you - you want them to help you. If I miss my flight to see my granddaughter on Christmas, it will be your ass."

Paine left the courtroom on a dead run. Strickland trotted behind like a faithful pup.

CHAPTER 75

E veryone knew Paine wasn't going to be able to get Strickland a new uniform in a few hours. On Army installations, only one store sold official uniforms, Military Clothing Sales, a place notorious for undependable hours and slow service. Government employees enjoying long lunches and even longer smoke breaks made uniform shopping more of an expedition than an experience. Even if the store was open, the chances they could (or would) rush to tailor a uniform defied common sense.

At 1358 hours, Gianelli was back on the bench. Before he called the jury, he addressed Paine. "Did you get the uniform situation squared away?"

"Yes, Your Honor," Paine replied.

I'm sure my jaw dropped. Gianelli's eyes widened perceptibly. He turned to the bailiff and said, "Recall Specialist Strickland and bring in the jury."

When the courtroom door opened, all eyes shifted to Strickland. Gianelli shot me a glance and smirked, ever so slightly. Half of the jurors snickered. The others cringed like they'd stepped on a pile of dog shit. "The pickle suit" hung on Strickland's rail-thin frame with all the form-fitting elegance of a caftan. Infamous for its hideous appearance, the Army Class A uniform was dark green, with a light green undershirt. Ugliest uniform on the planet.

The jacket almost reached Strickland's knees. His arms barely turtled their way out of the sleeves. Even from a distance, I could see the pins "tailoring" his sleeves and cuffs. Strickland had to slide his feet along the carpet to avoid slipping out of the oversized, patent leather shoes, probably Paine's spare pair. They could have doubled as cross-country skis. In the stunned silence of the courtroom, the only sound was the scratching of the soles easing their way down the worn carpet.

Once Strickland sat, Gianelli leaned forward, squinted, and eyeballed his chest. "Colonel Paine, where's his nameplate?"

"I couldn't get one made in time," Paine said. "I had to borrow a uniform."

"No kidding." Gianelli then addressed the jury, "As you can see, this soldier is out of uniform. We are going to proceed because I don't want to waste any more of your time. Let the record reflect that the prosecution has failed to ensure its own witness was in the proper military uniform. You shall not hold this against Sergeant Jefferson." He let the words hang for a moment. "You may proceed, trial counsel."

Paine hurried to get started. "Specialist Strickland, let me remind you that you are still under oath."

"Okay." Strickland nodded and wiped his nose with his sleeve.

Paine cringed but continued his questioning, "In 2002, were you deployed to Afghanistan?"

"Yeah."

"Were you deployed with Sergeant Tyler Jefferson?"

"Uh-huh."

"What was your job, over there?"

"I worked at the prison, the front desk, usually the night shift. Ya see. I have knee problems, so I had to work a desk job."

"When you worked at the front desk. What were your duties?"

"Uh, when new prisoners came in, I in-processed 'em."

"Were you working the night shift when a prisoner kneed Sergeant Jefferson in the groin?"

Strickland giggled. "Yup. I was there."

"Please walk us through the events of that evening."

"Sure can. Just like we practiced."

Major Hanna Weiss sighed. Paine acted like he didn't notice. "Go ahead." He motioned with his hand, encouraging Strickland to move along.

"I got on duty at midnight, my usual shift. I'm kind of a night owl, on account of all the Red Bull and shit, so I don't mind being up at all hours. The other guys liked that, 'cause they'd rather get sack time or talk to their families back home, you know, 'cause of the time difference and all. And I don't have much family. Well, I do, but we don't get along real good, so we don't talk much. And I sure as hell wasn't going to call them from Afghanistan since I don't call them from across town-"

"Specialist, stop." Gianelli held up his hand. "Colonel Paine, can you please ask questions that don't require the recitation of an epic poem?"

"Of course, Your Honor." Paine nodded at Gianelli and resumed his examination, "Specialist Strickland, on that night, did you have any contact with Sergeant Jefferson?"

"On that night? Hmm." Strickland leaned back, put his right hand on his chin, and stared at the ceiling as if formulating a new theory of physics. Thirty seconds later, he said, "Yeah, yeah. I seen Jefferson that night."

"Please tell the jury what you saw."

Strickland seemed confused. "You mean with Jefferson?"

I heard Weiss sigh again, this time much louder.

"Yes, with Sergeant Jefferson. What happened with Sergeant Jefferson?" Paine was losing his patience. He and his team had spent days preparing Strickland to answer these same questions. They didn't consider the appalling number of brain cells the man had destroyed with his recreational drug activities.

"Anyways," Strickland said, "sometime after midnight, the OGAs come in. Ya know, the guys that went out and caught the terrorists. They brung in a guy, like always. They never missed, always got somebody. Might have been a goat herder or somebody, but they always snagged someone probably 'cause they got paid by the capture' - that's what I was told - ya know, on 'count they wuz private contractor types and not reg'lar Army. Well, could have been CIA, FBI, KGB. Not sure, but them guys wuz badasses."

"Specialist Strickland," Gianelli said, "please listen to the question and answer the question you are asked."

Despite Paine's best efforts, his questioning of Strickland dragged on for hours. Finally, he got to the end of his examination.

"Do you remember the prisoner's name? The one they brought in?"

"Didn't at the time. Found out his name wuz Zamfir Naval." Strickland raised his eyebrows and glanced at Paine. "I say that right?"

Weiss's exaggerated eye-rolling caught the attention of some of the jurors. Nineteen hours of prep time, right down the toilet.

Paine said, "You mean Hamza-?"

I was on my feet. "Objection. He's leading the-"

"Sustained," Gianelli said before I could finish. "Colonel Paine, who is testifying? You or the witness?"

"I'm refreshing his memory," Paine said.

"No, you're leading the witness. Now, ask your next, non-leading question."

Paine continued, "Specialist, what was the prisoner's name?"

"It was Zamfir or somethin' like that?"

"Does Hamza sound right?" Paine started to nod but stopped when he realized Gianelli was watching him like a cobra watches a mongoose.

But it was too late, Strickland had caught Paine's cue. "Yeah, Hamza, that's it. And his last name has a couple of s's in it. Nassle, nope. Nasal, nope. Nassar - that's it! Hamza Nassar."

"What happened when Mr. Nassar came into the prison?" Paine asked.

"He hit Jefferson in the sack."

"Excuse me?" Paine cupped his ear like he was hard of hearing.

"He drilled him in the nut sack. Right in the family jewels - pow - in the balls. Jefferson crumpled like a double-wide in a windstorm."

Paine quivered. It was all for show. "Then what happened?"

"Well, the other fellas got him all chained up and stuff, and they took him off to his cell. They let Jefferson lie 'til he got his nads back in order. Took a while. It looked like that raghead crushed his nuts." Strickland laughed so loud he hiccupped. Gianelli glanced at me, waiting for me to object. I didn't, not while Strickland was making a fool of himself.

Paine drew closer, a conspiratorial glint in his eye. "After Nassar struck him, did Jefferson say anything?"

"He sure did. I've never heard nothin' quite so cold-blooded in all my life."

"What did he say? And, Specialist, try to remember exactly what it was. Be precise. This is important."

Paine had set the stage the way he wanted. And, somehow, Strickland delivered his most important line perfectly. "He looked right at me and said, 'So help me God, before the night is over, I'm going to beat that towel-headed motherfucker to death.'"

Paine almost bowed - a master thespian at work. "I pass the witness." As Paine swaggered back to his table, he flashed me an arrogant grin.

"This seems like a good breaking point," Gianelli said. "We will reconvene tomorrow at 0800. Have a nice evening."

CHAPTER 76

As I drove to my motel, my phone rang. It was a South Carolina number I didn't recognize.

"This is Max O'Donnell."

"Ma-yax." The caller actually pronounced my name with two syllables.

"Who is this?"

"Max, this is Trey." The voice sounded vaguely familiar, but I was tired and couldn't place it.

"Who?"

"Trey. Trey Kline."

My mind was blank.

The caller cleared his throat and said, "It's David Weathersby Kline, III. My father is David Weathersby Kline II of-"

I interrupted, "Stanford and Kline. I know who you are. How can I help you?" I didn't have time for this taint bucket, but his call piqued my interest.

"Oh no, Max. It is I who wants to help you. I have not had the pleasure of speaking with you since your job interview with our firm."

"I've been in trial, David."

"Please, call me Trey."

I swallowed and spit it out. "Trey, sorry for skipping lunch at the Club. Something came up with the Army."

"My father mentioned that. That's quite all right, and completely understandable." He spoke so slowly I wanted to finish his sentences for him. During the long pause, I could hear his breathing. I also heard paper shuffling.

"Max, I wanted to personally call you with our offer."

Offer - what offer? I thought.

"Considering the high-profile nature of our practice," he said, "these sorts of negotiations are always delicate and need to be handled with both sensitivity and civility."

"Indeed," I said. I never used "indeed."

"There are some details we need to hammer out. I mean, smooth over. Small matters (Trey actually said "mattahs") we ought to be able to move through with alacrity."

Good God, I thought. *He must be sitting at his desk with a thesaurus.*

Trey kept drawling away, "I am so pleased you concur with our assessment. Negotiations often break down over the most minuscule issues. Actually, more often than not, parties cannot come to a meeting of the minds regarding financial considerations. However, I knew you'd be a team player."

Was he offering me a job? "How can I help you - ah - Trey?" I asked, kicking myself for fumbling his name.

"Well, Max," he said, "we have a figure in mind. Normally, I would write it on a slip of paper so that you could peruse it for a moment. Much less crude than an actual discussion, you know. Filthy lucre and all that nonsense."

"Yes," I said. *What the hell was lucre, and what the hell was he talking about?*

He kept on speaking with the speed of a 38-year-old tractor in a muddy field. "Given the constraints put upon us by your current geography, I guess we will have to set good manners aside and talk to one another about money."

He could have said all that in about four seconds. Still, given I was about to become an employed civilian lawyer, I was not about to tell him to quit speaking like Jefferson Davis. "What do you have in mind?" I asked, then added, "if I might be so indelicate."

Two can play.

"We were thinking," he paused.

I could see the new seven-series Beemer: Midnight blue, black leather interior, working air conditioning. I had tried on an Armani suit once, just for fun. A perfect 46-long. I could feel the cool, silk-lined sleeves on my arms. I would get blue - no gray pinstripe. A Cremieux patterned tie. A custom-made shirt, monogrammed cuffs.

Then, Trey muttered something. It didn't sound right. "Excuse me?" I said.

He replied, "I said, '$2,500 a month.'"

The blood pounded in my head. I know I stopped breathing because I was dizzy after about 30 seconds. "Trey, that's half of what I make right now in the Army."

"I know, Max. It's only for a trial basis. In about a year, we can make adjustments, depending on how your career progresses."

I tried to keep my voice measured. "Let me get this straight. There might be a bad connection, and I don't want to offend you."

"Oh no, Max," he said, "clarity is paramount in these situations."

I took a breath. "You want me to come work for one of the most prestigious law firms in the South, and you intend to pay me $30,000 a year?"

Trey's laugh startled me. A high-pitched snicker - like a pre-pubescent boy. "My, oh my, Max," Trey said, "you are laboring under a most egregious misapprehension here."

I waited.

"We had no intention of offering you a job. Truth be told, we never considered you at all. Father only interviewed you as a favor to Annabelle."

"Then, what are we discussing?"

"Your monthly support payments to Annabelle, of course. Her parents requested we draw up papers for a legal separation."

"Fuck you, Trey," I said. "We're not getting a divorce." I hung up before he could respond.

Chapter 77

fter Trey's call, I had trouble sleeping. So, I watched Sponge Bob reruns to help me unwind. As I nodded off, my phone rang. A ringing phone at one in the morning hardly ever brings good news.

"Sorry to bother you so late," Rose said, "but this is important."

I flicked on the light and sat up in my bed. "What's up?"

"Specialist Strickland called me a few minutes ago," she said.

"Specialist Strickland? How did he get your number?"

"From my blog. He's been following the story."

"What did he want?"

"He said he has information that will help Jefferson. He wants to meet with you."

"Seriously? In the middle of the night?" I rubbed my eyes. "I don't think so."

"Max, he said it could save Jefferson's life."

I thought for a moment. If there was even a small chance that Strickland could help Jefferson, I'd take the risk. "Alright," I said, "where does he want to meet?"

"His motel room. He's staying at the Coral Inn, off of Montana Avenue, Room 15."

"No way. That sounds like a setup. I'll meet him somewhere private."

"Name the place, and I'll bring him there."

"Okay. Go get him," I said. "I'll call you in a few with the meeting location." I hung up with Rose and called Reggie.

"What does this asshole have to gain by helping my son?" Reggie asked.

"I don't know," I replied. "But it's worth looking into."

"Meet me outside of your motel in 30," he said and hung up.

I pulled a map from my rental car. It covered Southwest Texas and had blowups of El Paso and Juárez. While I waited for Reggie to pick me up, I searched for a secluded meeting spot. Over 1.3 million people lived in Juárez, so finding a private area was challenging. I chose the sprawling Chamizal Federal Public Park because it was less than a mile from the border and had small picnic areas scattered throughout. I called Rose and gave her the location.

Twenty minutes later, Reggie picked me up at my motel. His Escalade burned rubber as we headed toward the Bridge of the Americas and into Mexico. The early morning crossing was uneventful. The border security waved us through.

Reggie steered the Escalade deep into the park and stopped in a gravel lot next to a picnic shelter. When he killed the ignition, it was pitch black, like the inside of a cave. We sat and waited in silence. No chit chat. No radio. The only noise was Reggie's stomach. It sounded like two feral cats were fighting to the death inside of him. As our eyes adjusted to the darkness, lights appeared in the distance, and a beat-up white Nissan Sentra lurched toward us. It wasn't Rose. She drove a Honda Civic. Without the slightest hesitation, Reggie slid a Glock .9 mm from his shoulder holster.

He slapped my shoulder with the back of his hand and pointed. "Grab the piece from the glovebox." I followed his orders. Using the dim illumination from the glovebox, I made sure the Ruger .38 Special Revolver was loaded. It was. "You know how to use that?" Reggie narrowed his eyes as he scanned his surroundings.

"Reggie, I'm in the Army."

He snorted. "Yeah, but you're a goddamn desk jockey."

"Fuck you." I cocked the pistol's hammer. "I've been shooting since I was 10."

"Just checking."

The lights from the Nissan illuminated our faces as it drew nearer. It was no more than a baseball throw away. Reggie turned the key in the ignition and revved the Cadillac's 345 horsepower engine. "This city's a war zone," he said. "Shit can go bad real fast." He flipped on the high beams and shifted into Drive. Suddenly, the Sentra stopped. Out of the shadows, a figure walked toward it and got into the passenger side. As soon as the door closed, the car drove off the way it came.

"What was that about?" I said.

"Probably a hooker. No sweat."

Five minutes later, Rose's Honda parked alongside the Escalade with Strickland in the front seat. Reggie hopped out and lunged toward Strickland's door in an impressive show of agility and speed, especially considering his size and age. He snatched the door open, nearly ripping it off the hinges. Reggie jammed his pistol into Strickland's chest and said, "Get out."

Strickland's skeletal body flailed like a rag doll having a seizure as Reggie yanked him out of the car. "I'm trying to help you," Strickland hollered.

"Shut the fuck up," Reggie said as he slammed Strickland, face-first, into the Escalade's hood. Reggie holstered his pistol and frisked Strickland from top to bottom. He pulled a cheap flip-phone from Strickland's jacket and crushed it with his shoe.

"What the fuck?" Strickland said. "That's my phone." Reggie ignored him as he continued his search. Aside from the phone, Strickland carried a Velcro Army wallet, a military ID, three dollars, and a Trojan Magnum condom. Reggie tossed Strickland's wallet on the ground. Then, he opened the Escalade's back door.

"Get in," he said, nudging Strickland. Reggie and I climbed into the back, sandwiching Strickland between us.

"Who knows you're here?" I asked Strickland.

"Nobody," he said. "I mean nobody except for you guys and th...th..."

"The what?" I asked.

"That, that, that broad that drove me," Strickland said with a smirk.

Reggie removed his toothpick. "What's so funny?"

"Homie, that bitch is smoking. Maybe she'll let us take turns."

Without warning, Reggie's massive hand clamped Strickland's testicles like a gator locking on a raw T-bone.

"Ahhh," Strickland shrieked.

Reggie twisted like he was wringing a wet mop. "Show some respect, redneck." Then, he let go.

"I'm just playin'," Strickland said, as he doctored his gonads.

"Specialist Strickland," I said, "we don't have all night. Does Paine or anyone else know you're here?"

"Nah." He shook his head.

"What the fuck do you want?" I asked him.

"I know what happened to Nassar," he said.

"You know who killed him?"

"No. But I know who made his camel-ridin' ass disappear." Strickland chuckled. An awkward, nervous chuckle.

"Go on," I said.

"Like I said in court. I worked the front desk, the night shift. Nobody came or went without me knowin'. Man, I seen it all. Night is when the action happened. They always came at night, like cockroaches."

"Who's they?" Reggie said to him.

"The OGA boys, man. Scary fuckin' dudes. It was ugly. I seen it all - every single disgustin' thing they did."

I thought I found a hole in his story. "Strickland, didn't the OGAs work in the VIP interrogation rooms?"

"Yep."

"How did you see what the OGAs were doing if you were at the front desk?"

Strickland hesitated. Reggie poked him in the ribs. "Spit it out, boy."

Strickland's hands covered his crotch, anticipating another assault. "Let's just say, a few of us knowed some places where we could, ah, relax."

"What does that mean?" I said.

"Get high. I ain't proud of it, but it is what it is. Up in the vents. That's where I'd go. You know, where the air moves around."

"The ductwork?" I said.

"Yeah, the ducks. No one ever looked there."

I didn't bother correcting him. It was all clear now. "And you could see what was happening below in the interrogation rooms?" I asked.

"Yup." He nodded.

"You saw what happened to Nassar?"

"Sure as Mary was a virgin. They tore that man up?"

"Was it my son, Tyler?" Reggie asked.

"No. It was a scary-ass dude. Don't know his name, but he was always wearing cowboy boots. Fancy ones. You know, the kind with the silver toes. He was with the OGA's."

I glanced at Reggie. He nodded at me as he chewed on his toothpick. "Why am I hearing this for the first time?" I said. "You just testified, and you made no mention of this."

Strickland shrugged with one shoulder. "Nobody asked." He had a point. Paine didn't ask him about the OGA's.

"So why now?" I said.

"That prick double-crossed me," Strickland said.

"What prick?" Reggie asked.

"That cocksucker in charge."

"Colonel Paine, the prosecutor?" I said.

"Yeah." Strickland nodded. "He said 'cause I fucked up, the deal's off."

"What deal?" Reggie asked.

"He said if I helped him, he'd get me VA disability, ya know, for my PTSD."

"PTSD, my ass," Reggie said. "Boy, I know a junkie when I see one."

Strickland hung his head. "It's a disease, man. I need help."

Reggie and I were unmoved. "Did he put this deal in writing?" I asked.

"No."

Of course not.

"So, why did he break this deal?"

"Paine said I fucked up his case. That my testimony sucked, and the jury hated me. He was real pissed about the uniform thing. I told 'em, 'I said what you told me to say.' That's when he said, 'There's no deal.' I didn't know what to do, so I called my Uncle Ray, my mother's brother, and he told me I was a dumb ass for not gettin' the deal in writin'. That's when I thought I got hosed. So, I went to the prosecutor's office after court. That Jew bitch lawyer was the only one there."

Strickland protected his family jewels as he peered sideways at Reggie. He never saw my fist before it slammed into his solar plexus. As Strickland gasped for air, Reggie grabbed him by the throat and said, "Boy, get to the fuckin' point, quick, or we're leavin' your ass here, in cartel country. And good luck makin' it across the border without your wallet."

"Sorry about the Jew slur," Strickland said. "I was just sayin' that she was all friendly two, three days ago when she was tellin' me what to say, but now she's all, 'No one promised you nuthin',' and shit like that. That's when I figured out I ain't gettin' a deal."

I grabbed a fistful of his shirt and pulled him close to me. "What does any of this have to do with Jefferson?"

"I wanna fuck that prosecutor up," he said. "I want your guy to walk."

"Hard for me to believe you're switchin' sides out of the blue, even if you want to mess with Paine," Reggie said.

"Well." Strickland rubbed his thumb and index finger together. "A little appreciation goes a long way, ya know." There it was.

"How much appreciation?" Reggie asked.

"Not much," Strickland said. "Ya know, I'm gettin' outta the Army soon. Momma's got the bad sugar. I ain't got paid recently 'cause of a little misunderstandin'.."

"You mean your AWOL?" I said.

"Yeah, that," Strickland said dismissively. "I need a little cash 'til my disability kicks in."

This poor sap wasn't going to get disability. Folks with Dishonorable Discharges don't qualify for benefits.

"How much?" Reggie asked.

"I figure three large, plus a new phone."

That did it. "Fuck you, Strickland," I said. "We're not buying your testimony."

"Counselor." Reggie pointed out the window. "Why don't you step outside and get some air. I need to have a discussion with this soldier." It was not a request. I got out and closed the door. A few minutes later, I heard a knock on the window. When I crawled into the back seat, Strickland was grinning.

"So, tell us, Mr. Strickland," Reggie said, "what are you going to testify about tomorrow?"

"I'm gonna hook ya boy up," he said. "I'll tell the world about how the prosecutor made me lie and how he promised me bennies."

"Go on," Reggie said.

"I'm gonna tell them about how I seen that guy with the boots, that OGA, how he ass-kicked that Muslim motherfucker. Waterboarded him too. That's some nasty-ass shit. He's a mean sumbitch."

The moment of truth. "Did Jefferson kill Nassar?" I asked.

"Hell no, man. Those OGA fuckers disappeared him."

"What does that mean?"

"I heard 'em talkin' one day after they'd stomped that Tali's ass. They said one of our 'boys' needed to come home."

"Boys?"

"Yeah. Like a prisoner or somethin'. Said he needed to come home, and that Tali was their ticket."

"Go on."

"Next night, they bring in Doc Needham. He takes a syringe and jabs it in Al Whatshisname's leg. Damn camel jockey sat up like someone stuck a 220 line up his ass."

I looked at Reggie and said, "Epinephrine?"

Reggie nodded. "Yeah, sounds like it."

"Anyhow," Strickland said, "it juiced that guy up so much he walked out the door. Doc Needham was right behind him."

I pointed my finger in Strickland's face." How much of this is true?"

"All of it. I swear."

"This is important," I said. "After they took him out of Sangar Prison, did you ever see Hamza Nassar again?"

"No, siree." Strickland shook his head. "That boot-wearin' joker came back a few times, but that A-rab disappeared."

To be sure, we went over the whole thing again. We told Strickland to tell the truth about his drug habit and to take responsibility for his previous lies. At four o'clock in the morning, we cut Strickland loose. He got into Rose's car, and they drove off. Reggie was hungry, so we stopped at La Pecadora, "The Sinner," an all-night taco truck where we got an early breakfast before our last day of testimony. After we finished eating, Reggie dropped me off at my motel. Walking toward my room, I couldn't shake the nagging thought of what would happen if Strickland's testimony fell apart in front of the jury.

CHAPTER 78

The next morning, I entered the courtroom and found Paine sitting on his desk with his arms crossed. As our eyes locked, Paine stood and shouted, "You. In the judge's chambers, now." His face was as red as a maraschino cherry.

I took my time unpacking and then faced Paine. "What's this about?"

"This." Paine's hand clenched a stack of papers.

"I cannot see what you're holding, and I'm not a mind reader."

"Oh, you know what I'm talking about, O'Donnell. Follow me. That's an order." Paine stormed off toward Gianelli's chambers with me in tow. He barged in without knocking. "We have a problem," he said, waving the papers in Gianelli's face.

Instinctively, Gianelli's left arm swiped upward, knocking the papers from Paine's hand. Simultaneously, Gianelli cocked his right fist. I waited with anticipation for the judge to punch Paine in the face. It didn't happen. Gianelli slowly lowered his arm. Paine picked the wrong day to barge into his office. At this point, the judge was in no mood for drama. The Jefferson case had become a circus, and Gianelli knew the jury wanted to wrap this case up and take leave. No one wanted to spend Christmas Eve in court.

"Have you lost your mind?" Gianelli asked Paine.

Paine replied, "Captain O'Donnell and his co-conspirator, Rose Sanchez, should be held in contempt of court."

"What the hell are you talking about?" Gianelli said through clenched teeth.

"Have you read this article?" Paine pointed at the papers Gianelli had knocked from his hand.

Gianelli shook his head. "Court starts in five minutes. I'm not delaying this case anymore over your petty bullshit."

Paine collected the papers and handed them to Gianelli. "I beg of you. You need to see this."

Gianelli snatched the papers from Paine's hand and read them. "What does this have to do with Captain O'Donnell?" Gianelli said. "It's your witness, Specialist Strickland, who's been running his mouth to the press."

"Your Honor, there is classified information in the article," Paine said, "for one, the name of a CIA operative."

Gianelli shook his head. "So what? Besides, if Johnston is his real name, I'm Brad Pitt."

Paine's eyes nearly bulged out of his head. Yet, he continued, "There are details about CIA activities at Sangar, all of which are Top Secret. It's all over the internet. My staff tells me the story has been picked up by CNN. There is no way Specialist Strickland could have known about any of this unless Captain O'Donnell told him."

"Or you," Gianelli said. "Or a member of your staff. Or any number of other people who might have gained access to the information. I've seen your setup here. It's not exactly Fort Knox in your office."

Paine began to sputter. "I run a tight ship," he said, "and I resent the implication."

Gianelli slammed his hand on his desk, splashing coffee from his mug. "Aside from the fact that the Army has nothing to do with ships, lose the attitude. You can resent my implication all you want. What you cannot do is prove Captain O'Donnell had anything to do with the story you just shoved in my face. How do I know you can't prove it? Because no one has arrested the man. You do not have any evidence. You have demonstrated a raging hard-on for Captain O'Donnell since this trial began, starting with your infantile display with the papers on my courtroom floor."

Paine flinched.

"I have a long memory," Gianelli said, "and I am well aware that you and Judge Rake were up to your sleazy little necks in ex-parte communications about this case. You are lucky no one has filed an independent complaint."

Paine scoffed. "What are you insinuating, Tony?"

Gianelli stood and poked Paine in the chest. "Counsel, if you do not shut up and let me continue this trial, I will have a team of investigators down here before Santa gets into his sleigh." Gianelli's voice had never risen a decibel. He put both fists on his desk and leaned toward Paine. "Have I made myself clear?"

Paine did not respond. Instead, he snapped to attention, executed a perfect, parade ground about-face and exited the room. I was right behind him. I hadn't needed to say a word.

Reggie sat in the front row when we got back to the courtroom, chatting with Jefferson and his guards. I scanned the courtroom for Rose. She was absent. I wasn't sure what she wrote in her article, but I was concerned that Paine would use it to discredit Strickland. I called Rose on my cell phone. It went straight to voicemail. I walked over to Reggie. "Strickland ran his mouth to Rose about Johnston," I said. "She published an article this morning."

"What do you want me to do?"

"Find Rose and get me a copy of that article."

"Consider it done." Reggie stood and walked out of the courtroom.

CHAPTER 79

W hen we reconvened, Judge Gianelli addressed the jury. "Welcome back, everyone. We are scheduled for Specialist Aaron Strickland's cross-examination. Bailiff, please recall Specialist Strickland to the stand."

The bailiff left the courtroom and returned alone. "Your Honor," the bailiff said in a sheepish tone, "he's not in the witness waiting room."

"Check again, and make sure he's not in the bathroom." The bailiff left and came back five minutes later, empty-handed. That's when Gianelli blew his top. "Trial counsel?"

Paine was on his feet by the second syllable. "Your Honor, Specialist Strickland appears to be-"

"Colonel, if the next word out of your mouth is 'unavailable,' you might want to consider a career in the Merchant Marines."

Paine looked so obviously lost. I almost felt sorry for him. "This witness was told to be here by 0730 hours. Now, he's not answering his phone."

Gianelli said five words, "Find him. Now. Or else."

Paine, Weiss, and Bronson skittered from the room like rats. Nelson must have drawn the short straw - he had to stay. So did I. Judge Gianelli remained on the bench. Any whisper, cough, or yawn ran headlong into a withering gaze from the bench. Waiting in a courtroom with an angry judge is never fun. But, waiting in a courtroom with an angry Judge

Antonio Gianelli felt like agony. Forty-five minutes later, the bailiff handed Judge Gianelli a note. His brow darkened as he read it.

"Ladies and gentlemen," he said, "we are in recess until tomorrow morning at 0800 hours. I need to see counsel in my chambers - now."

On most days, the noise of the crowd filing out of the courtroom approximated the sound of junior high kids leaving for summer vacation. Today, something in Gianelli's tone warned everyone into silence.

Nelson and I walked into Gianelli's chambers. Gianelli sat. We didn't. Not enough chairs. Ten minutes later, a lathered trio of Paine, Weiss, and Bronson joined us. They didn't get to sit, either.

Gianelli held the note in his hand, a tiny sliver of white in his enormous paw. "Specialist Strickland is dead," he said.

I looked at Paine. He looked at Bronson. *Odd. Shouldn't he have looked at me?*

"Your Honor, the defense moves for a mistrial," I said.

"Save it, Counsel," Gianelli said, with a wave of his hand. "You are not getting a mistrial. I know you were unable to cross-examine Specialist Strickland. As such, I will order his testimony stricken and will instruct the jury to disregard it."

"The bell's been rung," I said.

Gianelli locked his eyes on mine. "Captain O'Donnell, the jury will do as instructed, and will disregard the testimony when so ordered."

I continued, "Sergeant Jefferson has been denied his Constitutional right to a fair trial. If there's a possibility that Strickland or Johnston could have provided exculpatory evidence, then you must remedy this situation. And the only remedy is a mistrial."

Gianelli rubbed his dimpled chin. "I'll take this under advisement."

"Your Honor, what was Strickland's cause of death?" Paine's prosecutorial DNA was in high gear.

"Says here he was found in his motel room with a needle in his arm. Apparently, he OD'd on heroin. Sounds a little fishy to me."

I couldn't think of anything to say. I wasn't alone. Finally, Gianelli spoke, "Take the day to reorganize. We'll start tomorrow at 0800 hours. That is all."

After Gianelli dismissed us, Jefferson and I double-timed it to our small office. I turned on my phone and called Rose. Again, it went straight to voicemail.

"What's going on?" Jefferson asked.

"Strickland's dead, and Rose is missing."

"Huh?"

"Last night, Strickland changed his testimony. He was going to help you. But this morning, he OD'd."

"He's a junkie. What'd you expect?"

"I expected him to show up, alive, and save your ass."

"How?"

"He was going to testify that you couldn't have killed Nassar because he was removed from the prison in August. Some kind of prisoner exchange."

Jefferson smirked and rocked back in his chair.

What the hell? I thought.

"You really think he OD'd?" Jefferson asked me.

I shook my head no. "There must have been foul play. Last night, Strickland told Rose about the prisoner swap. She wrote an article outlining the details. I haven't heard from her since. I sent your dad to look for her."

Jefferson paused for a long moment like he was struggling to come up with an idea. "Can't we just show the jury Rose's article?" he said.

"No. Newspaper articles are hearsay. They're not admissible."

Jefferson shrugged. "Now what?"

"I have some work to do. Head back to the brig and get some rest. I'll see you tomorrow morning." Jefferson gave a weak nod, and I handed him back to his guards.

On the way to my motel room, I got a call from a blocked number.

"Hello."

"Max, this is Rose. I'm using a burner phone." Her voice reverberated when she talked - lousy connection.

"Where are you?"

"Doesn't matter."

"Are you safe?"

"No."

"Strickland's dead," I said.

"I know."

"What happened?"

"This morning, he called. He was freaking out. Said someone was outside his room. I thought he was paranoid. Then, I heard a crash and a struggle."

"And?"

"A man's voice came over the phone."

"Who was it?"

"Don't know."

"What did he say?"

"'You're next, cunt,' and hung up."

"You have to go to the police."

"No way. I'm going underground until this blows over."

"What about the trial?"

"Fuck the trial, Max. The verdict doesn't matter if I'm dead. And whoever did this won't stop - these guys don't mess around. And they hate to lose." Then, the phone went dead. Every time I called back, it went straight to voicemail.

CHAPTER 80

I spent the night alone, thinking of how to proceed with Jefferson's case. We were almost at the finish line. My thoughts wandered to Strickland and how he could have saved the day, or not. I knew he was a loose cannon. His testimony could have easily backfired. Now, it didn't matter. His secrets would never see the light of day.

Then, I thought of Rose. My gut told me she was next. I replayed the Juárez meeting in my mind. Why did I trust her? From the start, she was only out for herself. And where the hell was Reggie? I had not heard from him since he walked out of the courtroom in search of Rose. I called him multiple times. He never answered.

After a restless night, I climbed out of bed, took a long shower, and headed back to Fort Custer. At 0800 hours, Judge Gianelli called the Court to order and said, "Members of the jury, due to unforeseen events, Specialist Strickland is unavailable to be cross-examined by the defense. Therefore, I am striking his entire testimony from the record. You must completely disregard his testimony. It cannot be considered for any reason. Is that understood?"

The jurors slowly nodded.

"All right then. Government, you may proceed."

Paine stood and faced the jury. "The United States rests."

Gianelli never looked away from the jury. "Before the defense proceeds with their case, I must inform you that I am dismissing Charge I, the premeditated murder charge, with prejudice. You are not to speculate as to why. You are not allowed to consider that charge, for any reason."

I thumped Jefferson on the leg underneath the table. This was an unexpected victory.

"Still," Gianelli said, "there are several charges yet to be adjudicated." He turned to me. "Defense, call your first witness."

I stood. "The defense rests." As I took my seat, I heard murmurs and papers shuffling at Paine's table. By calling no witnesses, we surprised them. They expected us to call character witnesses to say Jefferson was a good soldier. Then, Paine would call another dozen witnesses to prove the contrary.

"Captain O'Donnell," Gianelli said, "what is the status of the stipulation that we discussed?"

"Given the dismissal of the murder charge, the stipulation is unnecessary."

Paine let out a loud, dramatic sigh.

"Since the defense did not put on a case in chief, there will be no case in rebuttal," Gianelli said. Paine and Weiss whispered back and forth for a minute. It sounded like they were arguing. As the whispering grew louder, Gianelli cleared his throat and said, "Is there a problem, Government?"

"We wish to reopen our case," Paine replied. "We have a few more witnesses to call."

"I don't think so. You rested, and the defense rested. The case is over. I'm not allowing you to reopen your case because you supposedly forgot to call some witnesses."

"Your Honor," Paine said in a whimper, "it was an oversight."

"Don't go there. You have three experienced lawyers at your table and a team of paralegals sitting in this courtroom. You cannot tell me with a straight face that you forgot you had more witnesses. If that's true, which I doubt, then you have assembled a team of nitwits."

Gianelli turned to the jury. "You have now heard all of the evidence in this case. Before you hear closing arguments and begin deliberations, we're going to take a short recess."

CHAPTER 81

During the break, Paine cornered me in the bathroom and racked me against the wall. Veins bulged from his neck and forehead. "I know you fucking did this, O'Donnell!" he said in a rage.

"Did what?"

His red-rimmed eyes searched my face for the truth. "Don't play games with me, you piece of shit. Last night, you sent photos to my wife."

I knew precisely what he was talking about. It was my parting gift. During his surveillance, Reggie put GPS tracking devices on the prosecutor's cars. He compiled the data and noticed Paine took detours after work. So did Major Weiss. Instead of going to their homes, they headed north toward the Devil's Triangle, a high crime neighborhood known for drugs, prostitution, and cheap motels. Reggie followed Paine with his trusty Canon 7D camera and zoom lens when he noticed the detours.

Reggie snapped dozens of photos. He took pictures of Paine entering a motel room, and the couple embracing outside. But Reggie was a pro. He didn't stop there. He approached the motel's assistant manager, Javier Delgado, and asked for his help. At first, Javier refused. But everybody has a price. Javier allowed Reggie to install a discreet video camera in one of the rooms for a small fee.

On their next visit, Javier upgraded Paine and Weiss to "The Lover's Suite," for their regular patronage. The suite featured a heart-shaped hot tub, a vibrating bed, and a disco ball. The next day, Javier handed over the video, in exchange for $500 and an ounce of Royal Kush.

Back in the restroom, Paine's face twitched like a crackhead craving his next fix.

Time to end this standoff, I thought.

I gripped Paine's throat and slammed him into a restroom stall. "Listen, asshole," I said, "your wife got the G-rated version." His eyes widened. My left hand pulled his phone from his pocket. "You're going to call my wife and apologize for the lies you've spread. If not, your wife's getting all the videos, including the footage of Major Weiss getting you up the ass with a strap-on dildo."

Paine's face turned from red to green as he raced toward a toilet. After he finished puking, he dutifully called Annabelle. He explained everything, the photos with Rose, the bogus CID report, and the lies spread by Dill. I knew it wouldn't completely fix my marriage, but it was a start.

CHAPTER 82

At 1030 hours, Judge Gianelli announced to the jury, "Now, you will hear closing arguments." He motioned to the prosecution's table. "Government, please proceed."

Paine, who still looked a little nauseated, stood with the solemnity of a priest preparing to break bread. "Abraham Lincoln, the martyred sixteenth President of this country we hold so dear, once said, 'We are not enemies, but friends. We must not be enemies. Though passion may have strained, it must not break our bonds of affection. The mystic chords of memory will swell when again touched, as surely they will be, by the better angels of our nature.'"

Jefferson pushed a legal pad over toward me. I read the note. "What is he talking about?" I responded with a shrug.

Paine continued a rambling message. He quoted Aristotle, John F. Kennedy, Steven Hawking, and Dr. Martin Luther King, Jr. When Paine harkened back to the testimony of Needham, Cullen, Rickard, and the others, he paced the floor like a nervous father waiting outside a delivery room. When he got to the OGAs, his tap-dancing would have made Bill "Bojangles" Robinson jealous.

"The defense's case was nothing but smoke and mirrors," Paine said, shaking his finger at the jury. His delivery was so melodramatic it reminded me of a high school play. "They are trying to distract you. To confuse you. You need to keep your eye on the ball. These poor victims did not deserve the treatment they received, the abuses they endured." Paine turned and pointed at Jefferson with a quivering finger, tears welled in his eyes. "At the hands of that man. Nobody deserves that. U.S. soldiers cannot use prisoners of war as punching bags."

Paine moved closer to the jury, so close a few members leaned back to avoid being sprayed by his spittle. "The defense repeatedly brought up whether Other Government Agencies were in the prison. Who cares? What matters is that Sergeant Jefferson was in the prison and that he committed these crimes."

Paine could smell the finish line. "The issue in this trial is not the intelligence service of our great land. It is the standards by which we conduct ourselves as Americans. We stand for fairness and justice and righteousness. Despite our enemies' malicious intentions, we will not allow our servicemen and women to stoop to their low levels. We will not encourage, nor will we permit our military personnel to abuse those in the custody of the Land of the Free and Home of the Brave. Though we may despise everything our enemies stand for, we will not descend into the madness of their barbarous behavior."

The bailiff smiled at me and rolled his eyes.

Paine returned to the podium and took several swigs from his giant water bottle. When he quenched his thirst, he continued, "The defense has spun an elaborate spider web of misdirection. Yet, they cannot get past the fact that credible witnesses revealed Sergeant Jefferson as a violent, uncontrollable man. These witnesses, I might add, did not hide behind the mantle of secrecy, but felt honor-bound to give their damning testimony in the broad light of the Texas sun."

In a move he'd obviously practiced in the mirror, Paine pirouetted like a young Patrick Swayze, and pointed to Jefferson. "That man is a disgrace to the uniform we all wear, the tunic of bravery, worn with courage and integrity for centuries. Through our witnesses and exhibits, we have proven these heinous accusations beyond any reasonable doubt."

Paine paused, listening to the thunderous applause in his head. Then, he swept across the room, Julius Caesar ascending to the Emperor's seat before the Roman Senate, hesitated momentarily - and sat. How Gianelli kept from snickering at the pomposity of it all defied my imagination.

My turn. I gathered my notes and walked to the podium. "Members of the jury," I began, "Sergeant Jefferson is not guilty. Not - guilty. And the prosecution has not proven its case beyond a reasonable doubt. Not even close."

I stepped from behind the podium. "What *have* they proven?"

I held up a finger. "They've proven that Sergeant Cullen is a backstabbing liar who can apparently see through walls. I guess that immunity deal he got gave him superpowers."

A second finger. "They've proven that Doctor Needham has selective amnesia, and he was coached. I counted every time he said, 'I don't recall,' when I asked him a question. Sixty-seven times in total. Sixty-seven!" I stomped my foot for emphasis.

A third finger. "They've proven that unidentified civilians were running the prison like a medieval dungeon."

A fourth finger. "They've proven that nobody documented any abuses at the time."

"Last, but not least," I said, holding up five fingers, "the prosecution spent several *days* trying to prove that Sergeant Jefferson is an unpopular asshole." I stopped talking and let it sink in.

"Think about it," I said, "they called a dozen witnesses that witnessed no crime. They called them to sling mud on this man's character." I walked over to Jefferson and put my hands on his shoulders. "Being unpopular is not a crime.

Being rude is not a crime. Being an asshole is not a crime." A First Sergeant in the back row of the jury nodded. I took it as a good sign.

I returned to the podium and pressed forward. "Proof beyond a reasonable doubt is the highest standard of proof in America. To convict a person, the prosecution must present overwhelming, uncontradicted, powerful evidence."

"All of the proof must come from them," I said, pointing at the prosecution's table. "Their case is weak. It rises and falls on biased witnesses, known liars, and missing evidence."

"Read between the lines. A lot of shady stuff happened at Sangar. But it wasn't Sergeant Jefferson that did it. He's a scapegoat," I said, motioning toward Jefferson. "If someone should be on trial, it should be the CIA goons that were running that prison, not him." I expected Paine to object. He didn't.

I went on to address every witness and every piece of evidence, raising doubts, and calling out inconsistencies. Then, I reminded the jury about the evidence they did not see, the witnesses they did not hear from. The flight logs. The logbooks. The OGA civilians that were roaming the prison unchecked. Who were these OGAs? Where are they now? What were they doing to the prisoners?"

After 45 minutes, I made my final point to the jury. "I am about to sit down, but the prosecutor gets a second chance to stand up and convince you that he has proven his case. I am not allowed to respond to his final arguments." Some might think I paused for effect. I was making sure I got the last few sentences right. "But *you* can respond to his final arguments," I said, making eye contact with each juror. "You can go into the deliberation room and answer on behalf of Sergeant Jefferson. Answer in a voice that is loud and clear. Answer with a finding of not guilty. Not - guilty."

I sat down, expecting another Shakespearian soliloquy from Paine. Didn't get one. I think he was exhausted. He stood and delivered about a half dozen laborious sentences claiming he had, indeed, proven his case beyond a reasonable doubt. There was no final rousing call for truth, justice, and the American way, just a weary plea that he deserved to win.

After Gianelli charged the jury and sent them off to deliberate, Jefferson and I retreated to our temporary office and shut the door. I reached in a cooler I had brought, took out two cans of Diet Coke, and handed one to Jefferson. Each of us took a few sips.

"Now, we wait," I said.

"How long does this usually take?" he asked me.

"Could take hours. Could take all day."

"Hmmm." Jefferson nodded and took another sip. He broke the awkward silence. "So, whatcha think?"

"At least the murder charge was dismissed, but you may go down on some of the other charges."

"What am I lookin' at? A few months?"

"Paine's out for blood. He'll ask for the max. I'd guess years."

"Damn." Jefferson shook his head. "I thought you blew up their case."

"I did, but only the murder charge."

Jefferson's expression saddened like he was about to cry.

"I'm sorry," I said. "We didn't have much of a case."

"How long do they usually deliberate?" Jefferson asked.

"Every jury is different. Usually, the longer they're out, the more confused they are. The more confused they are, the better your chances-"

Suddenly, the door swung open, startling me. It was the bailiff.

This couldn't be good. "What's up?" I asked him.

"We're going back on the record," the bailiff said and walked away.

Jefferson's face turned a weird shade. He was shaking, like a 40-year-old virgin in a brothel.

"They probably have a question for the judge, or they want to take a break," I said.

"So, what do we do?"

"We go back in and listen to their question. The judge answers it. Then we come back here and wait. No problem."

Jefferson relaxed a little. As I opened the door, he whispered, "What if it's a verdict?"

Time for brutal honesty. "Oh. Then, you're likely screwed."

CHAPTER 83

B ack in the courtroom, Gianelli tapped his gavel, and the room fell silent. "Ladies and gentlemen of the jury, do you have a question?"

The jury president stood. "No, Your Honor. We have a verdict."

The courtroom murmured. Jefferson looked at me and mouthed, "What the fuck?"

Quick verdicts often mean a conviction, and this jury had deliberated for less than 15 minutes. The president of the jury handed the bailiff a paper with the verdict. The bailiff meandered over to Judge Gianelli and gave it to him. The whole process was excruciatingly painful. A minute felt like an hour.

Gianelli read silently to himself. He reached for a giant yellow highlighter, popped off the cap, and began highlighting the portions of the verdict the jury president would read. The highlighter squeaked as the judge dragged it across what seemed like too many lines. Finally, he stopped, folded the paper, and handed it back to the bailiff, who then returned it to the jury president. If Gianelli was surprised, he didn't show it.

"Accused and counsel, please rise," the judge said. "The panel president will announce the verdict."

Jefferson and I stood and faced the jury. No member looked at us, not one. I wondered if anyone could hear my heart pounding like Secretariat down the stretch at The

Belmont. The jury president took his good, damn time. My body surged with adrenaline, the same feeling one gets right before going over the edge on a roller-coaster. "This court-martial finds the accused, Sergeant Tyler Jefferson, of all charges and specifications," he paused. "Not Guilty."

Jefferson bear-hugged me as members of the press rushed out of the room.

"Maintain your bearing," Gianelli said, with a slight tap. It was over. Possibly a record for a military trial verdict, but it was over. "I'd like to thank the jury for their service, I wish you all happy holidays. This court-martial is adjourned." Gianelli smacked his gavel twice.

I gathered my stuff quickly. Time to get the hell out of Dodge. The prosecution team moved like bugs on a pest trap. As I closed my briefcase, I heard Gianelli say, "Colonel Paine and Major Weiss, I need to see you in my chambers. We need to discuss a delicate matter." During the deliberations, Gianelli must have found the XXX-rated material of Paine and Weiss I had slipped under his door earlier in the day.

Paine glared at me. "How could you do this to me?"

"You drew first blood," I said and walked out into the bright, winter Texas sun.

CHAPTER 84

In the end, Colonel Bradley Rake would be fine. The rape victim turned out to be a runaway meth addict who'd run "honey pot" schemes throughout the Southwest. Her specialty was picking up married men in bars and seducing them. Then, she extorted them for cash. She could spot wealth in the first three minutes, and no one ever asked for ID. She looked 25.

The guys without money were the lucky ones. Sure, they didn't get laid, but they also never got the day after phone call threatening rape charges unless they came up with five large.

Her scams worked beautifully, until one of her conquests, a cross-eyed trucker from Abilene, refused to play ball. Rather than pay her ransom, he strangled her to death and dumped her body behind an abandoned billboard just south of Agua Dulce, Texas.

She died two weeks after she'd taken money to bed Rake. Bad luck for her, good luck for Rake. No complaining witness, no case. So, Rake would be fine, but not unscathed. He received a Letter of Reprimand from the Commanding General and was "encouraged" to retire. No ceremony, no pictures. No one ever wants a photographic record of a handshake with an accused rapist. In the end, the Honorable Judge Rake was nothing but collateral damage.

Rose, on the other hand, would not be okay. An hour after her last call with Max, her Honda was found at the bottom of a steep ravine a few miles east of Truth or Consequences, New Mexico. She died on impact. No one could have survived that 200-foot drop.

The local sheriff labeled the wreck an accident and attributed it to reckless driving. It was just one of many crashes that occurred annually on Route 51's hairpin turns. Because of his rush to judgment, the sheriff failed to properly investigate. If he had, he would have noticed the dent in her rear bumper.

✕

A day after Jefferson's acquittal, Mr. Johnston (aka Thomas Fischer), stopped by the Pearl Spa, an Asian Massage Parlor outside the gates of Camp Peary, Virginia. While he lay face down and naked, awaiting a rub and a tug, Johnston was shot through the temple with a low caliber silenced pistol. His murderer remains at large.

CHAPTER 85

Since the first flight wasn't until early the next day, I decided a small celebration was in order. I agreed to meet Jefferson for a drink. The air inside the honky-tonk bar carried the usual late-night stench of sweat, beer, and hormones. I walked to the bar and ordered a rum and Coke before searching the place for Jefferson.

I raised my drink. "To victory."

My eyes roamed past my glass, and then, I saw him. A handful of men with crewcuts circled the corner pool table. They were obviously soldiers. Several women, varying degrees of skanky, leaned against the wall or clung to whatever grunt showed the most promise. At the table, cue in one hand and a beer in the other stood Sergeant Tyler Jefferson.

The song on the jukebox ended, so people quit singing along with Garth about his "friends in low places," and a momentary quiet settled across the bar.

"Jefferson!" I hollered at him.

He recognized me and waved. After he excused himself from the game, he lumbered over to me. "Max," he said, extending his hand.

I shook it. "What are you drinking?" I asked him.

"Nah, I got yours, counselor. It's the least I can do."

I nodded in the direction of the pool table. "You brought friends?"

"Me and my boys decided to shoot some pool before we make our way home tomorrow."

I recognized some of the people he was with. They were witnesses from his trial. One of them was Cullen. I pointed at the gaggle. "Sergeant, why are you playing pool with those assholes? They testified against you?"

He shrugged. "Hell. I've known some of them since elementary. Let bygones be bygones."

"Maybe you need new friends."

He smiled and slapped me on the back. "Nah. We're just having fun."

I nodded. "Where's your dad."

"He had to take care of some business back in Dallas. He said he'd be in touch."

I noticed his glassy eyes. "Why don't you let me get you a cab?" I said. Jefferson hesitated and looked with unconcealed lust at one of the females waiting at the pool table. I tapped him on the shoulder. "Sergeant, you just dodged a bullet. Let's not give Paine another target quite so soon. Time to go."

Cabs idled outside the bar, a ready-made customer base. Sitting in a well-lit parking lot listening to a West Coast ball game, beat cruising the streets and hoping your next fare hadn't just killed a hooker.

I gave instructions to the cabbie and handed him a $20. "Keep the change. Just make sure he gets in safely."

The cabbie nodded. "Sure thing, buddy."

Jefferson sprawled across the rear seat. I waited for him to buckle-up before I moved to close the door. "Hey," he said. "Hey. Hey!"

"What?"

"Two things, Max. I want to tell you two things."

"Okay."

"Thanks for my freedom. No one's ever stuck up for me before. I love you, man."

"My pleasure. Just stay out of trouble from now on."

"Yes, sir." I moved to shut him in, but Jefferson stiff-armed the door. "I said, 'two things.' There's something else."

"I thought, 'I love you, man,' was the second one." It was really time for him to be headed back to his life.

"Nope. That was all the first."

"What's the other one?"

Jefferson motioned for me to get closer. When I did, his hand shot behind my head and pulled me down. "It was Cullen," he said, exhaling alcohol-laden breath in my ear. "He killed that bastard."

"You're full of shit. Nassar wasn't in the prison."

Jefferson burst into laughter. "That's the crazy part," he said. "The CIA took him out for the prisoner swap. Stupid motherfucker got caught again three weeks later. They brought him back. He was goin' to GITMO early the next day, so no one logged him in. That's when it happened."

"Why didn't you tell me earlier?"

"I ain't no fuckin' snitch."

I could feel my blood pressure rising. "Cullen testified against you. He tried to put you in prison."

"Nah. He gave some real shit testimony. Just like we planned. X-ray vision?" He let out a booming laugh. "That's some funny shit."

"I risked everything for you, and you lied to me."

Jefferson's eyes blazed with a maniacal, almost evangelical fervor. "So? We won," he said and pulled himself out of the cab.

"At what cost?"

"Fuck the cost. I got my freedom!" He poked me hard in the chest. Too hard. "And that's all that matters."

Without hesitation, I shoved him back toward the bar. "Enjoy your freedom," I said. "Next time, you won't be so lucky." I climbed into the cab and headed for my last night at the Motel 6.

CHAPTER 86

After a long flight back, I pulled the Malibu into my driveway just before midnight. Standby is an agonizing way to fly. The only way to make it worse is to try it over a holiday. I sat in the driver's seat for a while with the motor running. It had been a long seven weeks. I had a lot to think about, but my only care at that moment was my family. I wanted to make things right.

Annabelle called me when she heard about Jefferson's acquittal. She had changed her mind and dismissed the petition. We would be able to begin anew. "Come home for Christmas, Max," she'd said. "The kids miss you."

I hoisted my suitcase out of the trunk, grabbed the two shopping bags full of presents I'd bought at Walmart, and walked toward the front door. No place like home.

My heel had just touched the top step when the door opened. Annabelle must have been waiting, watching for me. She stood in the door frame, wearing jeans and a sweatshirt - radiant - the baby held against her chest. The house smelled like gingerbread cookies.

"Hi, honey. It's good to be home."

She smiled softly.

"Daddy!" Ethan and Eva pattered toward me, wearing Christmas themed footie pajamas. I dropped the presents and scooped them up, squeezing them for a long time.

"Daddy, we got you a surprise," Ethan said.

"Don't tell him," Eva said. "It's not Christmas yet."

"Come on, Daddy," Ethan said. "Come see the puppy Santa brought." The children pulled me inside, and Annabelle closed the door to the outside world.

Acknowledgments

I am grateful to the following people for their help with this book. My brilliant and beautiful wife, Alexandra, for her support and patience throughout this long process. My friend and mentor, Arthur Fogartie, for his unwavering assistance, guidance, and motivation over the past three years. Danelle Morton, for her help with the early stages of this book and for getting me started on my writing journey. Lucy González, for critiquing my drafts and helping me shape this story. Last but not least, Dean Wideman, for his insightful feedback and camaraderie.